TRUCK STOP RODEO

THE LEGEND OF KNOX CREED

BOOK - 1

GRAY WILDER

Warning: Gay erotic romance.

The material in this book contains explicit sexual content that is intended for mature audiences only. All characters involved are adults capable of consent, are over the age of eighteen, and are willing participants.

TABLE OF CONTENTS

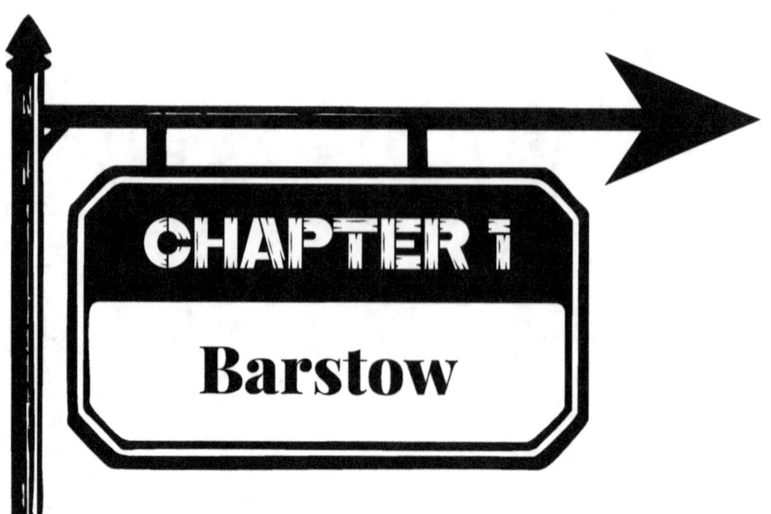

The sunrise over Barstow was not spectacular. The hues of purple and blue, tinged with dull yellow, slowly changed to a brighter yellow and muted orange as the dull and unassuming landscape failed to compete with the colors produced by the desert heat and the rising sun. Knox Creed stood naked in his living room, looking out the large window of his small house, admiring the contrasts that living in the California desert offered. He sipped at his hot coffee and allowed a sense of satisfaction to wash over him.

His joy was not rooted in the surreal sunrise nor in the afterglow of the prior evening's sex with the guy that he had picked up last night at Ricky's after the drag show. The guy, whose name he could not remember, was still asleep in Knox's bed. His joy this morning came from what sat in his driveway - a Volvo VNR Electric 6x4 tractor in Dark Gray Metallic. In small script on each side, the name Cyber Wolf was etched in a shade of gray slightly lighter than the color of the truck itself. The name he had chosen reflected the nature of the truck's electric motors and his self-designated status of being a lone-wolf on the road. He had purchased the new truck eight months ago, after years of saving for the substantial down payment on the expensive vehicle. Shortly after purchasing the truck, he obtained a contract with a local defense contractor to transport sensitive equipment across the country.

The truck itself was designed for regional distribution, but the unique requirement of his current contract made it a perfect fit. It was an opportunity that came along rarely for long-haul truck drivers. It was also an opportunity that changed Knox's life for the better. With the exceptional pay from the company and the lower operating costs of the electric truck, he would be debt-free in less than two years rather than the five years he had planned.

Knox liked living simply and efficiently. He didn't spend his money on things he didn't need. There were a few exceptions to this, the first being good coffee. It was a vice that he enjoyed, and he had invested in several high-end coffee systems to enhance this mild addiction. His favorite was his siphon system with its halogen torch base. It took time to make, but produced an exceptional cup of coffee. For his everyday cup, he had spent $1500 on a Gaggia Academia, which he cherished. His second vice was art. Occasionally, Knox would come across a painting or sculpture that made him feel happy. He often joked that his art was worth more than his house. It was not a true statement, of course, but it reminded him the value of surrounding himself with things that made him smile.

As he looked out on the truck, he admitted to himself that he considered his truck a piece of art. It was not only beautiful to look at but also served as an investment in his future. The all-electric truck had a base range of 275 miles, which extended to 350 miles with the regenerative braking and solar options that his employer had attached to the top of the short, 20-foot containers he usually hauled. The truck would charge to 80 percent in 90 minutes, just enough time for a bathroom break, a quick meal, or a quick blow job, or all three. He had opted for all the options with the truck, deciding that if he was going to make the investment, he would enjoy it. All the bells and whistles included a sleeper cab that would rival the finest Japanese pod hotel, with state-of-the-art entertainment systems, a mini fridge, microwave, and the most comfortable bed of any truck on the market.

Knox's typical run consisted of month-long hauls across the country to the East Coast and back. He rarely drove more than 300 miles a day, delivering small pieces of equipment along the way. All along the I-40 corridor. He didn't know much about the equipment that he delivered, only knowing that it was expensive, and the manufacturer insisted on extensive legal paperwork to go along with the locked trailers that he hauled. When he arrived at each of his delivery destinations, he would wait patiently while the truck was unlocked, unloaded, and re-locked. His evenings were spent in truck stop overnight lots. He loved the life this type of work provided. He loved the freedom and independence, as well as the absence of personal accountability to another person. Some might call him a lone wolf. He preferred to think of himself as self-aware. Though, in unguarded moments, a quiet corner of his mind wondered if self-awareness wasn't also a convenient excuse for avoiding true intimacy.

"Good morning." The voice came from behind him.

Knox turned, suddenly realizing that he was naked. Now he remembered why he had hooked up with this guy; trim, athletic, and very attractive in his dark green boxer briefs. He had a look that was reminiscent of a heritage that could be a mix of Mexican and Japanese. Hairless body, with dark black hair on his head and kind, soulful eyes that seemed to be constantly begging to be bent over and taken. The guy stared at Knox with a look of uncertainty about what to do.

"Good morning," Knox responded. "Coffee?"

"Yes, please." The guy answered as Knox made his way to the kitchen to grab a mug of fresh coffee for his guest and to refill his own.

Knox returned to the living room, handed the fresh mug of coffee to the guy, placed his own mug on a side table and walked casually to the bedroom to grab a robe. When he returned, the guy was seated on the sofa, carefully sipping at the hot liquid.

"Last night was really hot." The guy said.

"Yeh, it was pretty good," Knox answered, not wanting to ruin the mood by admitting to the guy that it was mediocre, at best. The guy was hot, that was for sure, but he had seemed rushed with the sex. Knox had wanted to take his time fucking the guy, enjoying his perfect body. But the guy had finished quickly and then had expected Knox to do the same. It was a reminder for Knox that a great body and a pretty face did not equate to a great fuck. Normally, Knox would have asked him to leave afterward, but the guy had fallen asleep quickly, and Knox had been sleepy from the three beers he had at the bar, so he let him stay over.

"Your body is hot. I'm really into the daddy type lately." The guy said as Knox settled into the opposite end of the sofa.

Knox realized that his body was a 'type' for the gay community. At one time, he had resisted being called a Bear but had settled into it over the past few years of his 38-year existence. He carried some excess weight for his six-foot height. He was sort of fit, something his doctor called 'fat-fit,' meaning that he was technically overweight but otherwise healthy. During his last medical exam, the doctor told him that he could stand to lose ten to fifteen pounds. His substantial body hair, very slight beer belly, and collection of tattoos on his upper arms and top of his back gave him a look that was only complemented by shaggy brown hair, facial scruff, and green eyes. Knox did admit that he had an attractive face. He would often look at himself in the mirror with gratitude for his rugged good looks.

"You're not so bad yourself," Knox replied to the guy.

"I, uh, I didn't get your name last night." The guy stated hesitantly.

"Knox. But my friends call me KC. You can call me Knox for now." Knox responded.

"You mean your trucker buddies call you KC?" The guy asked.

"Yep," Knox responded.

"I've heard long-haul truckers have a lot of stamina?" The guy said.

"True," Knox responded. "Speaking of which, you up for another round."

"Sure." The guy answered. "I'm Tom, by the way."

"Don't really care, but okay, Tom, put your mug down and come over here and straddle me." Knox was sincere and demanding in his response as he opened his robe to expose his erection. Knox opened the drawer of the nearby side table and pulled out a packet of single-use lube. He kept these stashed everywhere. They were handy for situations like this.

Tom stood, dropped his underwear to the floor, and walked over to stand directly in front of Knox. Tom's dick was nice. Seven inches with a slight curve downwards, which made it look heavy when erect. Knox reached out with his left hand and stroked Tom's dick, pulling hard and causing Tom to lose his balance and fall towards Knox. Tom steadied himself by placing his hands on Knox's shoulders. Knox's right hand was on his own hard, thick, eight-inch cock. Knox released Tom's dick and grabbed this packet of lube, which he had been holding by the corner between his teeth. The corner of the packet tore as he pulled at it, releasing a generous amount of lube into Knox's palm.

Knox reached his lubed hand under Tom, depositing most of it along his ass crack as the remainder dripped onto Knox's own cock that was begging to be massaged by Tom's tight hole. Tom had his knees placed on either side of Knox's thighs as Knox grabbed Tom's cock with his lubed hand and stroked as Tom lowered himself onto Knox's waiting, throbbing dick. Remembering how quickly Tom came the previous evening, Knox stopped touching Tom's cock and placed both hands on Tom's hips. Tom had taken Knox's large cock with the ease of a bottom that was well practiced in taking well-endowed men. As Tom rocked his hips, Knox pulled him further down onto his lap, making sure he was as far into his ass as possible.

This time, it did not take Knox long to get there. His mind was preoccupied with his trip the next day, and he just wanted to get his nut off and get this guy out of there. With a loud grunt, Knox thrust up and deposited his load in Tom's ass. As soon as he came, he grabbed Tom's dick and pumped it quickly, causing Tom to shoot on Knox's chest before Knox's own erection had subsided. Tom collapsed onto Knox's shoulder and started kissing there.

"You are so fucking hot!" Tom whispered.

"That was just what I needed to wake up," Knox said as he pushed Tom away and stood up. "You can shower with me if you want, but then you'll need to leave. I need to get my day started. I've got a long haul starting tomorrow."

"Okay. Thanks." Tom replied, seeming to decide if he wanted to do this since his attempt at affection had been casually rebuked. "Actually, I think I'll just go. I need to get ready for work."

"Sounds good." Feel free to have more coffee before you go. "Knox offered as he walked to the bedroom to shower.

When he had showered and dressed – jeans, work boots, his favorite Guns n Roses shirt and a well-worn ball cap - Knox returned to the living room to find Tom looking out the window, mug in hand, admiring the truck in the driveway.

"That's a nice truck," Tom said.

"Thanks. I'm super proud of it." Knox replied. "It took me many years and a lot of hard work to get it. But now it's mine."

"How long do you stay on the road?" Tom asked.

"About twenty days or so for each run. I generally do one run a month." Knox answered as he took Tom's mug and walked it to the kitchen, gently motioning Tom towards the door.

"Will I see you again?" Tom asked.

"Probably," Knox replied. "I go to Ricky's occasionally for the drag show. Maybe I'll see you there."

"Should we exchange numbers, just in case?" Tom asked, knowing the answer.

"No," Knox said firmly. "I'm not the exchanging numbers kind of guy.

Sorry, bud." Tom looked mildly disappointed.

"Got it. Can we do this again if I do see you around?"

"There's always the possibility." Knox did not like to commit to seconds with one-night stands unless the encounter was exceptional.

Tom left, and Knox started preparing for the trip that was coming up. He wondered what he would encounter on this one. Whatever it brought, his track record indicated that it would be memorable.

Knox spent the rest of his lazy Sunday packing his duffle bag for the trip. He made a quick run to the Stater Brothers market nearby to get snacks and a few travel toiletries for the trip. Knox drove a 1969 Mustang Mach 1 for his local driving. He had considered getting rid of the car when he bought the new truck, but he needed a run-around-town car, and the 'stang was paid for. He had bought the car ten years ago. He had been in his first full-time job driving a truck that he didn't own for a corn and alfalfa distributor that paid well but didn't care about Knox or any of the other 80 drivers that drove long distances in an unrealistic time frame for pay that seemed good but turned out to be not worth the stress.

The gas mileage on the Mustang was abysmal but worth the attention it got when he drove it. He was convinced many hook-ups had happened because of that car. He also considered the car a piece of art with its Calypso Coral color and black stripes. It looked fresh off the showroom. Knox took exceptional care of the car, keeping it clean and garaged when he was traveling.

T he next morning, Knox woke at 6am, walked naked to the bathroom, peed in the toilet, and shook his ample cock well before walking to the kitchen to make a cup of coffee. He pressed the wake button on the Gaggia and checked the water level and bean hopper while the machine warmed up. His penis gently rubbed the edge of the counter as he took one of his favorite double-walled glass mugs from the cabinet above the coffee maker. The friction caused a slight engorgement, which he gently stroked with his right hand while the coffee machine finished its start-up process. When it was ready, he removed his hand from his crotch and pressed the button for his favorite brew - a double espresso lungo.

As the coffee brewed, Knox turned around to the fridge behind him and grabbed three eggs, the butter dish, and whatever veggies were in the crisper. Today, the selection was limited to a tomato, remnants of an onion and bell pepper that he had wrapped together in foil, and a small bag of shredded cheese. At the last minute, he noticed a takeout container from his dinner two nights ago, which contained a small piece of grilled chicken breast and a generous portion of mashed potatoes. He placed all items on the cutting board that took up the small section of counter space between the fridge and the stove.

Knox turned back to the coffee machine, took the mug of fresh coffee, paused for a moment to take a sip, and turned back to the counter where the mound of ingredients sat in a haphazard pile on the wooden cutting board. He liked how easy it was to cook in this small and functional kitchen. He could easily do anything by simply turning in a circle.

Suddenly remembering an unfortunate splatter incident from the past, he took an apron from a hook on the wall by the fridge. He liked being naked around the house, but cooking naked posed its own set of challenges. He popped his head through the top loop of the apron and quickly tied the waist strings behind him, enjoying the way the fabric felt against his bare body and the way the loose strings tickled his butt cheeks and ass crack as he moved. Knox broke the eggs into a bowl and whisked them gently with a fork, adding the cheese and stirring gently before grabbing a knife from the drawer under the counter and turning his attention to the other ingredients.

As he chopped the veggies and chicken into a fine dice, Knox thought about the upcoming haul that he would start today. The company had told him there would be ten stops, all along I-40 and ending in Goldsboro, NC. After his last equipment drop, He could make his way back to Barstow at his leisure to return the trailer. According to his contract, he had a full 30 days to return a trailer after picking it up. This allowed him to take some rest and relaxation time after the trip. It also meant that there was no real hurry to get back to Barstow. He would see where the road and his adventures might take him.

He scooped up the diced veggies and meat and tossed them into the bowl with the eggs and cheese, stirring gently and adding salt and pepper before turning the electric stove burner to medium to allow the pan to heat. The pan lived perpetually on the stove. He washed it after each use and put it back in place for the next time. He had other pots and pans, but this large non-stick frying pan was the one he used the most. Using a spatula from the same drawer as the knife, Knox scraped all the egg mixture into the hot pan, gently moving things around while the eggs cooked. When everything was sufficiently cooked, he moved the food from the pan to a plate that had been waiting patiently in the dish drainer by the sink. A dash of hot sauce and a clean fork from the drawer under the coffee machine completed his breakfast preparation.

Knox liked to walk around while he ate. He walked back to the front window and looked out at his truck as he ate the scramble. He still could not believe how far he had come from just 5 years ago. After finishing high school in Riverside, he found himself aimless and confused about his future. His parents were no help. His father had made a career with Pacific Bell as a repairman, and his mother had been content to make an entire career being an administrative assistant at Riverside Community Hospital. Their lack of initiative and odd contentment at simply doing one thing for a very long time had prevented them from offering any useful advice to Knox. As an only child, he was taught to be content with what they had. It was a good childhood for him, but he did not realize until much later that there could be much more to life than what he saw in his parents.

Six months into a job after high school working the line at a plastics manufacturing plant, Knox joined the Navy. His short time in the Navy opened his eyes to what the world might offer him beyond his sequestered life in Riverside, CA. Two months of Navy boot camp at the Great Lakes Naval Training Center near Chicago, followed by nine weeks of Logistics Specialist school in Meridian, Mississippi, showed Knox a part of the United States outside of California that he wanted to explore. His first duty station was at the Naval Air Station, Pensacola, Florida. There, he made new friends, learned to drive a truck, and discovered his sexual preferences.

His encounters with other guys in the Navy started as awkward and exploring, evolving to refined over the four years of his service. He didn't consider himself easy, but he did embrace trying new things. He liked topping and bottoming equally as much, depending on the partner, of course. Sex with multiple people was fun, but it had to be the right mix to make it worth his time. Other kinks - like piss play and bondage - were just not his thing. He learned to revel in the pleasure of the simpler acts of sex. Touching, caressing, and kissing intermingled with some roughness seemed to be his forte. He loved having his dick sucked and loved sucking dick. The guys that were into that were into him.

By the end of his enlistment, Knox had obtained his CDL and had decided to take a job offer from a company that distributed auto parts to the Southeastern U.S. The company itself was good, but Knox felt unfulfilled with the day trips to the adjacent states of Georgia and Alabama. He craved something that would offer him more freedom. Freedom from schedules, sure, but also from the complicated knots of human expectation. A quiet truth he hadn't fully unpacked yet.

So, six months after separating from the Navy, he developed a plan for his future. He would move back to California, work for a company that provided trucks or allowed him to use a leased truck and save enough money to buy his freedom.

He packed up his few belongings in his older Nissan Pathfinder and headed to his family home in Riverside. His parents were more than happy to let him live with them while he looked for work. It only took a week to find a job with a local corn and alfalfa distributor. Living with his parents, on the other hand, was short-lived. Knox quickly learned that it was difficult, to say the least, to bring guys home. He had come out to his parents a few years ago, and they were accepting and supportive. Having sex in his childhood bedroom as an adult with his parents in the next room, however, was more challenging than he thought it would be. He brought a guy home one night, and the guy just could not keep his mouth shut. Knox repeatedly told him that they had to be quiet, but the guy was undeterred, riding Knox's cock with wild excitement and vocalizing the way it felt. Knox attempted to cover the guy's mouth with his hand, but it only made him louder.

After the guy left, Knox's father told him that it might be time for him to find his own place. Knox agreed. And shortly after, he found the house in Barstow where he now lived. The following year had been difficult. The job paid well, but he struggled to pay the mortgage, insurance, and other cost-of-living expenses while also having a social life. When the company offered him a chance to buy his own truck, Knox realized that this might be the beginning of his path to freedom. He took the leap, accepted the offer of the company-financed truck, and mapped out a plan to turn that situation into something better.

The truck offered by the company was a piece of shit that required regular repairs and unrealistic maintenance. Knox suffered through it, doing most of the work himself, until he had paid off enough of the debt to trade it in for a newer model with better financing. His new, well, slightly used, truck was a Peterbilt 384 in white, with no sleeper cab, no real upgrades, and not his favorite color. But the A/C worked, and it was reliable. He loved that truck and was able to pay it off in a few years, which allowed him to start saving for the electric one that proudly sat in his driveway.

Knox moved his duffle and the bag of snacks to the truck, arranging everything neatly in the ample storage compartments. His immediate neighbor, a kind older woman named Beth, who occasionally invited him over for dinner, had commented on the new truck.

"I like having you as a neighbor, Knox, and this new truck is so quiet! I'm not going to miss you starting up the old truck. Beth had been kind about Knox and the noise caused by the old truck. He had tried to be courteous and not let it run for long in the driveway before heading out with it. It was an unavoidable annoyance when living next to a trucker.

Knox settled into the driver's seat and reached to the left to quickly flick the key to the right to engage the electric motors. There was a soft hum as the truck came alive. The only true indication that the truck was ready to drive was the screen in front of him that indicated the battery status. He engaged the transmission and slowly backed out of the driveway. He smiled in joy at the precision the electric motors offered. He could back up or move forward half a mile per hour. A slowness and accuracy that was unheard of with standard transfer trucks. His current employer had mentioned in the interview that the electric truck provided them with an enormous benefit since the equipment that he would be hauling would only be complemented by such advanced technology. Knox thought it an odd comment at the time, but now realized that being able to back up that slowly in tight situations could prevent unacceptable bumps and jostling that might harm delicate equipment, no matter how well packaged.

With these various thoughts running through his head, Knox started his 15-minute drive to BarsTech Industries.

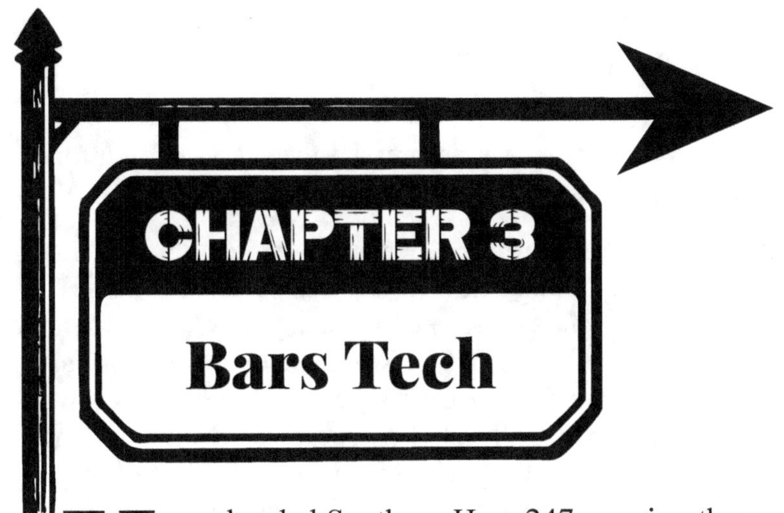

Knox headed South on Hwy 247, passing the regionally famous SlashXRanch. His thoughts briefly recounted the good food and cold beer at the café there, sometimes followed by a hook-up. Some of the hottest and horniest bikers stopped at the SlashX while traversing Southwest California. Just before the turn-off to the BarsTech complex, he noticed a road sign informing him that it was 28 miles to Big Bear City. He made a mental note to set aside some time to go back there. Several years ago, he had a very memorable week at the Big Bear guest house in Big Bear City with some big bears, a few cubs, and an otter. The thought made him laugh. You just couldn't make up a connection like that.

With a smile on his face at these good memories, he made the left turn onto an un-named paved road that seemed to lead to nowhere. Two miles of barren landscape later, Knox approached a small building incorporated into a massive security gate. A 15-foot fence topped with concertina wire stretched out to the right and left of the gate. The plethora of cameras and warning signs informed anyone approaching that this place was only accessible to those who had permission to be there. Knox knew better than to ask too many questions. When signing his contract, he had also signed several variants of non-disclosure agreements and had been informed by the company's attorney that his background check had returned satisfactory results. Knox had always kept his nose clean, even in the Navy; he always followed the rules. At least the ones that might have consequences.

On approach to the gate, Knox grabbed his company-issued ID from the tray just below the climate controls to his right. He rolled down his window as the truck quietly pulled up to the building. The guard checkpoint was located about twenty feet from the gate itself. The door to the building opened, and out stepped a woman in a black uniform that reminded Knox of the Navy working blues uniform with a few tactical elements added, including a utility belt complete with two guns, ammo, and what looked like grenades.

"Morning, Janet." Knox smiled as he pressed the one-touch button to roll down the window.

"Good morning, Knox," Janet replied, her bright smile complementing her brown eyes and dark hair tied back in a ponytail under her BarsTech-labeled ballcap. The *Cyber Wolf* is looking extra clean today." This friendly exchange at the gate was the only interaction Knox had ever had with Janet, but he had been seeing her like this for over a year now. She was always friendly, and they would occasionally chat as she cleared him for entry. Knox guessed Janet to be in her thirties. She had disclosed to him that she was a former U.S. Marine and had gotten out specifically for this job. She must have been special forces, Knox guessed, although she had not disclosed more about her time in the service.

"You're looking good," Knox said, smiling as Janet blushed. He had zero interest in women, but if he did, Janet would be his type.

"Thanks, Knox. You're such a charmer, but I know I'm not your type." She laughed.

"You're just missing one crucial thing, darling." Knox teased as they both laughed.

"Can't grow one and don't want one, thank you very much," Janet said through the laughter. "You ready for this run?"

"Yep, I'm all charged up and ready to go," Knox replied.

"Okay, stud. You're all cleared." Janet said, tapping on the tablet she held by the strap on the back. "Be careful, and don't do anything I wouldn't do."

"Well, that leaves me a lot of room to get into trouble." Knox joked.

"You just be safe. I'll see you when you return the trailer.

Knox gave her a salute with his right hand and pulled up on the switch to roll up the window with his left. Janet pressed the screen on her tablet, and the gate swung open towards Knox's truck. Knox waited for the gate to open completely before engaging the electric motors and moving the truck forward into the BarsTech Industries compound. The road continued in front of him with no buildings in sight. After a mile or so, the road started a gradual downward slope, and the actual compound of the company appeared in a clearly man-made depression.

The compound was comprised of three rectangular buildings, side by side, with the short end of each building facing the approach. The tan-colored buildings matched the color of the dirt around them and were separated by a space of about twenty feet with no noticeable connection between them. There did not seem to be any doors or windows in the two buildings to the left. The building on the right had a single, very large roll-up door almost to the edge of the right side of the building. To the left of that door, a regular door sat almost unnoticeable and unassuming. The approach road curved slightly to the right and ended at the roll-up door. There was a small parking lot to the left, with a walkway leading to the smaller of the doors. Solar panels provide shelter for the vehicle parked there.

Other than the loading area inside the roll-up door, Knox had never seen inside any part of the building. His interview for the job and all subsequent meetings had taken place in the guard shack building, which had several offices, a bathroom, and a small conference room. The loading procedure had been explained to him in painstaking detail in that conference room. There were pictures and videos describing the approach and exit, as well as what to do in case of an emergency. Which was basically to do what he was told by anyone else on the compound. Knox was fine with this. He did not feel the need to know more. They were paying him well to do a very simple job. A job that provided him with the life he wanted. He pushed down the flicker of curiosity that occasionally surfaced. Knew some questions were best left unasked, especially when the answers might complicate his carefully constructed peace.

Knox pulled his truck up the roll-up door and stopped. Engaging the park function of the truck but leaving the motors engaged. Within seconds, the door rolled up quickly. He was always shocked by the speed of this door, having never seen a roll-up door move that fast. He engaged the motors and moved the truck through the door. Ahead of him, he could see the entire length of the building. A second roll-up door mirrored the first at the other end of the building. To his left, about halfway down the long space, a regular door and another roll-up door were all that occupied the entire left wall. This roll-up door was smaller than the one he entered, looking more like a traditional garage door. To his right, four 20-foot containers sat on their chassis, with a bright green forklift that was used to position the containers behind the tractor. Each of the four pairs of wheels under each container had been placed on a low platform with some sort of ball-bearing system that allowed the container to be moved easily into position behind the truck itself. The entire space was a bright white. Everything looked sterile and new, the only contrast being the containers and Knox's truck.

As was the procedure he was taught on his first day, Knox pulled the truck to the far end of the space and stopped at a line that was marked on the floor in black. He engaged the park function of the truck and turned off the power. He then exited the truck and walked quietly in the eerie silence to the side door. Inside the door, he was greeted by Chuck, who smiled kindly and extended his hand towards Knox. Chuck was about Knox's height, mid-50s, balding, and always dressed in khakis, a button-up shirt, a light sweater vest - usually argyle, and what Knox called old man shoes. His glasses and his thin frame made him look older than he probably was. He wasn't unattractive, but seemed to Knox to be the type that spent way too much time at work and not enough time having fun.

"Knox Creed." Chuck greeted him." So good to see you. How have you been since the last run?"

"Hi, Chuck. I've been good. Living my best life." Knox smiled back as he shook Chuck's hand.

"Let's have a seat and talk about the route." Chuck motioned towards a small conference table nearby.

The room was comfortable and had the appearance of the living room in a high-end home. There were two leather sofas facing each other, with a low table between them. Each sofa had two end tables, with expensive-looking lamps positioned in the center of each one. At the end of the two sofas, two cloth club chairs were angled slightly towards one another, with a small round table between them. A wet bar to the side of the conference table looked well stocked with a variety of snacks and non-alcoholic beverages in a small, glass-front fridge. A single door on the far wall was the only indication that there might be more to this room than it appeared. Knox had never been further than this room.

"May I get you something to drink?" Chuck asked. "We have a new coffee machine. It's called a Gaggia Magenta. I don't personally drink coffee, but I've heard it's good."

"Seriously?" "Knox reacted. "I have a Gaggia at home. It makes the best coffee. And… in that case, I'll have an espresso lungo. A double, please."

"Perfect," Chuck said. "Give me a second to figure it out, and we will get started while it brews."

"Actually, do you mind if I do it?" Knox asked.

"Be my guest," Chuck replied and smiled at Knox.

Know walked over to the Gaggia, pressed the power button, and checked the water and hopper while it completed the initial startup and rinse. After a few moments, he pressed the button for the espresso lungo, changed the setting to make a double, placed a nearby mug under the spout, and pressed start. While the machine did its thing, Knox walked back to the table and sat across from Chuck.

"So, what's the route?" Knox inquired.

"Easy one this time," Chuck answered. "Here are the stops." Chuck pushed a piece of paper toward Knox. The page had ten stops outlined with addresses and instructions for each one, as well as the best window of time to arrive.

Kingman, Arizona

Flagstaff, Arizona

Gallup, New Mexico

Albuquerque, New Mexico

Vega, Texas

Oklahoma City, Oklahoma

Fort Smith, Arkansas

Little Rock, Arkansas

Nashville, Tennessee

Asheville, North Carolina

Goldsboro, North Carolina

"This is an easy route," Knox stated as he stood up to get his coffee. He took a slow sip before returning to the table. "Whatever beans you are using, make an excellent cup of coffee."

"I'm not sure what they are, but I'll find out and have some sent to your house if you like." Chuck was sincere.

"You'd do that for me, Chucky." Knox teased. He had known for some time that Chuck had a small crush on him. Of course, Chuck would never act on it since it would mean losing his job. And he was so far outside Knox's type. But Knox was curious. Chuck just might be the greatest sex machine in the West. Nevertheless, it would never happen.

As Knox slowly sipped his drink, Chuck started the same speech that he did before every haul. "You know the rules, Knox. The container is locked. It can only be unlocked by the person accepting delivery. The name of this person is on the manifest for each delivery. You are not, under any circumstances, to attempt to access the container. The container is equipped with sensors and cameras, both inside and out, that deliver a constant feed to the BarsTech cloud servers. There are redundancies for power, signal, and security. If any authority should inquire to a degree that you are not able to manage, you should give them the envelope that is included with the manifest in this binder."

At this point, Chuck slid a narrow three-ring binder across the table in front of Knox. They went through this exact procedure before every haul. The only difference this time was the coffee, which Knox continued to enjoy slowly.

Chuck continued, "Knox, the security of our products and the strength of our reputation with our customers depend on your plausible deniability. Do you understand this?"

"Yes, Chuck, I understand." Knox had learned after the first haul that it was not advisable to be sarcastic, funny, or ask questions. What Chuck required, presumably for the cameras that covertly recorded their exchange, was a simple affirmation and acknowledgment.

"Good. Now, let's go over the route again." Chuck opened the binder and turned to the second tab, which had a copy of the stops that he had shown Knox previously. With each stop, Chuck informed Knox about the details of delivery, as well as any challenges with the approach to each facility. He had satellite images and diagrams of each one. Knox had a few questions about tight turns. Knox usually waited in the cab of the truck while the equipment was being unloaded, but Chuck had told him that at the Albuquerque location, he would not be allowed to wait in the truck. Knox had inquired about where he would wait, and Chuck told him not to worry about it. Evidently, according to Chuck, someone would be escorting him to a place where he would wait. This was a new procedure for Knox, and he was curious to see how it would play out. Nevertheless, he knew his role, and he knew his place.

When they had finished their discussion, Knox took the binder as he drained the last bit of foamy goodness from the bottom of the coffee cup, being mindful of licking the residue from the rim as he looked at Chuck over the rim of the cup. Chuck was staring at him with a slack countenance, his mouth slightly open. Knox maintained eye contact with Chuck as he placed the cup on the table.

"Please don't do that," Chuck said as he laughed nervously.

"Do what?" Knox laughed, turning to walk out the door to his waiting truck.

Chuck did not follow him out. Knox's rig was ready to go. The 20-foot trailer had been attached to his tractor, and he was alone in the loading bay. He walked to the truck, hooked four fingers on the door handle and pulled firmly to open the door. After climbing up in the cab, Knox settled in his seat, took a quick glance over his shoulder to examine the space and placed the binder in the pocket of the driver's door within easy reach. Knox never knew what he expected when he returned to his truck after these equipment pickups. He had left the cab configuration in the "café" mode, which looked like a table with two comfy seats instead of the bed. The secrecy surrounding whatever it was that he was transporting always left him feeling unnerved until he was completely off the compound.

He flicked the key to power the motors and engaged the gears to move forward. With slight pressure on the accelerator, the truck inched towards the roll-up door. As he approached it, the door quickly rolled up, allowing him to exit the building. The exit road curved to the right to join back with the approach road closer to the gate. As he exited the building, Knox noticed another approach road that seemed to disappear under the third building. So that must be how they get things in and out. He wondered how extensive the underground part of the facility was. He also knew that he would never know. And he was okay with that. He liked doing his job, and he especially liked the pay and freedom that it provided.

As he approached the gate, Janet stood waiting for him. The gate remained closed. He rolled down his window and handed her the binder, as was protocol. No words were exchanged on the outbound trip. Janet looked at the binder, scanned a few bar codes with her tablet, and did a complete walk-around of the vehicle. This process took way too long for Knox's comfort. When she had finished with her inspection, Janet handed the binder back to him, winked and gave him a salute before pressing the screen on the table to command the gate to open. Knox took the binder and placed it back in the door pocket, rolled up his window, and focused his gaze on the road ahead as he started his journey.

K nox headed back to Hwy 247 and made his way North to the I-15/I-40 junction. Twenty minutes later, he was trucking along at a good speed of 70 mph for the three-hour drive to Kingman, AZ. BarsTech insisted that he not exceed 5 mph over any posted speed limit. This violated every aspect of trucker life, but he had learned to accommodate the request. He actually found it relaxing to be able to take his time with these deliveries. Sometimes, he would listen to audiobooks, but mostly, he just put on a music streaming service and enjoyed the superb sound system that had come as a standard feature in the truck. Country was his go-to music, but he liked a wide variety, often choosing to listen to a mix that made his friends shake their heads in confusion. Today was a favorite of his, Knox's playlist #7 - a little EDM interspersed with recent country hits, a few Broadway musical numbers, a hip-hop song or two, and some Johnny Cash thrown in for balance.

It was almost lunchtime when he got on the road, and he didn't want to waste time stopping, so he reached into his snack bag, which he had placed neatly beside his seat, and retrieved a Slim Jim. He devoured his favorite snack, chasing it with a long drink of cold water from the large, insulated cup in the cup holder. He reached back into the snack bag and grabbed the big bag of trail mix, which he plopped firmly in the other cup holder where it extended over the edges but was secure, nevertheless. He liked the mix that was predominantly nuts, with dried pineapple, mango, and shaved coconut.

Singing along at the top of his lungs to Burning Ring of Fire, his mouth frequently full of nuts and fruit, Knox traveled happily along until he exited the highway in the small town of Drake, AZ. Following the directions he had been given, he traveled East on a paved road, passing a seemingly defunct and very large cement production plant. The sign on the large structure labeled it as the Cedar Glade Cement Company. He continued for several miles past the defunct cement plant until the road emptied onto a large industrial warehouse complex.

Knox drove past several large cement warehouse buildings before arriving at his destination. The complex seemed to have a diverse group of businesses - a food distributor, a real estate office, several machine parts manufacturing companies, and even a coffee shop and café. When he arrived at the address on his paperwork, he noticed the sign on the door: Administrative Offices of Cedar Glade Cement Company. Odd, he thought, considering the plant itself seemed abandoned. But again, he knew not to ask questions.

He turned into the parking lot in front of the entrance and parked the truck along the side of the building. He exited the truck, making sure to lock the doors, and walked a short distance to the glass door labeled as the main entrance. On entering the office, he was greeted by a heavy-set woman in her fifties, hair dyed a brilliant red, make-up that was too heavy, and expertly done acrylic nails. The rhinestones on her turquoise glasses completed the look.

"Good afternoon! Welcome to Cedar Glade Cement. You must be Knox." The woman greeted him before the door could close.

"Uh, yes. I'm Knox. I have a delivery." Knox responded as he handed her the paperwork associated with this location.

She politely took the papers from him, scanned them quickly, looked up with a smile, and handed them back to him. "Pull the truck to the back, reverse to the loading door, place the truck in park, and wait in the cab until someone brings you confirmation. Understood?"

"Yes, understood." Knox liked that these deliveries usually went quickly. He anticipated this one would take less than 15 minutes.

He walked back out to his truck, unlocked it, opened the door, climbed inside, and drove to the back of the building. He reversed to the single loading dock door, engaged the parking brake and shut down the motors. In the side mirror, he could see a black canopy extending out to shield the gap between the truck and the building. A few minutes later, Knox could feel the slight jostle of the container door being opened. Ten minutes passed before the same motion indicated the container door being closed. A man approached the driver's side window of the truck. He looked to be around

Knox's age, dressed in Dickies work clothes in dark gray. Close-cut hair under a ball cap and a clean-shaven face offered a friendly greeting above the two labels on his shirt that indicated his name was Carl and that he worked for the Cedar Glade Cement Company. He was attractive and looked fit, causing a fleeting naughty thought to cross Knox's mind. Carl made circles with his finger, indicating that Knox should roll down his window. Knox complied.

Carl grabbed the support handle, stepped on the entry step, and pulled himself up with ease to be on the same level as Knox. With his free hand, he extended a single piece of paper through the window.

"All done. Here's the proof of delivery." Carl said.

"Thanks," Knox responded, giving him a smile.

"You staying nearby?" Carl asked.

"Probably just park at the TA and get something to eat. Why?" Knox was curious.

"Tacos and Beers has good food. And a good vibe. If you like Tacos. And beer." Carl winked, jumped down, and started walking back to the building. In the side mirror, Knox noticed Carl looked briefly back over his shoulder before going back into the building.

Knox started the truck, engaged the motors and headed back to the highway. Once on I-40 East, it was a short twenty minutes to the TA Travel Center just West of Kingman. He pulled up to the EV chargers, which were inconveniently but safely located a long distance from the fuel stations, plugged in the truck to charge, and walked to the main building to use the restroom and check out what amenities they might offer. He was pleased that the restrooms were clean and private shower rooms were offered, for a fee, of course. Knox paid for a membership to all the major truck stop brands, so showers were discounted, and most of them had driver's lounges that offered free coffee and other amenities. Knox found an empty stall, locked the door, dropped his pants, and scrolled through social media feeds while he did his business. When he was done, he washed his hands well before exiting the bathroom and perused the aisles of the store and the menu in the restaurant before heading back out to the truck.

The truck had charged 70%, which was enough for the night. He would complete the charge tomorrow while he showered and had breakfast. As he moved the truck to the bullpen, where he would stay overnight, his thoughts turned to Carl's suggestion. Tacos and Beers did sound like a good plan for dinner. Once he had parked the truck in the well-lighted lot, he put up the window shades for privacy and looked up the place on his phone. The menu looked good. He opened the Uber app on his phone and typed in the address. Ten minutes was close enough to make it worth it.

Knox ordered the Uber and walked to the main entrance of the restaurant to wait for pickup. The app said the car was 2 minutes away. Soon, he was in a small SUV with his driver, Jenny, for the short ride to Tacos and Beers. Jenny prattled on tirelessly about how good the tacos were at the restaurant, but the real treat - according to 23-year-old Jenny - was their quesadillas. She regaled Knox for at least five of the ten minutes on the deliciousness of a crispy grilled tortilla stuffed with steak, onions, peppers, and lots of cheese. He was glad when the drive was over and was seriously considering having a quesadilla instead of tacos.

The interior of the place was exactly what Knox had expected. Colorful décor accented wooden tables and chairs typical of a Mexican restaurant. The main dining room extended to a bar area that was darker and had tables and chairs made to resemble beer barrels adapted for eating. The atmosphere made Knox feel instantly like he could settle in and have a relaxing evening with beer and good food. He ordered at the bar - steak quesadilla and a Dos Equis - and found a high-top table in the corner. As he settled in with his beer while he waited on the food, he observed the mix of people in the bar. The main dining room had been occupied primarily by families and groups, but the bar had a mix of couples, guys by themselves both at the bar and at tables like him, and a few groups of three. Everyone seemed to be content to be in the space they occupied.

The food arrived, and it was every bit as delicious as Jenny had said. Three bites into the hot, gooey, cheesy quesadilla, Knox took a swig of his beer and happened to look up in the direction of the entrance to the bar. A very attractive man stood in the doorway, looking around as if scanning the room for a familiar face. Was that Carl? Knox could not be sure in the absence of the labeled shirt and ball cap. The guy saw Knox, smiled, waved, and headed in his direction. It was Carl. Well, this is an interesting turn of events, Knox thought to himself.

"So, you decided to give it a try," Carl said. "Mind if I join you?"

"Hey…Carl, was it?" Knox replied." Sure, I'd love the company."

"Let me order some food. I'll be right back." Carl turned without waiting for a response and walked to the bar.

Knox stared as he walked away. Carl had changed into jeans, cowboy boots, and a western shirt with snaps, like what Knox was wearing. The jeans accented the most perfect ass Knox had seen in a long time. Carl's tight shirt and narrow waist hinted at a physique that was only achievable by a combination of working out and genetics. Carl soon returned with a beer and took the barrel-like stool adjacent to Knox.

"What'd ya get?" Knox asked.

"Steak quesadilla. They're amazing." Carl answered.

"I'll agree with that. My Uber driver told me I had to get it. After five minutes of her describing it, I knew what I was ordering before I even got here." Knox chuckled.

"I'm Carl, by the way." Carl extended a hand.

"Yep. I remember the shirt. Knox."

"Yep, I remember the manifest." Carl smiled and winked.

"So, you were hoping to see me here?" Knox was feeling forward.

"Yes. I actually had a hard time focusing at work. I kept thinking about what would happen if you I did see you here." Carl admitted.

"And what were those thoughts? I like directness, by the way, so don't hold back." Knox winked back and smiled. He knew his smile usually took guys to a place where they were headed.

"Uh, okay. Well, after seeing your rig, I was hoping you might show me the inside of it. It looks pretty special." Carl stammered.

"It is special. And yes, you can see the inside. Anything else?" Knox pushed.

"Uh, uh, I'm not used to guys being so forward, but here goes." Carl lowered his voice. "I was hoping you would bend me over and fuck the shit out of me. I also want to suck your cock, because I imagine it's pretty close to perfect. And I want to kiss you and touch you all over. And now I'm rambling like an idiot, and you're thinking that you've encountered the crazy guy at the truck stop."

Knox moved his hand under the table and placed it softly on Carl's knee. "Calm down, buddy. We can make all that happen." Knox looked directly into Carl's eyes. "I had the exact same thoughts when you handed me the papers through the truck window. So, now that we've established that we're going to have super-hot, mind-blowing sex in the cab of my rig, let's enjoy dinner and get to know one another." Knox winked and smiled again as he took a bite of quesadilla.

Carl reached over covertly and touched the front of Knox's jeans, feeling the push of his erection against the zipper.

"Yes, Carl, that's what happens when guys talk to me about getting fucked in my truck." Knox laughed as he took a drink of beer, letting Carl's hand linger in anticipation.

"I'm so fucking hard right now," Carl said. "I don't know if I can finish eating."

"You can finish eating, buddy. This is a sure thing for you, so don't worry about it. When I get started with you later, your dick is going to be even harder than it is now. Now tell me about yourself." Knox reassured him.

They talked and ate for another 15 minutes. Carl grew up in Kingman, studied physics at Northern Arizona University in Flagstaff, moved back to Kingman to teach high school, and got recruited to work for Cedar Glade. He had been there for almost ten years now. Knox told him a very glossed-over story about his upbringing, military service, and his journey to owning the truck and working for BarsTech. They did not discuss what Knox was hauling, but Carl seemed to think that Knox knew. Carl paid the tab for both of them, which Knox was only too happy to concede, and they walked out of the restaurant without speaking.

Carl walked them to his newer, black Toyota Camry, and they rode in silence back to the truck stop. On the drive, Knox reached over and slowly massaged Carl's crotch, feeling the erection return with force. Knox liked to tease the guys he picked up. He liked getting guys turned on - repeatedly - before letting them explode. It made for very memorable encounters, and he considered it one of his strongest sexual skills. A guy once had told him that what Knox did was considered 'edging' by most. So, Knox had eased into that practice when it suited him, like it did tonight.

Carl parked beside Knox's truck. Knox unlocked the cab and started the climate control on the truck's app before getting out of the car. He climbed into the truck and moved to the passenger seat, motioning for Carl to join him. Carl climbed into the driver's seat, and Knox locked the doors from the passenger side.

"Ever been in one of these?" Knox asked.

"No, give me a tour," Carl answered.

"Well, this is where you engage the motors," Knox said, pointing with his right hand as his left hand flicked open the top snap on Carl's shirt. "And this tells the battery level." Knox pointed to the gauge on the dash as he unsnapped the second button. This tutorial continued as Knox moved his face closer to Carl's, eventually running his hand under Carl's shirt and feeling the soft hair that covered Carl's chest. Carl moaned with each set of information. Eventually, Knox stopped talking and kissed Carl firmly on the lips, pulling away slightly and letting his mouth brush lightly across Carl's. As he kissed Carl's neck, his hand deftly unbuckled Carl's belt and the button of his jeans, slowly moving the zipper down. Knox hooked his fingers in the waistband of Carl's underwear and slid his fingers down to rub the head of Carl's throbbing, erect cock. Carl groaned with pleasure.

Knox abruptly stopped his affections and moved to the back of the cab, where he quickly converted the table to a bed, allowing the mattress to fold down. He sat on the edge of the bed, legs spread and motioned for Carl to join him. Carl exited the driver's seat and stood, facing Knox. Knox pulled him close and dropped Carl's pants to his ankles, releasing his erection. Carl's cock was six inches and fat, tapering to a cut head that was begging to be sucked. Knox took Carl's dick in his mouth, inserting it with one quick motion. He circled the head with his tongue and applied pressure with his cheeks as he moved his mouth along the shaft. The sounds emanating from Carl let Knox know he was doing something right.

Carl pulled his hips back to extract his cock from Knox's mouth.

"My turn." He said as he dropped to his knees between Knox's legs. He frantically unbuckled Knox's belt and unbuttoned his jeans to access Knox's pulsing hard-on. "Now that's what I'm talking about."

Carl went at Knox's cock with wild abandon. Knox had to stop him after a few minutes. "If you want to be fucked, you're going to have to stop this. Take off your shirt and pants and get on the bed." Knox's tone was commanding.

Knox himself stood and undressed as Carl did as he was told. Knox enjoyed looking at Carl, his tan skin telling of some southwestern heritage, his hairy body partially obscuring the cut of his athletic physique, and his smile making Knox feel like he was going to cum before he could get started. Knox lowered himself onto Carl, kissing him passionately as they ground their erect dicks into each other. Knox raised himself up and told Carl to turn onto his belly, grabbing a packet of lube from the shelf nearby.

Carl flipped over, his back arched, presenting his ass for Knox to take.

Knox squeezed the lube into his palm and gently massaged it into Carl's hairy ass crack before lightly stroking his own dick to get it ready. As Knox positioned the head of this thick cock against Carl's ready hole, he lowered himself onto Carl's back, hooking his right arm under Carl's neck and pulling his head back as he entered him. Carl gasped as Knox's cock spread his hole open. Once inside, Knox did not pause, his strokes slow at first and getting quicker, and Carl begged him to fuck him harder. Knox reached under Carl and grabbed Carl's dick as he thrust. When Knox shot his load up Carl's ass, his grip on Carl's neck pulled back harder as his grip on Carl's throbbing erection became tight. Carl shot his jizz onto the mattress mere seconds after Knox came. They both collapsed in exhaustion as Knox rolled off to the side, pulling Carl's backside into him to spoon him as they recovered. Knox softly kissed Carl's neck.

"That was better than I expected," Carl whispered, breaking the silence.

"Yep, you've got one hot ass. Made me cum super quick." Knox said.

"Thanks. Your dick felt great up there."

"Sorry, buddy, as much as I like this, I need to get some sleep. So, you're going to have to leave soon." Knox whispered softly, trying to be kind.

"Okay, I get it," Carl responded. "Can I have your number for the next time you are in town?"

"Uh, I really don't exchange numbers. Sorry." Knox was trying to be gentle but direct with this guy. He definitely wanted to keep it open for another time. "But I know where you work, so I'll look you up when I'm in town again."

"Okay. Please do. I could get fucked by you over and over." Carl seemed disappointed, which was the story of Knox's life after fucking guys like this.

They got dressed, and Carl exited the truck. Knox noticed that he sat in his car for a few minutes before driving off. When Carl was gone, Knox got out of the truck, locked it and went inside to use the bathroom and wash up.

Back in the truck, Knox stripped down to his underwear and climbed under the sheets. He turned on the TV, tethered the WiFi to his phone, and picked a retro sitcom to watch while falling asleep. As he lightly rubbed his chest hair, he thought back on what a good fuck Carl had been. If this first encounter was any indication, this was going to be one good trip.

Knox woke at 6 a.m., stretched his arms above his head, and looked down to see the sheet tented above his crotch. He knew he needed to pee, but he reached down and enjoyed a few soft and slow strokes just to get the morning started. Once his erection had subsided, he sat up on the edge of the mattress and reached for the portable urinal he kept in a cabinet nearby. Once his bladder was empty, Knox tightly closed the lid on the urinal and placed it in one of the cup holders by the driver's seat. He threw on a pair of sweatpants and a t-shirt and settled into the driver's seat before slipping on his boots with no socks.

He engaged the motors, not bothering to buckle his seat belt, and moved the truck to the charging stations, which were on the other side of the lot from where he had parked for the night. After plugging in the truck, he shouldered his duffle bag, which held toiletries and clean clothes, locked the truck, and started walking to the main building to shower. Knox paid the clerk for the shower key and started walking toward the hallway that led to the shower rooms. On his way, as he passed the coffee station, he heard someone call his name.

"Knox?" Carl said, dispensing coffee into an extra-large travel mug. His uniform was pressed and clean, looking just as dapper as he had the previous day during the delivery.

"Morning, Carl. You stalking me?" Knox laughed

"You should be so lucky." Carl chuckled. "I stop here every morning to get coffee. I thought you'd be on the road by now."

"Nope. It's only 150 miles to my next delivery, so I have the luxury of time this morning. Besides, I need to shower and get some breakfast."

Knox said.

"I don't have time for breakfast, but I can help you in the shower if you're interested." Carl sounded hopeful.

"Yeh, that might be nice." Knox leaned in close to Carl and whispered, "I was pitching quite the tent this morning, thinking about your hot ass. How about you give me a blow job in the shower?"

"Lead the way," Carl responded, gesturing with his hand towards the shower rooms.

Knox turned and started towards the shower rooms, looking at the key in his hand to make sure he went to the right one. Carl finished filling his travel mug, making sure the lid was screwed on tightly and followed Knox. Knox reached the shower room six, unlocked the door and entered, being mindful to not allow the door to close all the way. Carl entered soon after and closed the door firmly behind him. Knox dropped his bag on the wood bench by the door, kicked off his boots, stepped into the shower stall, and pulled his sweatpants down to his ankles. His erection stood tall, a clear message to Carl that the attraction from the night before was still present. As Carl approached, Knox extended a hand, palm forward.

"Stop. Take off your uniform. I don't want you to mess it up. And I want to see all of your gorgeous body." Knox commanded.

Carl stopped and slowly started removing his uniform. He unbuttoned his shirt first, pulling the tails out and allowing them to hang loose while he unbuckled his belt and unbuttoned his pants. Shoes were next. Carl placed them neatly on the bench beside Knox's duffle, removing his socks and placing them in the shoes. He removed his pants and shirt, hanging them on the hook above the bench. Carl stood before Knox in a tight black undershirt and black boxer briefs that could barely contain his erection. The undershirt came off next. Knox stroked his cock as Carl's muscles rippled under the layer of body fur. He dropped his underwear to the floor and kicked them to the side.

"This good?" Carl asked, smiling.

Knox stepped forward, wrapped his hand around Carl's thick dick, and kissed him deeply, pulling them together with the force of the action.

"Suck my cock and make me cum in your mouth," Knox said, placing his hands on Carl's shoulders and guiding him to his knees.

Carl knelt, took the head of Knox's hard cock in his mouth and slowly rotated his tongue around it, making small motions so that his lips massaged the ridge of the head of Knox's engorged and now throbbing dick. Carl wrapped the fingers of his left hand around the base of Knox's dick, removed his mouth from it long enough to spit in his right hand, then pushed it up between Knox's thighs as his hot mouth started back at working Knox's shaft. Carl's wet finger found Knox's tight hole and probed it lightly, gathering intensity and pushing deeper as his lips moved more quickly up and down a cock that was ready to explode.

"Jesus fucking Christ!" Knox said breathlessly. "You're going to bring me fast today."

Carl worked faster as Knox grunted and thrust his dick all the way into Carl's hungry mouth. As he came, Knox grabbed Carl's head and held it in place to make sure all his essence made it down his throat.

"Damn, you're good," Knox said.

"Glad you liked it." Carl stood, wiping at his mouth before kissing Knox deeply, exchanging some of Knox's own jizz. Knox reached down and started stroking Carl's dick, kissing him harder, pulling him in closer. He could feel Carl's balls tighten, so he dropped to his knees and took all of Carl's erection into his mouth. Reaching around and placing both hands on Carl's furry butt cheeks, Knox pulled Carl into him as his throat worked Carl's cock. Carl shot his load quickly. Knox swallowed every last bit, licking the head clean before standing up and kissing Carl deeply.

"Shower with me, and I'll give you my phone number," Knox said.

"Deal," Carl replied.

They showered, soaping each other up, kissing lightly, caressing each other's bodies. When they were done, Carl dried off first, took his phone out of his pants hanging on the hook, and texted his boss that he would be late. He then created a new contact and pretended to enter his number as Knox told it to him.

"It might just be me, but it looked like you weren't really doing anything on the phone," Knox stated.

"Yeh, you caught me. I already have your number entered. It was on the manifest." Carl admitted. "You mad?"

"Nah, you get points for creativity." Knox laughed. "I'll be back this way in a couple of weeks. Want to have dinner and do this again?"

"Yes, please." Carl smiled as he got dressed.

"Cool. I'll text when I know my ETA." Knox replied.

"Be safe. See you soon." Carl said as he exited the shower room and pulled the door closed behind him.

Knox smiled at this guy's persistence. Did he really stop here to get coffee every morning? Knox doubted it but was flattered either way. Now, he had a regular in Kingman. He got dressed, turned in the shower key to the clerk, who gave him a smirk of acknowledgment, and walked back to his truck. Once he had disconnected the charger, he spent a few minutes making the bed, not bothering to truss it up this time. This next leg was short, just 150 miles or so to Flagstaff. From the directions Chuck had given, this delivery might take longer, and he wanted time to have another enjoyable evening.

Once on I-40 going East, Knox put on an audiobook. He loved the science fiction work of Colton Taylor and was excited to start the second book in the Volywr series. The two-and-a-half-hour drive was pleasant and easy. Traffic was heavy, but the weather was good.

Knox took the exit for Bellemont, just West of Flagstaff. He continued along the frontage road until it ended and then turned South into the parking lot of the small, two-floor office building. The sign at the entrance to the parking lot read Flagstaff Research Labs: a Division of BarsTech Industries. There was a sign indicating that deliveries were to take the road around to the back side of the building. Knox maneuvered the truck out of the parking lot and along the side road to the back of the building. The road sloped down, revealing a lower level with a loading dock that was not visible from any other approach. Knox backed the trailer up to one of the two doors with their built-in shrouds. He placed the transmission in park and switched the truck's power to off. Then, he waited patiently in the truck.

After 15 minutes had passed, Knox started to consider that he might have to walk around to the front of the building to let someone know that he was there. Just as he was going to exit the cab, a tall man in khakis and a royal blue golf shirt approached the cab. He waved at Knox and motioned for him to exit the truck. Knox opened the door and hopped out of the truck.

"You must be Knox." The guy said, extending his hand in greeting.

"Yes. And you are?" Knox asked, reciprocating with the handshake.

"Brad. Sorry for the wait. We thought you might be arriving later. But we're happy that you are here." Brad apologized. "You can wait inside if you want. Grab what you need from your truck and follow me. This should take under an hour."

"You have coffee in there?" Knox asked.

"Yes. Really good coffee, actually." Brad smiled.

"Cool. Let me get my phone and mug." Knox replied, handing Brad the papers that he had been holding.

Brad waited patiently while Knox climbed back in the truck, grabbed his phone and travel mug, and climbed back down. Knox did not bother to lock the truck. He followed Brad in through a regular door to the right of the two roll-up doors. Inside, Knox found himself in a small but comfortable waiting room. A door on the far side presumably allowed access to the warehouse. The recessed can lights in the ceiling provided an amber glow that was a welcome calm to the typical lights found in offices. Two overstuffed chairs flanked a small side table and water dispenser that served both hot and cold water. The table held a single-serve Lavazza coffee machine, a variety of pods, a selection of teas, and packets of sweeteners and creamers. A shelf above the table held generic white mugs.

Knox slipped his phone in the front left pocket of his jeans and removed the cap from his mug, quickly realizing that it would not fit under the spout of the European coffee machine. It was a challenge that he had at home with his Gaggia. When he needed coffee in his travel mug, he would make several batches in a regular mug and pour it into the travel mug. So, that's what he did here. He had had coffee from this brand of machine once before and found it good but not exceptional. The variety of pods offered here, though, intrigued him. He selected a super crema from the bowl of pods and was very pleased with the result. Coffee in hand, he settled into one of the chairs to wait.

As he took a sip of the delicious coffee, his phone vibrated in his pocket. He had to stand up to remove the phone from his front pocket, checking to see who might be texting him as he sat back down in the comfy chair. It was Carl. He had some time, so I might as well chat with him.

(Carl) Hey Knox. How's the road?

(Knox) Good. Waiting while they unload. How r u?

(Carl) Day is good. Better after this morning, haha

(Knox) Yeah, that was a good way to start it

(Carl) Stopping in Flagstaff for the night?

(Knox) Yep

(Carl) It is only 2 hrs drive for me

(Knox) Keep your options open

(Knox) I'll let you know my plans once I'm parked

(Carl) Sounds good

Knox didn't usually allow repeat encounters with guys while on the road, but he was willing to make an exception with Carl. He slowly sipped his coffee and had almost finished it when Brad re-entered the room.

"All done," Brad said, handing the paperwork back to Knox.

"Thanks. Have a good day." Knox replied as he walked out the door and back to his truck. Once back on I-40, Knox took his time on the 20-minute drive to the Little America Travel Center. This stop was one of the nicest truck stops in the country, catering to tourists as well as truckers. He knew that they would have clean showers and even special rooms set aside for drivers in the hotel adjacent to the travel center. Knox usually ran into friends here, which made him both nervous and excited. Some encounters were best not re-visited.

As Knox performed his usual routine of getting himself settled while the truck charged, his thoughts turned back to Carl. Maybe he would get a room tonight instead of sleeping in the truck and see what extended time with Carl might look like. The thought made him both horny and scared. Scared, not of the sex, but of the unfamiliar pull of something deeper, something that threatened the carefully constructed walls around his heart. That was new.

After organizing his stuff in the cab of the truck, Knox shouldered his duffle bag and walked to the main building of the large truck stop complex. The EV charging stations were located closer to the hotel than to the truck stop itself. The weather was pleasant, and he enjoyed the stroll, taking his time to appreciate the scent of the pine trees and the sounds of the birds chirping in the afternoon sun. He headed for the driver's lounge, hoping for the serendipitous chance to see an old friend or two.

The lounge reserved for drivers was a large room conveniently situated in the hallway that led to the shower rooms. The shower rooms at this place were well known because some of them also had soaking tubs, a rare treat for weary drivers. Several dark brown leather sofas and matching chairs dominated the space. A very large television had been conveniently hung on the far wall so that the movie playing on it could be viewed from any point. A variety of small side tables and round dining tables with straight-back chairs accented a long counter next to a row of vending machines that sold everything from drinks and snacks to condoms and toiletries.

Knox took a quick inventory of the few guys and one woman in the room and settled into one of the large, comfy chairs to check his email and social media feeds. A few minutes later, a tall, fit, black man entered the room. His close-cropped hair had a hint of silver to it, which only enhanced his muscular arms and shoulders that were bulging, along with his hairless, broad chest, in his tight, low-cut t-shirt. The 3-inch inseam shorts, earbuds, and gym bag slung over his shoulder told the story of a man who spent his leisure time at the gym. Knox recognized him immediately and smiled brilliantly as the guy walked quickly in Knox's direction.

"KC!" The guy said, dropping his bag to the floor and embracing Knox with a big bear hug, lifting him slightly off the ground.

"Bubba!" Knox responded, hugging back tightly. "I was hoping I'd run into you on this run."

"Man, it's been, what, at least a year, maybe more. What've you been up to, handsome?" Bubba's smile showed his genuine joy at seeing Knox.

"Oh, you know, living life to the best, like I do." Knox smiled back. "I got a new rig and a new contract. It keeps me busy."

"Wait. Is that your EV plugged in out there?" Bubba asked as he sat down in the chair next to Knox. "The one with the pup trailer?"

Knox sat back down in his own chair and crossed his legs at the ankle, his knee pointing towards Bubba. "Yeh, that's all mine. I'm super proud of it. Top of the line. All the options."

"So, what are you doing in Flagstaff?" Bubba continued. "I thought those electric rigs were only good for short runs."

"Nope. It charges to 80% in 90 minutes. But I only drive about 300 miles a day. This new contract has me making small deliveries along I-40. It's a dream job." Knox explained. "The short box is not heavy, which makes the range good. Plus, the company I work for installed a special solar booster on the roof, so which helps.

"That's amazing, man. I'm so happy for you." Bubba said. "Eat with me tonight. Let's catch up. I've never really gotten to spend time with you." Bubba winked at Knox. "I got a room for a couple of nights while my rig has some work done on it. The restaurant here is pretty good."

"Sounds good. I'd like that. What's wrong with your rig?" Knox asked.

"That old piece of shit. I need to get a newer one, but I'm attached to it. It's the radiator. That bitch goes through hoses like nobody's business. But I don't want to talk about that." Bubba went on, "I'm going to the gym for a quick pump. Meet me at the Silver Pine, that's the restaurant at the hotel, in two hours. It's been a good month, so food's on me."

"Deal," Knox said. "I'll get my stuff situated in the lot and walk over in a couple of hours."

Knox walked back to Cyber Wolf, disconnected the charging cable, and moved the rig to the lot. He spent the next hour cleaning himself up in the cab and re-packing his duffle. He had never hooked up with Bubba, but after seeing him today, he realized that this might be an option tonight. Or at least he was hopeful that it might be. On the walk to the restaurant, he thought about Carl. Would Bubba be open to a third? Even if not, Knox could easily entertain Carl by himself.

It was still 15 minutes until he was supposed to meet Bubba, so Knox settled on a bench along the path to the restaurant to text Carl.

(Knox) Hey. What r u doing tonight?

(Carl) Hopefully, driving to Flagstaff?

(Knox) Yep.

(Carl)

(Knox) Heads up, there might be a third.

(Knox) You okay with that?

(Carl) Sure

(Carl) As long as ur part of it, haha

(Knox) You'll get a lot of attention from me

(Knox) been thinking about you all-day

(Carl) same

(Carl) be there in an hour

(Carl) drop me a pin

(Knox) pin dropped, Silver Pine at Little America

(Knox) see u soon

(Carl) can't wait

(Knox) btw if you can stay the night, I'll get a room

(Carl) yep, that would be nice

(Knox) done

Knox realized that Carl had started the drive to Flagstaff before hearing from him. This made him smile. He diverted to the hotel front desk and quickly got his own room. He asked for the trucker discount but asked if they could put him in the non-trucker section. The front desk clerk was hesitant, but Knox told her that he had a family member visiting and wanted it quieter, so she complied with a smile. He walked the short distance to the restaurant, not bothering to go to the room first. He noticed that Bubba was already seated in a circular booth in the corner of the restaurant. The Silver Pine restaurant itself was very nice, not your typical truck-stop hotel place. It had clearly been recently renovated in muted neutral tones of gray and brown.

Bubba stood and gave Knox another big hug. Bubba had showered after his workout and changed into jeans and a fresh light gray t-shirt. They sat down and quietly perused the menu. They both ordered a beer while deciding what to eat. The server, a young, nervous man in his twenties, brought the two beers and took their order. Knox opted for the chopped steak, one of his all-time favorite meals. Bubba ordered the grilled chicken with a salad and steamed veggies, a meal that was predictable considering his physique.

"So, let me get something out of the way." Knox started the conversation. "You know I'm hoping something happens tonight? Right?" He was direct in his usual way, but there was a hint of hesitancy in his voice. "And if you're not into it, then that's cool. We can just eat and catch up."

"I was kinda planning on that," Bubba said, staring at Knox. "When I saw you in the lounge, it dawned on me that I regret not making this happen sooner."

"Here's another complication. Or maybe not. I've got someone driving in to see me. Carl. Hooked up with him yesterday. You good with a third?" Knox asked matter-of-factly.

"Hell yeh, always up for that," Bubba responded. "But hey, what's up with you and having a guy twice on the road? Isn't that against your rule? The KC I know never has seconds."

"I know, I know. This guy seems worth a second helping." Knox said. "Actually, this will be a third helping of this one."

"Well, if you liked it that much, I'm sure I will too. Does he know there might be three of us? Or is he expecting just you?" Bubba asked.

"I texted him and told him. He said he is okay with it." Knox answered. "I also got a room so he can stay the night. I might stay with him."

"Man, you are getting soft!" Bubba laughed. "But it's cool, my friend. You be you. That's what I always say. I'm not one to judge."

They laughed together at Bubba's comments. The food arrived soon after, and the two men enjoyed catching up about their lives on the road. As the server cleared the table, Knox's phone buzzed on the table, the preview of a text from Carl appearing on the screen.

(Carl) Just parked

(Knox) in the restaurant. Come in

"Carl just parked. He'll be in soon. You're going to like him." Knox smiled at Bubba.

Carl entered the restaurant, spotted Knox, smiled brightly and walked towards them. As he approached, Bubba looked at Knox and winked.

"Carl, this is my old friend, Bubba." Knox introduced them as Bubba extended a hand, which Carl firmly shook.

"You want some food before we go back to my room?" Bubba asked kindly.

"No, thanks. I had something before I left." Carl replied, not bothering to sit down with them.

"Okay, sounds good. I'll take care of the check on the way out and meet you two outside. Bubba stood and made his way to the cashier near the door. Knox and Carl exited the restaurant and waited outside.

"Good to see you," Knox said.

"Same," Carl replied. "I'm a little nervous. I've never been with two guys before."

"Bubba's a gentle giant. It's going to be fun." Know reassured him. "But you can tap out any time. No pressure and no judgment. Just let me know, okay?"

"Okay. I don't know why, but I trust you." Carl said.

Knox smiled at him and put his hand on Carl's shoulder, giving it a squeeze. "After we're done with Bubba, I want some time with just the two of us."

Carl smiled at Knox as Bubba came out the door and motioned for them to follow him. The three men walked in silence on the five-minute stroll to the building that the hotel had designated as driver rooms. Bubba's room was on the first floor. He pulled out a key card and opened the door to the simple but comfortable room. Two queen-sized beds, a console with a large television, and a small sofa made for easy accommodations.

Bubba entered first, kicking off his shoes, followed by Carl, then Knox, who closed the door behind him and removed his own boots quickly, leaving them by the door. Bubba motioned for Carl to have a seat on the sofa. As Carl sat down, he followed the other two and removed his shoes. Bubba pulled Knox to him and looked at Carl. "Knox and I have never been together, so the tension has been building for years. Watch for a bit, and then we'll include you. Okay?"

Carl nodded as Bubba pulled his t-shirt over his head, revealing a perfectly chiseled, hairless chest with small silver rings in each nipple. At the age of 48, Bubba's body looked better than most guys in their twenties. Bubba slid the four fingers of his right hand into the waistband of Knox's jeans and pulled him forcefully close. Bubba's lips met Knox's with a passion that had been building for years. Knox pressed his hips forward, feeling his own erection pressing against Bubba's hard cock, which extended down his leg under his jeans. Knox fumbled at Bubba's belt and pants, wanting to get his mouth on the monster pressing against him. Opting for a more direct route, Knox pushed himself away from Bubba and ripped open the snaps on his own shirt, letting it fall to the ground behind him as he knelt to face Bubba's crotch.

"Take off your shirt and unbutton your pants," Knox looked sideways at Carl as he unbuckled Bubba's pants and pulled them down around Bubba's muscular legs. "And then come join me."

Carl worked on following Knox's instructions as Knox turned his attention back to his target. He yanked Bubba's white briefs down to join his pants. Bubba stepped out of his pants and underwear, releasing a long, black cock that swung from side to side with Bubba's movement.

"Now, that's what I'm talking about," Knox commented as Carl joined him on his knees.

Before Knox could get to it, Carl's mouth was on Bubba's hard dick. With a mouth full of Bubba's cock, Carl's eyes looked at Knox's. "Take your pants off. I want to stroke your cock while I suck him." Carl said and resumed working Bubba's long, hard dick with his tongue. Knox complied, allowing Carl's hand to wrap tightly around his cock. Carl and Knox took turns licking the entire length of Bubba's shaft and sucking on its engorged head. Bubba's head arched back in pleasure.

"Fuuuuck, you two have magic mouths," Bubba exclaimed.

Knox and Carl continued working Bubba's dick, one hand of each man on Bubba's smooth, firm ass cheeks and their other hands massaging the cock of the other.

"Time for everybody to be naked," Bubba said, stepping back slightly and reaching a hand under the chin of both Carl and Knox, pulling them gently to standing. Their three sets of lips met as Carl and Knox finished removing their few remaining pieces of clothing. When Carl had removed his pants, Knox remembered why he was so into this guy. His body was beautiful, and his cock was nice and fat. Knox noticed Bubba admiring the same thing and gave him a wink as if to say I told you so.

Knox looked at Carl. "I want to fuck you. And I want you to fuck me." He looked at Bubba." Both Carl and Bubba nodded and smiled, understanding Knox's request to be the lucky Pierre.   Carl moved to the bed nearest him and positioned himself on his back, his knees bent and splayed, presenting both his hard cock and waiting hole to Knox. Knox knelt on his knees between Carl's legs, his own ass high in the air, presenting itself to Bubba. He started with circles of his tongue in the space just under Carl's balls. Carl moaned in pleasure as Knox's tongue slowly moved up the crease of his balls and up his shaft until Carl's throbbing head was fully in Knox's wet mouth. Knox worked Carl's cock with slow deliberation, taking a bottle of lube that Bubba had thrown on the bed and using one hand to wet Carl's hole while the other arm rested the forearm on the bed, his hand reaching under Carl's leg to cup his buttock.

Bubba stood to the side of the bed, enjoying watching the scene playing out before him. His hand ran softly over Knox's furry bottom, occasionally allowing his fingers to drift to the crack and tease Knox's hole, which quivered with each touch. When Knox had finished with the bottle of lube, Bubba squirted some into his own hand and liberally lubed up his own cock before resuming the attention to Knox's crack. As his slick hand moved slowly up and down Knox's hairy crack, he moved it all the way down to Knox's balls and onto his cock. Reaching between Knox's thighs from behind, he helped get Knox ready to penetrate Carl.

Positioning himself behind Knox, his feet still on the floor, he let his erect penis rest at the top edge of Knox's ass, gently sliding the head back and forth, enjoying the friction of the hair and skin. As Knox pressed his cock into Carl's hungry hole, Bubba let his own cock fall to Knox's tight hole, easing it in while Knox moved back and forth, working his own pleasure from both sides. As Knox entered Carl, Carl arched his back and pushed his hips forward, forcing Knox all the way in. Knox remembered this move as extreme waves of pleasure washed over him from the feeling of Carl's tightness massaging his dick while Bubba entered him from behind.

Once all three men were fully involved, Bubba placed his left hand on Knox's hip and his right hand on the center of Knox's back, keeping himself steady as Knox rocked slowly back and forth, working his own dick in Carl while working Bubba's hard cock from behind. Knox placed his palm on Carl's beautiful cock and let it slide against it. Knox's fingertips massaged the head of Carl's dick, occasionally venturing up his furry belly. Carl's body hair turned Knox on to a level he had not experienced in a long time. Knox's hand wandered up to Carl's cheek, his fingers threading through the thick hair until he reached Carl's shoulder. Knox moved his other hand to Carl's other shoulder and pulled himself entirely into and onto Carl's body. This motion caused Bubba's feet to lose traction on the floor. He fell onto Knox, his rock-hard cock making its way fully into Knox's ass. Fully flat on Knox, who was prone between Carl's legs, Bubba ground his hips in a circular motion, massaging deep inside Knox's hole.

"I'm very close, buddy," Bubba said breathlessly in Knox's ear as his eyes met Carl's.

"Fill my ass," Knox commanded, thrusting his hips back harder and faster. This motion made Knox shoot his load in Carl. Knox's hole tightened and quivered as the orgasm wracked his body. The pulsing sphincter around Bubba's dick made him cum. He pulled out quickly, pushed back to his knees, grabbed his dick with his right hand, and pumped streams of hot, milky jizz onto Knox's back.

Carl's hands, which held a tight embrace around Knox, became covered in Bubba's ejaculate. The feeling of warm jizz, combined with the continued pressure of Knox's hand on his penis, made him cum. As his balls tightened, Knox moved his fingers to encircle Carl's thick dick. Carl shot his load between them. Exhausted, Bubba collapsed on the bed beside them, reaching out to rub Carl's chest as Knox rolled off Carl's other side, nearly falling off the queen-sized bed. They all three laughed at this mishap.

"Okay, boys. That was fun, but Daddy's gotta get some sleep. You can shower, but then you have to leave." Bubba said.

"No worries," Knox said. "I got a room, so we will shower there. "Let's get dressed." He looked at Carl, gave him a quick kiss on the mouth, and rolled off the bed to a squatting position before standing. He helped Carl up. They both looked at Bubba's magnificent body as they dressed. Bubba had fallen asleep and was starting to snore gently. Knox and Carl left, quietly closing the door behind them. It was a short walk to the adjacent building and their private room.

"Did you like that?" Knox asked as they walked to the room.

"Yep. It was super hot. But I'm looking forward to some one-on-one time with you." Carl answered.

"Me too," Knox replied.

They walked in silence to the room. Once they were inside, Knox removed his clothes and walked to the bathroom. "Shower with me." He looked at Carl, an order more than a question. Carl quickly undressed and followed Knox into the bathroom. Knox turned on the shower to a warm but not too hot temperature, slid the glass door to the side and stepped in under the water in the walk-in shower. Carl followed Knox into the shower, standing in the back and allowing Knox to rinse himself off. Knox stood under the water, not acknowledging Carl's presence in the tight space. He faced the showerhead, letting the warm water run over his head and face. He ran his fingers through his hair and down his chest. He could feel Carl's hard cock occasionally brush against his ass as he moved under the stream of water. He turned to face Carl, pulling him close to him, feeling Carl's erection pressing into Knox's slowly growing one. He rotated them both so that Carl was fully under the stream of warm water. Then Knox kissed Carl. Slowly, gently, his lips barely brushed Carl's as his tongue darted in and out of Carl's mouth, exploring and teasing.

Their hard dicks fought for attention as the kiss became more passionate. Knox reached towards the pump bottle of body wash that was affixed to the wall of the shower, filled his palm with several pumps of soap, and rubbed his hands together before placing them on Carl's hairy chest. He softly caressed the soap into Carl's chest, moving his hands up to the shoulders, down the arms, around to the back and down to his buttocks. Knox's lips never lost contact with Carl's as he lathered him up.

Carl's soft moans and sighs let Knox know that he was enjoying this attention. Carl attempted to touch Knox's hard dick, only to find his hand brushed away each time. Knox moved his right hand down to Carl's dick, his fingers slick with soap, cupped the head with his fingers and ran them down the shaft slowly, pulling back towards the head, then grabbing both cocks together, Carl's on top of Knox's. Knox thrusts his hips forward fucking his hand as his erect cock massaged the underside of Carl's.

"Wash me." Knox directed, pulling back and looking directly into Carl's eyes.

Carl loaded his hands with soap and started with Knox's broad shoulders. Carl moved in to kiss Knox as he washed him, but Knox pulled away, maintaining eye contact. Knox liked the tease, and Carl was easy to get worked up. Knox would make sure that Carl's second orgasm of the night would be one to remember. Carl continued washing Knox, moving his hands to Knox's lightly hairy chest, then to his belly, and finally around to his hairy ass. Knox refilled his hand with soap and resumed washing Carl.

They continued to wash each other, enjoying touching each other's bodies under the warm water. Once they were sufficiently clean and rinsed, Knox turned off the water, grabbed a single towel from the rack on the wall and started softly drying Carl. Carl stood quietly, allowing Knox to enjoy providing the intimate attention. After Knox had sufficiently dried every inch of Carl's body, he dried himself with the same towel.

"Go to the bed, get under the covers, and wait for me there," Knox instructed.

Carl left the bathroom, walked to the bed, pulled back the solid white duvet and top sheet, and climbed in. He turned on his side, facing the bathroom door. Knox emerged from the bathroom moments later, his glorious body on display for Carl to see. Knox's heavy penis swung gently as he walked towards the bed. He stood at the edge of the bed, looking at Carl snuggled under the sheets. He allowed Carl a minute to enjoy looking at his body before he joined him. Knox settled in on his side, facing Carl. Carl reached out a hand towards Knox's chest, letting his fingers trace the hair before moving up to Knox's neck, where he let his hand rest softly.

Knox reached over and extended his arm around Carl's torso, pulling him close, their growing erections playfully touching under the sheet. Knox's hand caressed Carl's back, moving down to his furry ass, tracing his hairy legs with his fingers, then back up again. Once his hand was firmly on Carl's butt, Knox pulled him close, their lips meeting in a soft kiss that quickly escalated to passion. Carl's hands explored Knox's body with a frantic urgency that exposed his pent-up desire.

"Carl," Knox whispered softly into Carl's ear.

"Yes, Knox," Carl replied.

"Slow down. I'm not going anywhere tonight. I'm all yours till the morning." Knox reassured him.

Carl's motions slowed, allowing himself to enjoy what and whom he was touching. Carl's hands lingered on Knox's upturned thigh, enjoying the soft, light brown hair that covered Knox's legs. He slowly started moving his hands down to Knox's shin, then his ankle. As he moved his caressing hand, Carl used his other hand to push Knox flat onto his back. Carl moved himself to be prone on top of Knox, grabbing Knox's hands and interlacing their fingers as Carl gently moved Knox's hands above his head. Carl pressed into their hands as he kissed Knox. His kisses were forceful, locking their lips while exploring Knox's mouth with his tongue. He softened the kisses as his fingers released their lock on Knox's, his palms moving slowly down Knox's arms, enjoying every small tactile sensation of touching all parts of the man under him.

Carl's hands reached Knox's armpit and glided gently to his chest. With a slight push, Carl moved his body down so that his face was on Knox's chest. Carl allowed his face to rest softly on the bed of light brown fur as his hands continued down Knox's flanks until they rested on his hips. Carl buried his face in Knox's chest hair, breathing deeply and taking in the scent of soap and musk. He moved his face to the right, where his tongue extended to lightly flick Knox's erect nipple. Carl performed acrobatic moves of small, deliberate circles around the nipple, intermittently sucking and flicking with the tip of his tongue before returning to the circles. Knox's back arched in pleasure.

"You are so good at this!" Knox exclaimed under his breath.

Carl did not respond. He moved to the other nipple, pushing down with his hips as Knox thrust his own upwards in response to the sensation. When Carl had satisfied himself with Knox's nipples, he moved the focus of his very adept tongue to the rest of Knox's torso. He traced down the line of hair running from the patch at the top of Knox's body to his lower belly. Carl alternated soft kisses with movements of his tongue, stimulating Knox's skin with every touch. Carl paced himself, trying not to be too eager to get to his ultimate target.

That target was soon reached, however, as Carl's chin brushed inadvertently against the head of Knox's trembling cock. Knox took in a sharp breath at the sensation. He felt like he was going to explode. It had been a long time since anyone had been able to effectively edge him like this. Carl continued by rolling to one side, propping his head up on his hand, and using his other hand to trace the lines of Knox's hard cock with a single finger. Every touch of Carl's finger caused Knox's dick to flex. The sounds coming from Knox seemed like he was going to shoot his load. Each time Carl got a reaction from Knox, he pulled his finger away, watching with delight as Knox's cock bounced and throbbed.

With one single motion, Carl lowered his mouth onto Knox's thick cock, slid his lips to the base, then back up again, fully removing himself from it.

"Where's the lube?" Carl asked.

"Duffle. Couch. Front zipper." Knox could barely speak.

Carl rolled off the bed with a quick leap, landing on his feet and sprinting the few steps to the couch. He quickly found the small bottle of lube and had one hand greased up and rubbing his crack before he made it the few feet back to the bed. His super thick cock bobbing up and down as he moved. When he got to the bed, his lubed-up hand was on Knox's cock before his feet had left the floor. He straddled Knox, placing his feet flat on either side of Knox's thighs, allowing Knox's eager cock to brush against his taint before angling his ass to get the head in just the right place for insertion. With a swift motion, he lowered himself onto Knox. He sat there, Knox's hard, throbbing cock fully inserted into his hole. His hips did not move. He wasn't ready for Knox to cum yet.

Carl leaned forward, laced his fingers around the back of Knox's next, and kissed him, being mindful to move his hips as little as possible.

"How long can you last?" Carl asked, a smile escaping his lips.

"Not long. You've got me so worked up." Knox smiled back.

"Let me do all the work. Don't hold back. Just stay inside me until I cum." Carl instructed as he placed his left hand, palm down, in the center of Knox's chest, his right hand encircling his own cock. Carl started to fuck his own hand, causing his hips to rock back and forth, massaging Knox's erection with his tight hole. Carl's hand moved to the left, and his fingers playfully enjoyed Knox's nipple as he moved. The touching of his nipple took Knox over the edge. He moved his hips in rhythm with Carl's, emptying into Carl's hungry hole with just a few pumps. Knox, exhausted from the anticipation and final release, let his hands rest on Carl's chest as Carl continued stroking his thick cock. Knox reached one hand down to stroke the underside of Carl's balls. His fingertips brushed his own cock, where it remained inside Carl. This touch caused to Carl to shoot. Thick streams of jizz escaped his dick and arched across Knox's chest and face. Carl threw his head back in ecstasy as he orgasmed. The hand that remained on Knox's chest gripped tightly at Knox's pecs, clenching and releasing as he came.

Carl panted, his body heaving as the built-up tension exited his body. His hands fell back to rest on his own thighs. Their eyes met as Carl fell forward onto Knox. Their lips met, Knox's arms wrapping around Carl and hugging him tightly. Carl's hands gently caressed Knox's head, running his fingers through his shaggy, light brown hair. Knox softly massaged Carl's back as they kissed.

Eventually, Carl rolled off Knox and to the side, positioning himself with his head on Knox's chest, his arm draped over Knox's torso. Knox reached down with his free hand and pulled the covers up over them. They both fell asleep, feeling satiated in each other's company.

An hour later, Knox woke and carefully extricated himself from Carl's embrace. He walked to the bathroom, turned on the shower, waited for the water to get hot, stepped in and peed down the drain before washing himself. Once washed and dried with a fresh towel, he walked back into the room to find Carl watching TV.

"Didn't mean to wake you, just had to pee and felt like a shower." Know said.

"No worries. I need to shower, too. Will you be up when I finish?" Carl asked.

"Yes, I'll watch TV." Knox smiled and crawled back into bed as Carl walked to the bathroom and closed the door.

Ten minutes later, Carl emerged and got back in bed, curling up next to Knox.

"I don't know what all this means. I really like you." Carl admitted.

"I know," Knox responded. "I really like you too. I like our time together. You're different from the other guys I hook up with. But, Carl, I just don't do well with commitment. You need to know that. I want to see you again, but you know what I do for work. For right now, nights like this are the best I can do.

"I understand," Carl said as he burrowed deeper into Knox's chest. "I'm okay with it. Do I want more? Yes. But I knew what this was when I drove here yesterday. Is it okay if we keep in touch?"

"I'd like that. I don't have many people that I keep in touch with regularly. Just don't get upset if I don't reply right away. Being on the road can be tough for quick responses." Knox pulled Carl closer, enjoying the cuddling.

"Got it," Carl said. "Let's get some more sleep and then have breakfast?"

"Sounds good. As long as you let me blow you when we wake up. I missed my

chance to have so time with that thick cock of yours." Knox kissed the top of Carl's head with genuine affection.

Carl laughed, "Deal."

Knox turned off the TV and rolled Carl over so he could spoon him. They soon fell asleep and woke a few hours later. As promised, Knox gave Carl a mind-exploding blow job. Followed by Knox jerking off while Carl kissed him and fingered his hole – one of Knox's favorite things. They cuddled for a few minutes before admitting that they needed to get moving.

They did not speak much as they got dressed.

"Let's get some breakfast, then I need to get on the road," Knox said.

"Sounds good. Do you need to top up the Wolf while we eat?" Carl asked.

"Yes, I do. Want to help plug it in?"

"Yes, please." Carl smiled brightly. "Your truck fascinates me. I've never seen anything like it."

They packed up their small duffle bags and walked to the front desk to check out before walking to Cyber Wolf. Carl climbed in on the passenger side as if he belonged there. This made Knox smile but also a bit uncomfortable.

"What's your next stop?" Carl asked.

"Gallup, then Albuquerque," Knox answered as he parked the truck at the charging station.

Carl got out of the truck with Knox and watched him inquisitively as he connected the charging cable. Knox then opened the app and showed Carl how he could monitor the truck remotely. Knox locked the truck, and they walked to get breakfast while it charged. Back at the Silver Pine, Knox ordered biscuits and gravy – his favorite on the road – while Carl was happy with a bowl of oatmeal and fruit. Both had black coffee.

"So, give me some ground rules. I want to keep you as a friend, possibly with benefits, and don't want to push you away." Carl said.

"No rules, Carl. We're not a couple. I do want us to be friends. And I abso-fucking-lutely want the benefits." Knox smiled. "You can text me, call me, whatever you feel like doing. Just let me reply at my pace. Okay?"

"Okay." Carl smiled back, showing he truly seemed okay with this.

They finished their meal and walked back to Knox's rig. Knox unplugged the truck, stowed the charging cable, and motioned for Carl to join him in the cab. Carl climbed in and closed the door. Knox grabbed him and pulled him close, kissing him passionately before nestling his face in Carl's neck.

"I don't usually get this way over, guys, but I'm gonna miss you. Keep in touch. Just be patient with me, okay?" Knox was nervous admitting this to Carl.

"It's all good, Knox. You do what you are comfortable with. Let me know when you are passing through again, and we'll catch up." Carl reassured him.

"Thanks, Buddy," Knox said, giving Carl one last, tight hug.

Carl climbed down out of the cab and started the walk back towards the hotel and to his car. Knox watched him walk away, trying to sort out the feelings he was experiencing. Pushing everything down in true Knox Creed fashion, he engaged the engine and guided the truck onto I-40 East toward Gallup, New Mexico.

Knox settled in for the 3-hour drive to his next destination. Gallup was only two and a half hours away, but the notes that Chuck had made on the itinerary indicated that he should expect an additional 30 minutes to get to the delivery point once he exited the highway. The flat desert scenery and bright sun allowed him time to think about the past two days. It had been good to see Bubba. And the sex with Bubba had been hot. It's not as satisfying as the sex with Carl, though. This thought troubled Knox. Was he falling in love with Carl? Knox resisted this notion. He had enjoyed a night of extremely satisfying sex intermingled with emotional intimacy. Yes, the depth of the intimacy was more than he had experienced with other guys, but in his eyes, that did not equate to love. Love involves trust. And Knox did not know Carl well enough to truly trust him. Not yet, at least. Nevertheless, he would keep in contact with Carl. He could use a good friend, and he had a feeling that Carl could deliver on that over time.

Just a few miles before reaching Gallup, Knox exited and took Highway 491 North toward the small town of Gamerco. Fifteen minutes later, Knox had passed the town , according to the sign on the side of the road, was entering Navajo Nation Off-Reservation Trust Land. He made a mental note to look that up later, having no idea what it actually meant. Two miles later, he turned left onto a paved side road and drove the final mile to the delivery location.

The sign in front of the low-profile building read Navajo Nation STEM Education and Research Center. Interesting, thought Knox. The building itself looked like a very long, one-story adobe home. Painted the typical golden ochre of other pueblo buildings, there were no windows and only one door in front of the small parking lot. A sign situated near the approach indicated that deliveries were to the left and around the back. Knox slowly drove the truck past the building and noticed a narrow service road that circled to the back of the building. As he proceeded along the narrow road, Knox noticed that the building extended much further back than was noticeable from the front. Midway along the wall of the massive building, a two-bay loading dock was recessed into the building itself. A normal-sized pedestrian door separated the two roll-up doors. The shadow cast by the bright sun on the corners of the building made the alcove appear secretive and sinister in the desert heat. Knox loathed recessed loading docks. There was just too much room for error backing the short trailer along a tight wall to get it aligned with the roll-up door. Nevertheless, he had a natural gift for backing the rig and positioned it perfectly on the first try.

As usual, Knox remained in the cab until someone approached the truck with further instructions. Within minutes of docking the truck, the smaller door opened, and a woman approached the truck. Clearly native American, she was dressed in a light tan-colored pantsuit that complimented her stocky frame. Her jet-black hair was pulled back in a ponytail that extended down her back to her waist. She squinted against the bright sun as she motioned for Knox to roll down his window. Knox complied and returned her smile in greeting.

"Welcome. I'm Sarah. May I see your paperwork and ID, please." The woman asked as she climbed up on the running board, expertly grabbing the support handle in the process.

"Hi, Sarah. I'm Knox. Here ya go." Knox replied, still smiling as he handed her the paperwork and his driver's license.

Sarah looked at the papers, then a quick glance at the license before handing it back to him. She kept the paperwork and hopped down from the running board.

"This will only take about ten minutes," Sarah said. "I'm pretty sure we're your smallest delivery. Please wait in the truck, if you don't mind. I'll be back out soon."

Sarah turned and walked back to the building, not waiting for acknowledgment from Knox. She tapped a badge on the pad beside the door and entered a code on the keypad below it. In his side mirror, Knox watched her enter the building, then moved to the back of the cab, which he had converted back to the dinette configuration before he started out that morning. Settling into one of the comfy seats, he opened the texts on his phone to see a message from Carl.

(Carl) Hey!

(Carl) Just saying hi

Knox debated about whether to text back now or wait. He decided it would be cruel to purposefully keep Carl hanging. It was a novel feeling, this urge to respond. A tug-of-war between the self-sufficient Knox Creed and a nascent desire for something softer, something messy.

(Knox) Hey buddy!

(Knox) Easy drive today. Waiting at the delivery site.

(Knox) Going to sit here in Gallup for the night.

Knox hesitated. How much did he want to tell this guy about how nice it was to be with him. Fuck it, he thought. What's the worst that could happen?

(Knox) I enjoyed my time with you.

(Carl) …

Knox didn't have a lot of time to chat, and he didn't want to keep him hanging.

(Knox) Getting back on the road. Maybe FT tonight?

Knox hit send before thinking. What the fuck was he doing? FaceTiming with a hook-up? He must be getting soft in his old age. He chuckled to himself at the absurdity of this, considering his looks, stamina, and mental acuity told of anything but old age.

There was a knock on the side of the truck as Knox quickly moved to the driver's seat. Sarah was waiting with a smile as Knox rolled down the window.

"Here ya go. All set. Safe travels." She said, handing him a single piece of paper, which he deftly filed with the others. As Sarah walked back to the building and Knox engaged the electric motors, He noticed a preview of two texts coming in from Carl.

(Carl) Me too

(Carl) Yes, to FT. Text me first when you get settled.

The thought of offering to FaceTime with Carl made Knox both nervous and excited. He promised himself there would be no sex involved. He really did not want to lead the guy on any more than he already had. He got back on 491 going South and took I-40 back to the West to get to the Love's Travel Center, where he planned to spend the night in his truck.

By the time he had plugged in the truck, it was early afternoon, and Knox was hungry, so he decided to scope out the food in the travel center. His choices were limited to things that were frozen and could be microwaved or a hot section of fifteen varieties of fried foods with sides of mac and cheese or mashed potatoes. Nothing looked appetizing, and he was not in the mood to venture out to find anything better. He used the bathroom and walked back out to the rig. He would sit in the cab while it charged and grab some food to go after moving it to the bullpen for the night. His phone app told him that the truck still had fifty minutes to 80% - just enough time to check emails and texts and scroll some social media.

Back in the cab of the truck, he settled into a seat in the back and searched several social media apps to see if he could find Carl. Within minutes, he closed the apps and threw his phone on the opposite seat in frustration. What the fuck was he doing? This was not like him at all. Settling back in the chair, he laced his finger across his chest and closed his eyes to think. Carl was just a good fuck. That's all. Nothing more. His mind wandered to thoughts of Carl with his shirt off. That chiseled, hairy chest. The perfectly sized dark nipples. The way his neck muscles tensed when he came.

Without noticing it, Knox found his hand slowly rubbing the growing mound in the crotch of his blue jeans. His erection had grown quickly just thinking about this guy. Becoming more frustrated with his uncontrollable emotions, he moved back to the driver's seat and exited the vehicle. 78% was good enough for the night. He would top it off in the morning. He unplugged and stowed the charging cable, closed the charge port door, and got back in the cab. It was a short drive to the opposite side of the small truck stop to get to the lot, where there were only four other trucks parked. Knox chose a space in the middle of them, put the shades in the windows, exited and locked the truck, and walked back to the building.

Dinner consisted of chicken fingers, mac and cheese, and a two-liter bottle of Coke Zero. He added a big bag of popcorn to have a snack for watching Netflix later. He felt like having a night in. He would eat and relax, watch some TV, and possibly FaceTime with Carl. He walked back to the truck, food in hand, as his mind consistently wandered to Carl. Was he actually looking forward to talking to him?

Back in the cab of Cyber Wolf, Knox kicked off his boots and removed his pants. He switched out his typical button-up western shirt for a well-worn cotton t-shirt and settled in at the table to have his dinner. He turned on the small TV and navigated to a streaming show about people looking for homes. It was one of his guilty pleasures while eating in the truck. After finishing the four chicken fingers, with honey-mustard dipping sauce and all of the generous portion of mac and cheese, he bundled up the trash in a plastic bag and put it aside to take out later. The half-full bottle of drink fit perfectly in the small fridge. Knox did not like to collect trash in the truck unless necessary. He cleaned his hands with the industrial-sized pump bottle that he kept in one of the storage compartments, converted the dinette to the bed configuration, and settled back onto three propped-up pillows to find a movie to watch for the evening.

Selecting a Rom-com, since he seemed to be in a weird amorous mood – a thought that made him laugh, he opened the messages on his phone and clicked on the one for Carl.

(Knox) What r u doing?

He placed the phone beside him on the bed and pressed play on the TV remote. He was twenty minutes into the movie, a playful romance-comedy about a girl who wanted a guy but couldn't have him for reasons that were not yet clear in the plot when his phone vibrated next to him.

(Carl) just got home. U?

(Knox) had dinner in truck

(Knox) in bed.

(Knox watching movie

(Knox) have popcorn

(Knox) join me?

(Carl) gimme ten, I'll call

Knox thumbed up this last text, placed the phone back on the bed, and pressed play. He felt a slight nervousness in his belly as he waited for Carl to call. It had only been five minutes when his phone buzzed repeatedly, the screen indicating an incoming FaceTime call from Carl. Knox sat up, rolled his shoulders to loosen up, and slid the button on the screen to answer the call. Carl's face and shirtless upper chest appeared on the screen. He was in bed, pillows supporting his head, a broad smile on his face at seeing Knox smiling back at him.

"Hey," Knox said.

"Hey," Carl said.

"What was for dinner?" Carl asked.

"Chicken fingers, mac and cheese. You naked?" Knox asked, still smiling.

"Yep. Why would I call you with clothes on?" Carl chuckled.

"I'm not complaining," Knox responded.

"Take your shirt off." Carl requested.

Their conversation was interrupted by a knock on the side of the truck.

"Hold on a minute. I'll be right back." Knox said quickly, placed the phone on the bed. Maybe the police doing a check? Maybe someone recognized his truck? He pulled back the corner of the shade on the driver's window and saw a woman standing below. The worn mini-skirt, halter top, and heels gave her away as a desperate hooker trying to make a buck or two in the slim picking of the small truck lot. Knox opened the driver door, kneeled with one knee on the seat, his erection clearly visible.

"Hey, Honey. Looks like you're ready for me." She said.

"Nice try," Knox said with a laugh, "unless you've got a dick under that skirt, you're barking up the wrong tree."

"Sure, you don't want to give it a try anyway? I can make you feel real good." She was persistent.

"Nope," Knox said as he closed and locked the door, watching to make sure she had moved on to the next truck before turning his attention back to Carl.

"Everything okay?" Carl asked.

"Fucking lot lizards," Knox commented.

"That's a real thing?" Carl asked.

"Unfortunately, yes. And they are usually skanky in these parts." Knox laughed. "But enough of that. Where were we? I think I was going to take my shirt off."

Knox propped the phone the small shelf on the wall beside the bed, making most of his body visible in the camera as he stepped back toward the front of the cab. If Carl wanted a show, Knox would give him a show. He crossed his arms in front of him, grabbing the bottom of his t-shirt and pulling it slowly over his head. He tossed it on the bed as he adjusted the erection that was evident in his bright orange boxer briefs. Standing still and looking at the camera, he heard Carl release the breath that he had been holding. Knox reached down with his right hand and rubbed his cock, which extended in that direction against his thigh.

"Is this why you wanted to talk?" Knox asked.

"Not really, but I like this. Please continue. We can talk later." Carl replied, clearly stroking his cock.

"Position your phone so I can see all of you," Knox demanded.

"Okay, give me a minute," Carl said as he muted the call. When he returned, he had placed the phone on some surface to the left of the bed. Knox could see Carl's entire form, his hairy torso, his hairy legs, and of course, that thick cock. Watching Carl stroke his dick made Knox want to pump his own fast till he came.

"This good?" Carl asked, looking directly at the camera as he continued to touch himself.

"Oh yeah," Knox said, pushing his underwear down to his ankles and stepping out of them. "Keep doing what you're doing. Seeing you like this won't take me long."

"Stroke it for me," Carl said.

Knox encircled his thumb and forefinger around the head of this cock and made small movements up and down. As he got closer to orgasm, he grabbed his pulsing, hard dick with his entire hand and made long strokes, the motion becoming quicker as Carl licked his own lips and continued to touch himself. Carl stared directly at the video of Knox jerking off. His moans became louder, clearly getting closer to orgasm. Carl's moans brought Knox to his destination. With a final pump of his fist, Knox held the base of his engorged penis as his jizz shot across the floor of the cab, some of it ending up on the bed. Knox reached his left hand up to the roof to steady himself, his right hand still gripping his dripping cock. He looked up at the screen of his phone just in time to see the ribbon of cum shoot from Carl's dick. Carl pushed his dick forward as he came, causing the thick liquid to land on his thighs. Knox was overcome by a sudden urge to drive the five hours back to Kingman and drop a second load in Carl's tight, hairy ass. As he came down from his high, Knox grabbed a tissue from the box on the same shelf as the phone, wiped his dick and the small amount that had landed on the bed, and relaxed back on the mattress.

He grabbed his phone and brought it to frame just his face and shoulders. Carl had grabbed his own phone and did the same. They were both smiling.

"Now that that's out of the way, how was your day?" Knox asked.

"Hold up. That was super hot. Let's acknowledge that first." Carl laughed.

"Okay, okay. I admit. That was hot." Knox laughed with him.

"Thank you!" Carl said, grinning.

"So, tell me about your day," Knox said.

"My day was good. I pretty much do the same thing every day. It's work I like, so that's good." Carl offered.

"I'm not really sure what you do," Knox admitted. "And I'm not really sure if I'm allowed to ask."

"Well, you know what you deliver, so you can guess from there," Carl said.

"Actually, Carl, I don't know what's in my truck. It's one of the conditions of my contract." Knox said hesitantly.

Carl was silent for several minutes, looking off in the distance, not sure how to respond. "Oh, I didn't know that."

"It's okay. I don't want to know. It works better like it is." Knox said.

"Okay, let's go with this." Carl started. "My team does research using cutting-edge technology. You deliver a crucial part of that technology. Can we go with that simplified explanation?"

"I like that," Knox said. "I do want to know more about you, Carl. But I was serious when I said I need to take it slow."

"Yes, I remember. I'm okay with that. Let's share one thing about each other. It can be anything. Sound good?" Carl's voice was kind and gentle, which made Knox want to share more than one thing with him. "I'll go first. I'm an only child."

"Okay, let's see, I'll go with the same then. I also am an only child." Knox laughed.

"You're making that up." Carl grinned again.

"I'm not. Seriously!" Knox smiled at him.

"Cool," Carl said.

"Okay, buddy. I need to get some sleep. Tomorrow's delivery will be a long one. Short drive to Albuquerque, but a long wait time." Knox's voice drifted off as remembered that he would need to look at the paperwork again tomorrow before he hit the road.

"Okay, Knox. I may need to rub another one while thinking about sucking your dick." Carl said as a big smile appeared on Knox's face.

"Goodnight, Carl."

"Goodnight, Knox."

Knox ended the call, put on his t-shirt, grabbed the bag of popcorn, settled back into the pillows, and pressed play. He drifted off to sleep before the movie ended.

Knox was curled up under the blanket when he woke at 6 a.m. He stretched his arms above his head as his legs stretched in the opposite direction off the side of the bed. He sat up on the bed, his feet landing flatly on the floor as he looked down at the erection peering up at him. He had to pee, but he stroked it a few times anyway, just for the sensation, a ritual that he always enjoyed. Allowing a few minutes for it to go down while he grabbed the portable urinal from the compartment under the bed, he stood, urinated in the container, shook the remaining drops from his now flaccid penis, and placed the container on the front console shelf to dispose of later. It would be a short two-hour drive to Albuquerque today. However, Chuck had told him that the delivery itself might take a few hours. The truck batteries had maintained 74%, so he would not need to top it up before the short drive. The solar panels on the roof of the trailer utilized the hot New Mexico sun to keep them at an adequate level between charges.

Knox grabbed a t-shirt and a pair of gray sweatpants from the compartment to the side of the bed and took his time putting them on. He slipped his boots on with no socks and casually plopped one of his favorite ball caps on his head. He threw his toiletries kit and a fresh change of clothes into his duffle bag and headed to the main building to take a shower and have some breakfast. As he stepped out of the truck, the desert heat hit him in the face with a force that was unexpected. The low humidity and moderate wind added to the insult. He tucked his chin to his chest and walked quickly to his destination.

The shower rooms were simple but clean, and Knox was washed and dressed before 7:30 a.m. He bought a breakfast burrito – sausage, egg, cheese, and green chilli – and a large coffee, choosing to eat in his truck instead of the small seating area of the store. Back in the truck, he quickly raised the bed and converted the space to the dinette configuration. He turned on the small television and watched a home repair reality show while he enjoyed his breakfast. He was always looking for interesting projects to do at his own home in his downtime, and these shows provided ideas during his mealtimes in the truck. When he had finished the burrito, which was just the right amount of spicy, he gathered up any collected garbage and tossed it in the bin nearby before refilling his coffee and settling into the driver's seat to start his day.

The drive from Gallup to Albuquerque was easy. The landscape was surprisingly beautiful this time of day, highlighting the rich red and ochres of the mesas, which contrasted with the browns and sparse greens of the desert. Driving East into the rising sun, however, was challenging, and he had to carefully position the sun visor to complement his sunglasses so that he could have a clear view of the highway.

Knox drove past the downtown area and exited I-40 on Eubank Blvd, going South towards Kirtland Air Force Base and Sandia National Laboratories. Shortly before the entrance to the Air Force Base, he turned left onto Innovation Parkway and soon arrived at his destination. The nondescript three-story building looked like any other generic office building, except for the unusual amount of land that surrounded it. It looked like the industrial park had been planned for additional structures that had simply never been built. The sign out front read *Sandia Industries*. He followed the directional arrows for deliveries, which took him to the back to the building, where a concrete ramp led to a lower level and directly under the building. Knox encountered a large roll-up door head-on. As he approached it, the door rolled up, and a gentleman in a black tactical security uniform motioned him forward. The guard walked slowly backward as Knox silently moved the rig forward and into the dark hold. As he moved forward, Knox could tell that there was lighting in the space, but it was dim. His eyes adjusted as he tracked the directions of the guards, who motioned for him to stop, and the door closed behind him. There was another door ahead of him that presumably exited the space. Or at least he hoped so. Backing the trailer in the direction of approach would be a bitch.

The guard approached Knox's window and motioned for him to lower it. Knox complied.

"Good morning. Please sit in the truck. Someone will be out soon to provide further instruction." The guard said, waiting for Knox to acknowledge the request.

"Sounds good. Thanks," Knox replied.

He did not have to wait long for someone to greet him. A woman approached his window. She was blonde, maybe in her fifties, and very fit, as evidenced by her perfectly tailored tan suit. She wore a white silk blouse that was open enough to show a hint of breasts that would make a straight man curious. Her stylish eyeglasses added to the mystique of the possibility that she could be either an executive, a scientist, or both.

"Good morning! Knox, is it?" She greeted him, smiling.

"Yes, Ma'am," Knox replied, returning a smile that clearly caused a flutter in her otherwise professional demeanor.

"Welcome to Sandia Industries. I'm Sandy. Gather your documents and get out of the truck, please. We will go into the conference room, where I'll explain your options while you wait." Sandy instructed.

Knox already had the paperwork in hand and had stowed his phone, and the attached slim-line wallet in his front left pocket in anticipation of having to leave the truck for a few hours. He opened the door and climbed down from the cab.

"This is some rig," Sandy commented. "I've never seen one of these up close."

"Yep, I'm very proud of it," Knox said.

"You should be. BarsTech is very selective about their drivers, so you must be unique among other truck drivers." Sandy complimented him.

"I like to think so. It's a good gig. I like the route and the work. And I get to meet nice, cool people like you." Knox returned the compliment.

Sandy smiled. "Follow me, please." She walked in front of the truck and entered a door on the opposite wall. Knox followed.

The room they entered was similar to the conference room at BarsTech. Comfortable furniture, a conference table, and a small, well-equipped kitchen area. The only noticeable difference was a separate alcove that was sectioned off by a glass wall and door. The alcove held two leather club chairs and a large television. Sandy walked over to the conference table and casually took the paperwork from Knox's hand, spreading them out on the table's surface and giving them a quick look.

"I'll need to see identification, please." Sandy was pleasant, but her tone had changed to have a business-like edge.

"No problem," Knox said as he pulled out his phone and extracted his driver's license from the attached wallet. He handed her the license, which she took, looked at it closely for a short moment, and handed it back.

"This delivery will take about three hours. You are more than welcome to wait here. There is plenty of entertainment, and we can have someone bring lunch if you like. If you wish to leave, someone will escort you out of the building, where you would be on your own to explore and make it back in time to get your truck. Understood?" Sandy seemed to indicate that they preferred that he remain in this room.

"Understood." Knox acknowledged. "I'll stay here. I can entertain myself here with no problem. As long as you have good coffee, which I'm sure you do. And lunch would be nice."

"Excellent. Please make yourself at home. I'll send Brian to get your lunch order." Sandy smiled again and walked back to the loading area. There did not seem to be any other entrance or exit to this space. Other than the door marked as a bathroom, there were no other doors.

When he was alone in the room, Knox surveyed the kitchen area and noticed that they had the same coffee machine as BarsTech, which made him smile. He took a mug from the tray next to the machine – tan with the company logo in black - and made himself some coffee. He walked over to the alcove and carefully opened the glass door, being careful not to spill the hot drink. He settled into one of the chairs, placed his mug on the small table nearby, and took the television remote to see what was offered. All major streaming services seemed to be available, so he selected one of the home improvement shows and pulled out his phone to check texts and emails. He was not surprised to see a text from Carl.

(Carl) *GM. How's the drive to ABQ*

(Knox) *Morning. All good. At delivery. Waiting.*

As Knox hit send, the glass door opened, visibly startling him. An attractive man in his twenties entered. His clean-shaven face and close-cut dark hair told of someone who might have recently separated from military service. He was dressed in light blue slacks and a black golf shirt. The pants and shirt clung tightly to what was clearly a fantastically well-toned body.

"Knox?" The guy queried. "I'm Brian."

"Hey, Brian," Knox replied.

"Sandy said you might want lunch. Anything in particular?" Brrian asked.

"What would you recommend? Anything special to this area?" Knox really didn't care what he had for lunch.

"There's a local Peruvian chicken place that's nearby. We all go there a lot. Grilled chicken thighs and house-made fries with this delicious green sauce. And pickled onions on the side." Brian sounded excited about this option.

"Sold!" Knox exclaimed, smiling at Brian.

"Cool. I'll be back in about thirty minutes." Brian said as he turned and walked out the door.

Knox settled back into the chair and noticed another text from Carl.

(Carl) *plans tonight?*

(Knox) *Not yet. But the guy getting me lunch might change that* Knox could see that Carl was typing, and then the three dots went away. It was at least five minutes before he got a response.

(Carl) *sorry, just had a moment of jealousy, lol*

(Carl) *hopefully, that works out.*

(Carl) *regardless, I want to hear about it*

(Carl) *FT tonight?*

(Knox) *Yeah, you know how this works.*

(Knox) *Play it by ear?*

(Carl) That *sounds good; let me know*

Knox returned to watching the show and checking emails. Brian arrived not long after with the food.

"Join me?" Knox asked.

"Uh, sure," Brian said uncertainly.

"Don't worry. I'm mostly harmless." Knox laughed as Brian pulled one of the small side tables forward and placed the white plastic bag of food on it. He took out two Styrofoam containers, two sets of pre-wrapped plasticware and four small containers. Two held a light green liquid, and two held purple pickled onions. Brian doled out the goods and opened his container to reveal the food. Knox did the same. The aroma was intoxicating. Charcoal grilled meat with fresh, thick-cut fries. Knox copied Brian as he tossed the pickled onions on top of the chicken and then poured the green sauce all over everything. They both started eating.

"This is delicious. Good recommendation." Knox stated.

"Thanks. I eat this way too much. But it is good protein. The fries are a necessary evil." Brian laughed.

"Are you from Albuquerque?" Knox asked.

"Yes." Brian said, then added, "I did four years in the Marines, then got this job, so I moved back here."

"Marines. That explains the body." Knox waited for a response. Brian looked up and made eye contact, then smiled and went back to eating. "I'm a former Navy, myself."

Brian ate in silence for a few minutes, then asked, "Do you have plans while you are here?"

"Not really. It's just overnight, then on to the next delivery. Any recommendations? Knox probed, hoping Brian would offer to show him around.

"Look, I'm just going to be direct. I think we like the same things, so I'm just going to be direct." Brian rambled nervously.

"Please do." Knox was enjoying watching Brian figure this out.

"I was planning on going to The Albuquerque Social for a drag show. That interests you?" Brian asked timidly, still unsure if he was correctly reading Knox.

"Yes, Brian, that does interest me." Knox grinned at Brian.

"Whew, I thought I was misreading you," Brian said with relief. "I'm meeting some friends there around 9. What's your number? I'll text you the address."

Knox recited his number to Brian and received a text with a pin to the address.

"I'm sleeping in my truck tonight, so I'll Uber there," Knox said.

"Nice. Can't wait. My friends are going to love you!" Brian said excitedly.

Knox helped Brian clean up the takeout containers from their lunch and waited for Brian to leave before making himself another coffee. This might be fun, he thought to himself. However, it was clear that Brian was more interested in introducing Knox to his friends than he was interested in Knox for himself. A familiar, quiet sigh escaped him. The thrill of the chase, yes, but a flicker of something deeper felt conspicuously absent.

The delivery took just over two hours. The time passed quickly after his lunch with Brian. Sandy had seemed rushed when she brought back the delivery verification paperwork and ushered him, politely but quickly, to his truck. Once in his truck, the door in front of him rolled up, and the same security guard from before motioned for him to move forward. Knox drove the truck out of the secluded basement loading dock and up a similar concrete ramp that joined with the main road. The drive back West on I-40 to the TA Truck Stop at the I-25/I-40 junction was short, and Knox had Cyber Wolf plugged into the Tesla supercharger nearby within 15 minutes of leaving the delivery location. While the truck was charging, he walked to check out the facilities. The truck stop itself did not seem to be in the best area, but he had been in worse. The showers were clean but worn and in need of renovation, as were the bathrooms, in general. But the staff was very friendly and accommodating, which seemed to Knox to be typical of the people in New Mexico. Knox returned to his truck and waited in the cab for the short time that it took to finish charging before moving it to a space in the lot.

Knox gathered a fresh shirt, underwear, and socks and threw them into his duffle. Locking the truck, Knox did a complete walk-around the trailer before heading into the building to shower. After a quick shower, he dressed and perused the food options, knowing that he should have something to eat before heading out for the evening. His choices were limited to things that could be eaten as is or microwaved. He chose a protein-heavy frozen dinner, supplemented with a separate frozen mac and cheese. He would cook these in the truck later, rationalizing that the protein and carbs would be helpful if he had too much to drink. With two hours until he needed to leave, Knox settled into the seat in the back and decided to see if Carl could chat.

(Knox) *FT?*

Knox's phone buzzed with the incoming FaceTime call mere seconds after he sent the text. Knox smiled as Carl's face appeared on the screen. He was slightly disappointed that Carl had a shirt on.

"That was quick," Knox said.

"Just got home from work," Carl said, matching Knox's smile. "What are you doing?"

"Just showered. Still have a couple of hours before heading to the club. Thinking about you." Knox said casually.

"You didn't think to call me when you were in the shower?" Carl teased.

"Then I would not make it out tonight!" Knox teased in return.

"What club are you going to?" Carl asked.

"The Albuquerque Social," Knox answered. "A guy at the delivery site told me about it. There's a drag show tonight. I'm meeting him and his friends there."

"Sounds fun," Carl said. "So, you're meeting up with guys from the delivery sites now?"

"Hey, Hey!" Knox scolded. "Need I remind you what happened in Kingman?"

Carl laughed. "I'm teasing you. But, yes, I'm also jealous. Listen, Knox, I know you're going to have sex with other guys. I just like you and liked being with you. I'm not as naïve as you think. Just let me tease you and give it back to me. I'll be okay."

"You know I can give it to you." Knox teased.

They both laughed. Knox talked to Carl while microwaving his dinner and while eating it. He found conversation with Carl easy. They chatted about their day and the upcoming deliveries. They agreed to check in with each other the next day.

Knox cleaned up the trash from his meal and dropped it in the garbage on the way to the main building, where he would wait for the Uber. The car arrived five minutes after ordering it, and Knox had a pleasant chat with the driver, an older local man, during the 10-minute ride to The Social on Central Ave. The driver had evidently had fares here before and dropped Knox off at the back of the building where the entrance was marked but would not have been evident from the street. Knox entered the club and learned that a membership was required. Hesitant to pay the small fee, another group checking in kindly took him in as a guest. Once inside, Knox was happy to see this small capsule of gay life in the city. Everyone inside seemed happy to be there. A hallway led towards a large room, a bar to the right, an open space with a stage to the left, and tables scattered throughout. The mix of people was more diverse than he had anticipated.

Knox scanned the room and noticed a head pop up from a small group in the far corner. It was Brian who proceeded to wave his arms in excitement, motioning Knox to join them. Knox made his way through the crowd toward them, getting looks along the way. He had a clear impression that he could have his pick of guys in the room at this place.

"Knox!" Brian screamed, embracing Knox with a big hug, his demeanor evidently different from work. Brian was dressed in tight retro shorts and a tight tank top, both of which left nothing to the imagination. He wore makeup, including glittery eye shadow and dark red lipstick. Although Knox still found Brian incredibly attractive, it was a look that he was not expecting.

"Knox, these are my friends, Kevin and Steve." Brian continued as Knox shook hands with the two gentlemen. Steve was clearly much older than both Kevin and Brian. Knox guessed him to be in his late sixties. He was attractive and looked fit, with salt and pepper hair, a nice smile, and an average face. Steve was dressed in khakis and a light blue button-up shirt. His loafers and general dress were at odds with Kevin's, who was dressed like Brian. Kevin was blond, had clearly coordinated with Brian to wear complimentary outfits, and had an outgoing personality. He was not as muscular as Brian, but his trim body was covered with light blonde hair that only accentuated his attractiveness. Kevin's face had the classic look of a blond lifeguard. Chiseled jaw, full lips, and floppy hair falling softly on his forehead. Knox was immediately attracted to Kevin and was curious about the relationship between Kevin and Steve.

"I'm going to the bar. Rounds for everyone? Knox, what'll you have?" Steve stood and placed a hand on Knox's shoulder with the offer.

"Old Fashioned, if they can make it. Otherwise, any whiskey will do. Neat, please." Knox said.

"Got it," Steve replied and turned to walk to the bar.

"Just so you know," Brian leaned forward and whispered in Knox's ear, "Kevin and Steve are a couple, but Steve only likes to watch. So, they generally take someone home to take care of Kevin. Just in case you're interested. I can tell from their reaction that they are interested in you."

"Good to know." Knox turned his head towards Brian. "And what about you? Do you ever participate?"

Brian laughed. "Not with them. Kevin and I had a brief thing a few years ago, but it just didn't work. I would normally be all into you, but I just started seriously dating this guy, and I want to see where that goes. I hope you understand, Knox."

"My loss then." Knox smiled and laughed. "I suppose I'll survive."

They laughed together.

Steve returned with the drinks. Knox hated cocktails in plastic cups but understood the need for them in places like this. The old-fashioned, itself, however, was not bad. Kudos to the shirtless bartender. The drag show started soon after and showcased Albuquerque's finest. It was not the quality that you might get in larger cities, but the Queens went all-out, and the crowd was happy and supportive. Knox had purposefully brought a pocket full of one-dollar bills and supported each performer as they worked the crowd.

During the show, Knox noticed Kevin's hand occasionally brushed against him. Between the overt touching and the looks that Kevin was giving him, Knox perceived that his evening would be spent with Kevin and Steve in whatever bizarre arrangement they might have. Knox was excited to find out what this meant. The show ended, and Steve cornered Knox as the crowd congratulated the performers.

"I think Brian might have told you about the arrangement that Kevin and I have," Steve said quietly. "I won't bore you with the details of why we do this, but let's just say it works for us. Are you interested?

"Yes, I'm interested," Knox replied. Can I ride with you two to your place? I can Uber back to my truck after."

"Of course, of course. Kevin is going to be so excited. I can tell he's really into you. We will go over ground rules on the way to our place."

"Sounds good. I'm looking forward to it." Knox responded.

As the crowd thinned, Brad said goodbyes to the group and left. Knox, Kevin, and Steve walked to Steve's SUV in silence. When they got to the vehicle, Knox got in the back seat, where Kevin joined him. As soon as they pulled out of the parking lot, Kevin leaned over and kissed Knox slowly and deeply, his hand running along the crotch of Knox's jeans to feel the bulge growing there.

"I've been wanting to do that all night," Kevin remarked as Steve looked in the rear-view mirror and smiled.

"Easy, Kevin, let's at least get him home before you give it all away." Steve laughed.

"You said something about ground rules?" Knox asked, wanting to make sure he knew what his role was in all of this.

"Yes," Steve replied, "Kevin likes to get fucked. I like to watch. I also like to touch and play, but when you two get going, I'll just sit back and watch. Sound good?"

"Yep. "Knox said. "Just no filming. Okay?"

"We don't like to film any of our hook-ups," Kevin answered for them. "So don't worry about that. Although, I will tell Brian about it. Hope that's okay."

"I'm good with that," Knox answered.

They arrived 5 minutes later at a very large, older, adobe-style, one-story home in the North Valley area of the city. Once parked in the garage, Knox followed Kevin and Steve into the home. Steve offered Knox a seat on a leather sofa in the living room as Kevin disappeared into another part of the house.

"Kevin is going to get things ready in the bedroom. We'll join him in a few minutes. Do you want a drink?" Steve asked. "I make a much better old-fashioned than the club."

"That'd be great, thanks," Knox answered.

Steve walked to a bar nearby and prepared two *old fashioneds*, returning to the sofa and sitting at the opposite end from Knox as he handed him the drink. "This your first time in this particular situation?"

"Yes. I've had plenty of threesomes, but never one like this. I'm curious, though." Knox said.

"You're going to like it. Kevin is a delicious fuck. Just pretend I'm not there." Steve continued.

"You know, I'm happy for you to join us." Knox offered.

"I know, Knox, but watching really is my thing. It's a long story about how I came to learn that about myself, but it is what it is. Nevertheless, I'm going to really enjoy watching you. You're a much better specimen than what we usually get here in Albuquerque. And the trucker aspect of it is taking Kevin over the edge!" Steve seemed truly excited about watching Knox have sex with his partner.

"Whatever floats your boat. I'm not the judging type." Knox raised his glass towards Steve in a toast.

"Okay, Kevin should be ready. Bring your drink, and let's join him in the bedroom." Steve instructed.

The bedroom was unlike anything that Knox had seen. A large steel "bed" dominated the room. It looked like an open cube with many hooks and attachments. The mattress was covered in black waterproof sheets with a variety of pillows arranged neatly at one end. A leather sling had been attached to the top of the frame and hung towards the end of the bed. A counter along the wall adjacent to the bed held a variety of accessories, including poppers, various bottles of lube, dildos, and leather straps. On the wall above the counter, hooks presented harnesses and masks. Kevin had changed into a mesh thong and leather harness that framed the upper part of his athletic chest. He had washed off the makeup, his hair wet and slicked back.

"Let's get you a harness," Kevin said, walking to the wall and choosing a brown leather model with brass studs and rings. He also selected a matching mask that reminded Knox of the Lone Ranger. He threw these two items on the bed and grabbed Knox's hand, guiding him to the end of the bed near the sling. Kevin took the drink from Knox's hand and placed it on a small table nearby. Knox kicked off his boots in the process.

Kevin placed his hands on Knox's shoulders, running them down the arms, exploring the musculature under the shirt. He reached up and unsnapped the shirt, button by button, forcefully untucking it as he got towards the waist of Knox's jeans. Knox shrugged his shoulders back to allow the shirt to fall to the ground. Kevin took in a deep breath as he ran his fingers through Knox's chest hair.

Steve approached from behind, still fully clothed, and ran his hands across Knox's muscled back, eventually extending one hand around to play with the trail of fur on Knox's belly. Kevin leaned in and kissed Knox on the mouth, inserting his tongue to explore the taste of sugared whiskey inside. His fingers expertly worked at Knox's belt and the buttons on his jeans. Steve started kissing the back of Knox's neck, continuing to explore the masculine body between him and Kevin. Kevin's hand reached between the jeans and underwear and cupped Knox's hard cock, allowing his fingers to trace the lines of the head before removing his hand entirely and dropping to his knees.

Knox was enjoying the sensation of having dedicated attention from both the front and the back. Kevin's face was now level with Knox's crotch as he pulled down the jeans and underwear at the same time, freeing the burgeoning bulge that had been straining to escape. Knox's erect penis hit Kevin in the face as it escaped his clothing. Kevin deftly caught it in his mouth, massaging the head with his tongue as he moved up and down the shaft in quick motions before standing up and facing Knox.

Knox could feel Steve's erection pressing into him from behind. He turned to face Steve. He attempted to start undressing Steve, but found his hand brushed away as Kevin forcefully turned him back to face him. As Knox stood naked, except for his socks, Kevin fitted the harness on him and gently placed the mask, which was surprisingly comfortable. Knox moved Kevin to the side of the bed and pushed him back on it. He reached down and grabbed the front of the mesh thong, pulling hard as it ripped away from Kevin's hips. Kevin's head arched back in pleasure as his hard cock was forcibly freed. Knox knelt between Kevin's thighs and took Kevin's small, erect penis into his mouth. As Knox slowly worked Kevin's cock, Steve continued to rub and massage Knox's body. Knox found this sensation intoxicating.

Kevin grabbed Knox's head with both hands and pulled it to his own face. They kissed passionately for a few minutes before Kevin moved his mouth to Knox's ear. "I want you to fuck me in the sling. I like it slow out and hard and fast in. Be as rough as you want."

Needing no other instruction, Knox got to his feet, grabbed Kevin's hand and pulled him after him. When they were both standing, Knox grabbed the back of Kevin's neck forcefully and moved him to the end of the bed. Knox pulled Kevin's face close to his.

"Do you like verbal, as well?" Knox asked.

"No. Just action." Kevin responded.

"Get in the sling," Knox said as he pushed Kevin hard up against the bedpost, then released him. Kevin complied, quickly climbing into the leather seat and fixing the leather straps around his ankles. Steve had taken a seat in the leather side chair, his pants unzipped but not unbuttoned, his fat, long, erect cock in his hands. He touched himself slowly as he watched Knox take care of his boy.

Knox kneeled between Kevin's raised legs and used both hands to spread Kevin's ass cheeks. Kevin's hole was pink, hairless, and looked very tight. Knox usually liked bottoms that were more natural, but having one that was this prepared wasn't so bad occasionally. Knox performed slow circles and loops across Kevin's butthole, occasionally darting his tongue into the center with force. He paid attention to Kevin's moans, repeating a move when it got more of a reaction.

"Fuck me, please stick your cock in me," Kevin begged.

Knox ignored Kevin's pleas, continuing to tease him. Knox reached up to the bed and grabbed a bottle of lube that Steve had placed there while Kevin was getting into the sling. He lubed up his right hand and ran the palm across the underside of Kevin's hard-on. Kevin moaned louder, and Steve stroked his own dick faster. Knox moved his lubed hand to his own cock and got it slick. He stood, rubbed the remaining lube on Kevin's hole, and positioned the head of his penis against Kevin. He could feel the hole quiver and flex with the sensation of the head of his hard cock pressing lightly on it.

Knox reached forward and took a firm hold on the center of Kevin's harness. They made eye contact, and Knox nodded his head up and down to ask if Kevin was ready.

"Please shove it in. Please. Please. Please." Kevin begged again.

Pushing hard and fast with his hips and pulling towards him with the harness, Knox entered Kevin with force. Knox felt his balls slap Kevin's ass cheeks as he entered. Kevin arched his back, moving his hips in circles to get as fully on to Knox's thick cock as possible. As requested, Knox slowly pulled his cock out, allowing just the head to remain in Kevin's pulsing rectum. Knox let it sit there, pushing Kevin away and maintaining firm control with his grip on the harness as Kevin tried to push himself back onto the cock.

"Fuck, you're a tease," Kevin said angrily. "Now fuck me, goddamn it."

Knox remained still, watching Kevin squirm. Without warning, Knox removed his hand from the harness and grabbed the chains holding Kevin's legs. He pulled hard on the chains, forcing Kevin onto him. He repeated this movement a few times, in fact, out slowly. Then he pulled out completely and placed his dick on top of Kevin's, using his right hand to stroke them together while running his left hand up Kevin's torso. Knox liked the feeling of Kevin's chiseled frame covered in soft blonde hair. Kevin continued to writhe in ecstasy. Knox pulled back and repositioned his cock on Kevin's butthole. This time, when he shoved in, he grabbed the harness with both hands. In fast and out slow, as requested. His motions got quicker as he approached orgasm. Kevin could sense that Knox was close.

"Come inside me. Drop a big load in me. Give it to me hard." Kevin begged once more.

As Knox came, he placed one hand around Kevin's cock and stroked. Knox came with force and ground into Kevin as his huge load emptied into Kevin's waiting ass. He kept his still-hard dick inside Kevin while he stroked Kevin's cock. Kevin tried to grab his own cock as his orgasm approached, but Knox fought his hands out of the way. When Kevin came, his body jerked and convulsed, his back arching as the spray of jizz slung in all directions. While Kevin was emptying his balls, Kevin looked to the side to see Steve stroking his massive cock with both hands. His hand moved fast, and when he came, his hips pushed forward as thick cum oozed out of the head in an amount that Knox thought might choke someone if that dick had been in their mouth. Steve collapsed back in the chair, his dick going limp, and the jizz continued to ooze over the legs of his pants and onto the chair.

Knox looked at Kevin, who was playing with Knox's chest hair.

"Did you enjoy that?" Knox asked.

"Oh, my god, that was good," Kevin said. "And by the way, Steve usually doesn't cum, so this was a treat for him, as well."

"Seeing what came out of him, I don't know how anyone could take that." Knox laughed.

"Yep, the first time I blew him, it literally almost choked me." They both laughed.

Knox pulled out and stretched out on the bed. Kevin unstrapped his ankles, slid out of the sling, and joined him. Steve went into the ensuite bathroom and closed the door.

"Just you and me?" Knox asked.

"Yeah, he doesn't like to cuddle after. He'll shower and get dressed again, so we have some time." Kevin said as he turned to place his head on Knox's chest, continuing to play with the chest hair.

Knox pulled Kevin closer and whispered in his ear, "I can go again if you want to get on top."

"Seriously? Uh, yes, please." Kevin replied as he stretched out on top of Knox, kissing him in the process. Kevin dropped his knees to the side of Knox and felt that Knox's erection had returned. Kevin ground his ass against it, his lips remaining in contact with Knox's. Knox reached for the lube and applied a liberal amount to Kevin's crack, letting his motions grease up Knox's cock, which quickly slid into Kevin's used hole.

Kevin sat upright and slowly moved his hips in circles.

"I LOVE this position," Kevin said.

"Me too. What about the fast in, slow out?" Knox acquired.

"I really like that, but it's more for Steve than for me. This position is my favorite." Kevin admitted.

They fucked in silence, kissing, grinding, Knox thrusting his hips while Kevin rocked his own. They heard the shower running and could hear Steve singing while in there. Kevin came first this time, shooting his load on Knox's face, which he proceeded to lick off while Knox continued to fuck him. Knox fucked Kevin for a longer time and came quietly inside him for the second time that evening. Kevin rolled back to Knox's side and reclaimed a place on his chest.

"Will you tell Steve about this second round?" Knox asked.

"No. He wouldn't care. But some things I just like to have for myself. Is that okay?" Kevin replied.

"Yes, Kevin, that's okay. You need some things just for yourself." Knox reassured him.

Kevin fell asleep on Knox. Knox wasn't sure what he was supposed to do at this point, but he decided that he really wanted to get back to his truck. He gently moved Kevin to the side, got out of the massive bed, and put on his clothes. He took his phone from the pocket of his jeans and ordered a ride, which would arrive in 3 minutes. He quietly left the room and exited the house by the front door, where the driver was waiting. It was a short ten-minute ride to his truck, which sat patiently waiting for him in the lot. Knox gathered some fresh clothes and his duffle and went to the main building to take a shower before turning in for the night. He thought of texting Carl to tell him about this adventure, but decided to wait until the next day, when they would have more time to talk.

After the shower, Knox dressed and went back to his truck. He settled in with a bag of popcorn to watch TV while reviewing the plan for the next delivery. The drive tomorrow would be almost four hours, and he wanted to get some good rest. He quickly drifted off, thinking about the evening and about Carl.

The noise of trucks moving around the lot woke Knox as the bright New Mexico sun seeped in around one edge of the privacy shade, which had not been securely pushed into the corner of the windshield. He stretched, reached his right hand into his underwear, scratched under his balls, and ignored the morning wood sprouting between his legs. He pulled on a pair of gray sweatpants that he had tossed on the foot of the bed the night before and grabbed a fresh t-shirt from one of the storage compartments. After slipping on his boots, he walked the short distance to the building to get coffee. There was some trail mix left in the truck, and he would make that his breakfast after he got on the road. But first, he needed coffee. He sipped the surprisingly good brew as he walked back to the rig, deciding that he would top up the batteries before hitting the road.

Knox drove the truck to the nearby supercharger station and checked his texts and emails in the 30 minutes it took to bring the batteries to 95%. He was surprised that there was nothing from Carl. Hesitant to be the one to initiate the conversation, his need to connect got the better of him.

(Knox) *good morning*

(Knox) *getting on the road soon. Just wanted to say hi.*

Ten minutes passed before his phone vibrated with a text notification.

(Carl) *Hey*

(Carl) *how was last night?*

(Knox) *interesting*

(Knox) *chat while I drive?*

(Carl) *sure*

(Carl) *call when ur on the road*

(Knox) *cool. 15 min*

Knox unplugged the truck, staged the bag of trail mix in the cup holder next to his coffee, and got on I-40 East towards Amarillo. Once he was safely past Tijeras Pass, Knox used the voice command function of the truck to call Carl.

"Good morning!" Carl answered the call.

"Hey, buddy. How's your morning?" Knox asked.

"I'm good. The real question is, how was your evening?" Carl chuckled as he asked the question.

"It was…interesting," Knox replied.

"Tell me. I can't wait to hear about it." Carl said.

"Well, I went to the drag show, and it was good. Met a couple there, Kevin and Steve. Kevin's in his twenties, and Steve is in his sixties. They invited me back to their place." Knox started the story.

"I can tell this is going to be good." Carl reacted.

"You don't know the half of it." Knox continued. "On the short drive to their house, they told me that I needed to fuck Kevin while Steve watched. Kevin was hot, so no problem there. But their bedroom is unusual. They have this massive dungeon bed thing that accommodates a sling and many attachments. So, I fucked Kevin in the sling while Steve jerked off in a chair nearby."

"Sounds hot." Carl said. "Wish I could have been there to see it."

"I wish you had been the one in the sling!" Knox admitted. "But, yes, it was hot. Not sure it's something I want to do again. But it was hot."

"Did you exchange contact info?" Carl asked.

"Carl. You know me. We didn't even exchange last names. Steve went to take a shower, and Kevin fell asleep. So, I left and ordered a ride back to my truck." Knox reassured him.

"That is pretty interesting. I want to hear more about that next time I see you." Carl said. Knox remained silent for a minute, not knowing how to respond.

"Where are you off to now?" Carl filled the silence.

"Amarillo," Knox said flatly, knowing that he was hurting Carl by not addressing when they might see each other again and not knowing how to stop doing it.

"Well, be safe. Text me if you want to talk tonight." Carl said, taking the hint that Knox wanted to end the conversation.

"Okay, buddy. Don't be offended if you don't hear from me. Okay? It's going to be a long day." Knox attempted to let Carl know that he might need a night off from talking.

"Got it. No worries, Knox." Carl replied and disconnected the call.

Knox settled in for the remaining four hours of the drive. The bright sun and cloudless sky should help the solar panels to keeping the charge on the batteries stable for the extended distance, but he would keep an eye on the energy usage, nevertheless. The route was relatively flat, so he did not anticipate any problems. He toggled the truck's touchscreen to see what charging stations might be on the route. There were two supercharges between him and his destination so which provided the reassurance he needed to relax and enjoy the bland landscape that promised an uneventful journey. He changed the touchscreen back to the audiobook screen and pressed play to finish the Sci-fi novel he had started a couple days ago.

Knox exited the highway at Vega, Texas, about 45 minutes West of Amarillo. He took the two-lane road South, driving past a large cemetery on his left. Just past the cemetery, the road ended at an intersection. Knox turned left, as indicated on the directions to the delivery and pulled into the driveway of what looked like a small home. Knox verified the address and parked the truck parallel to the front of the house, the end of the trailer aligned with the front door. The door opened, and two men approached the driver's side of the truck. Both wore jeans, boots, shirts similar to the ones that Knox always wore, and casual straw cowboy hats. Knox rolled down the window as they got closer to the truck.

"Howdy!" One guy said. "You must be Knox. ID and papers, please."

Knox handed the requested items out the open window. The guy who had spoken grabbed the handhold on the side of the truck and lifted himself up onto the running board. He took the papers with his free hand, looked at them briefly, and handed them to the other guy. The other man took the papers but left Knox's driver's license in the hand of the guy on the running board, who handed it back to Knox.

"It'll take us about 15 minutes to complete the delivery. You okay waiting in the truck?" The guy asked.

"Yep, no problem at all," Knox replied.

The guy hopped down from the truck and followed the other man back into the building. Soon after, the door re-opened, and two other men appeared with what looked like a folded tent that you normally see in people's yards for family picnics and barbeques. They placed the large bag on the ground and quickly assembled a fabric box that connected the back of the trailer to the door of the house. Knox watched in his side mirror as the contraption was erected in just a few minutes. Knox could not detect any movement after the barrier had gone up. Five minutes later, he noticed the tent collapse on itself, neatly folding into a shape and size that slid neatly into the storage bag. The men dragged the bag back into the building, being passed by the original man who spoke to Knox, who approached the cab of the truck. Knox rolled down the window and reached his hand out for the papers he could see in the man's hand. The guy handed them to Knox without stepping up on the running board.

"Thanks for waiting. You're good to go." He said.

"Thanks," Knox responded. This was the most bizarre of the deliveries so far.

Knox engaged the motors and headed back to the highway. He still had enough energy to get to the truck stop in Amarillo, 45 minutes away. He drove past Amarillo, deciding to spend the night at the Love's truck stop on the East side of town. It was an easy off to get to the supercharger, which was within reasonable walking distance to the truck stop building. Knox was looking forward to showering and a good steak.

He grabbed his duffle and plugged in the truck, listening for the sound of the autolocking system as he walked away. The ten-minute walk to the truck stop's main building was easy, although dusty. He had forgotten how windy West Texas could be. He talked to the clerk at the register to get a shower room and find out where he might get a good steak. The clerk's name tag said her name was Jill. She recommended the Western Horseman Club for steak. According to Jill, it was the best steak in Amarillo and Texas, and maybe even America. She also told him that there was room to park his rig in the back of the building. While he showered, Knox thought about whether it might be better to just take an Uber rather than drive the truck to the steakhouse. He didn't plan on having more than one drink, so driving there seemed the best choice. After the shower, he walked back to the truck and pulled down the bed so that he wouldn't need to worry about that later with a belly full of meat.

He drove the short distance to the restaurant and found that there was, indeed, plenty of space to easily park the truck. It was too soon for an early dinner, so Knox kicked off his boots and stretched out on the bed to watch TV until the restaurant opened. An hour later, he slid his feet into his boots, grabbed his straw cowboy hat from the hook on the wall, and jumped down out of the cab. He liked wearing the hat, and it seemed fitting for the location.

The interior of the Western Horseman was exactly what you would expect from the name and location of the restaurant. Rustic wood was accented by walls covered in rich brocade and dim lighting. The occasional splash of neon created an environment that was comfortable and uniquely up-scale Texan. Knox noticed a U-shaped bar at the far end of the large space and asked the hostess if he could have dinner at the bar since it was just him. Since the restaurant had just opened, Knox perceived that he was the first guest of the evening.

"Of course, hon, you'll have good company. A lot of guys like to eat at the bar when they're by themselves." She responded in a thick Texas accent. "Choose any seat you want. I'll bring a menu over. Ricky'll get you a drink as soon as he gets back."

Knox made his way to the bar and chose a seat midway along the far side, giving him a clear view of the entrance and the main dining room. People watching would be fascinating tonight, he thought. The hostess brought over a menu, silverware rolled in a black cloth napkin, and a small paper card with the specials of the evening. The menu was extensive and included gourmet items that Knox had not expected. In addition to the obligatory shrimp cocktail, other appetizers included a sushi roll, foie gras, and homestyle fried salmon cakes. Knox skipped past the variety of starters and entrees to peruse the section with a Texas-sized variety of steaks and chops. Although the 40oz tomahawk sounded appealing, Knox knew that it would pose problems driving the next day if he ate the whole thing. He decided on a ribeye, closed the menu, and waited for Ricky to return so he could order a drink. Ricky showed up a few minutes later.

"Sorry for the wait, bud. What'll it be?" Ricky smiled. He was heavy set, with an attractive face, and wore a loose-fitting black western shirt with the restaurant logo on the breast.

"Old-fashioned, first, please." Knox started. "Then I'll have the 16oz ribeye, medium, loaded baked potato."

"Gotcha. Choice of whiskey?" Ricky pointed both forefingers at Knox and made an annoying clicking noise. "Want some fried pickles? They're on the house tonight for the first hour."

"Yes, please. That sounds good. I love fried pickles. And your choice of whiskey, just make it a good one." Knox said.

"Comin right up!" Ricky said as he turned and grabbed a bottle of whiskey that Knox did not recognize from the shelf. He returned soon after with the drink.

"Local whiskey. Good stuff. Let me know what you think." Ricky said. "Pickles be out soon. I put a delay on the steak so you could enjoy 'em."

"Thanks," Knox said, taking a sip of the drink. "This is really good!"

"Thought you might like that." Ricky grinned as he walked away to help another customer on the opposite side of the large bar.

The fried pickles were delivered by a short, petite waitress, who simply smiled as she placed them on the bar in front of Knox and quickly walked away. They were delicious. Crunchy on the outside and juicy on the inside. The house-made spicy ranch for dipping gave them an extra punch. As he enjoyed the drink and the pickles, Knox occasionally looked around the room to see the tables filling up fast. As a large group of people cleared the host stand, Knox noticed a gentleman walk in with a hat similar to Knox's. He was taller than Knox at maybe 6'2", wearing jeans, boots, a bright teal Ariat snap-up shirt, and a bolo tie that looked like a rare turquoise. The bolo itself almost blended in with the shirt, and Knox only noticed it because of the way the light caught it as the guy turned. He was clearly of Mexican heritage with a well-trimmed, close-cropped beard. His smile was intoxicating as he talked with the hostess, who was clearly flustered at his good looks. She motioned to the bar. He must be here by himself, as well, Knox thought.

The man started walking towards the bar and selected a stool to the left and two down from Knox. Ricky looked up from pouring whiskeys, waved and smiled as the guy sat down. They clearly knew each other. Knox assumed the guy must be a regular. Knox returned to his drink, glancing to his left at intervals to get a better look at the guy. The man's face was not the kind of attractive that would be labeled as that of a model, but had the rugged attractiveness of a masculine ranch hand. His nose was slightly too large for his face, but oddly, it only made him look better. Knox noticed dark, shaggy hair extending just an inch below the back of his hat, telling of a full head of hair. Knox had a thought run through his head of running his hands through that hair. Odd, he thought. He usually had initial fantasies of other body parts. He was immediately aroused at the change in his own thoughts.

Ricky approached, and the man ordered an old-fashioned, which Ricky made with priority over the other orders. The guy grabbed the drink with his right hand, looked to his right at Knox, and lifted the glass in an air toast. Knox did the same and smiled. They both took a sip, and the guy set his drink back on the bar.   He extended his hand towards Knox.

"Ryder." He said.

"Uh, Knox." Knox fumbled, then quickly centered himself. "They seem to know you here."

"Yep, I come here at least once a week when I'm in town. Food is good. Drinks are good. People are good." Ryder said.

Knox did not detect any accent under the West Texas drawl. "I'm just passing through. Jill, at the truck stop, recommended it for a good steak."

"She did well." Ryder continued. "Best steaks in Texas. And old fashioneds." He smiled and lifted his glass again.

Ricky returned with Knox's steak, placing it down in front of him. The smell of the grilled meat made Knox's mouth water.

"Ribeye. Good choice." Ryder said. "Hey, Ricky! I'll have the same as my buddy Knox here. Medium."

"Comin right up, Mr. Garcia," Ricky replied and hurried off to the kitchen.

"Mr. Garcia?" Knox laughed. "You are either very important, or they are scared of you here."

"Maybe a little of both." Ryder laughed. "No, seriously, they're just very respectful folk here. Please eat, Knox. Don't want your steak to get cold."

"Thanks," Knox said as he tucked into the juicy steak.

The steak was amazing. Without a doubt, the best steak that Knox had ever had. It was perfectly marbled, tender, and flavorful to a point that seemed ridiculous.

"What do you think?" Ryder asked.

"Un-fucking-believable." Knox said, chewing on a bite of tender steak. "This is literally the best steak I've ever had."

"Good to know," Ryder said with a smile.

Ricky returned with Ryder's steak, which had clearly been made a priority in the kitchen.

"Here ya go, Mr. Garcia. Anything else for you, gentlemen?" Ricky asked.

"Not at the moment," Ryder answered.

No, but this is the best steak I've ever had." Knox looked at Ricky, who smiled and then looked at Ryder.

"What did I miss?" Knox asked, pausing his chewing and looking back and forth from Ryder to Ricky.

"The beef here comes from my family's ranch," Ryder said. "That's all."

"Well, my new friend. Your family knows how to raise cattle. That's all I can say." Knox continued eating as Ryder started on his own steak.

They ate in silence for a few moments, each enjoying their own steaks. Ryder took a bite of the loaded baked potato, savoring the flavors of bacon, cheese, sour cream, and chives with the underlying rich, unsalted butter. After he had swallowed the delicious bite, Ryder slid his plate over towards Knox and moved to the seat next to him.

"Mind if I join you for dinner?" Ryder asked.

"Please do," Knox replied with a smile.

"So, you're a trucker?" Ryder asked.

"Yep. I live in Barstow. My contract has me doing short distances along the I-40 corridor. Which is perfect for my rig and a really great job for a trucker, in general." Knox added.

"Wait. Is that your VNR Electric out there?" Ryder asked with excitement.

"Yes, it is. How do you know about the VNR? Most people don't even know that electric rigs even exist." Knox asked.

"I've been trying to take the ranch into the more efficient era. My dad doesn't fully understand it, but he lets me do what I want with the business as long as the profit stays strong. That's a lot to say that I just research the hell out of things." Ryder laughed. "I'm looking at getting the 4x2 version for the ranch. I'm trying to figure out if it can be used for transporting things around the property. We have some solar farms in different areas, and I think we can use those battery banks to charge the trucks. But I haven't pulled the trigger on it yet."

"That's amazing," Knox said. "I've never thought about that application of the EV trucks before. I got mine because it increases my profit once I learned how to manage the energy usage, of course."

"Honestly, Bro, I have so many questions about your truck." Ryder seemed genuinely interested in sharing information.

"Okay. But be forewarned, I love to talk about my rig, so once I get started, it might be difficult to get me to stop." Knox smiled and released a low chuckle under his breath.

"I doubt I would ever get tired of hearing you talk about your truck." Ryder laughed. "Would it be possible for me to see it? When we're done with dinner?"

"Of course. I love to show it off. I splurged and got every single add-on that was offered. So, it's pretty sweet." Knox bragged.

"Can't wait to see it," Ryder said.

They finished their meals, and Ricky cleared their plates.

"Dessert?" Ricky asked.

"Not for me, thanks," Knox said.

"The usual, please. Two forks." Ryder said, winking at Ricky.

"What's your usual dessert?" Knox asked.

"Toffee cake with cinnamon ice cream. You're gonna want to try it." Ryder looked at Knox. He suspected Ryder wasn't just talking about the cake.

Ricky showed up a few minutes later with the toffee cake.

"So, tell me about this toffee cake," Knox said, picking up a fork and letting it hover above the dessert.

"It's basically the closest thing to an orgasm without actually having sex," Ryder said, looking directly into Knox's eyes. "Toffee cake made with local butter, cinnamon ice cream made with heavy cream from local dairy cows, and candied pecans on top."

"The pecans aren't from Texas?" Knox asked, trying to keep a straight face.

"They are," Ryder answered. "A small farm outside Waco."

Ryder had been pointing at each element with his fork as he mentioned it to Knox. After finishing his elaborate description, Ryder stuck his fork in the ice cream, picking up a small amount on the tongs, which he then stuck in the cake. He used the thumb and forefinger of his other hand to pick up a candied pecan and dropped it on top of what was on his fork. He then placed it in his mouth while looking directly at Knox.

"Mmmmmm," Ryder mumbled, chewing the delicious dessert and rolling his eyes back in his head to portray his enjoyment.

Knox mimicked Ryder's method, pulling the fork slowly out of his mouth as he maintained eye contact with Ryder. Knox was silent while he finished the bite.

"Okay, I'll admit, that's some pretty fucking good dessert," Knox said, digging in and getting another bite, this time managing to get all three elements on the fork with one swoop. Ryder did the same. They continued taking turns at the mess on the plate until it was all gone.

"Thanks for letting me share your cake," Knox said.

"My pleasure." Ryder grinned. "Let's go look at your truck."

"Let me get the check first," Knox said.

"No need. This one's on me." Ryder said.

"I didn't see Ricky being the check," Knox mentioned.

"He didn't. Knox… I have a private arrangement with this place. We settle things at the end of each month. And Ricky knows you're my guest. So, it's on me tonight. Now let's go look at that truck."

Knox followed Ryder out of the restaurant and around to the back of the building. He really hoped he wasn't misreading the signals. He had a gift for knowing when a guy was interested, but this one gave him a small amount of doubt. As they walked towards the truck, Knox noticed a Ford F-150 Lightning parked nose-to-nose with the Cyber Wolf. The Ford was the same color. It looked like his rig had birthed a baby electric truck.

"Well, that's cute," Knox said. "It looks like my truck had a baby. Wonder who that belongs to?"

"It's mine." Ryder chuckled. "When I saw your truck parked here, I couldn't resist. Of course, I had no idea who drove this thing."

"The Lightning is a great truck. I was thinking of getting one." Knox said as he unlocked and opened the door to his rig. He motioned for Ryder to enter first. He told himself that he wanted Ryder to get an unobstructed view of the cab as his first impression, but Knox knew the real reason was to get a look at Ryder's butt as he climbed up the running board. And it was worth it.

"Wow," Ryder remarked as he entered the spacious cab. "This is like a small apartment."

"Let me show you around." Knox motioned for Ryder to sit in the passenger seat as he himself stood in front of the bed. "As you can see, the dash has the latest tech." Knox motioned to the dashboard and the large touchscreen. "And there is a lot of storage, including a small fridge, microwave, and TV. The truck has Wi-Fi that uses its own LTE data plan and can tether to other devices." Knox pointed to each item as he mentioned it. "And I can raise the end of the bed." Knox pressed a button on the wall, and the head of the bed raised up, then back down. "The bed folds up, and this area converts to a dinette for two. Although I've never eaten in here with anyone else." Knox was rambling at this point.

Ryder moved to sit on the bed beside Knox.

"Thanks for the tour. It really is a magnificent vehicle." Ryder said, reaching his left hand up to remove Knox's hat, placing it on the crown in the passenger seat. At the same time, he removed his own with his other hand and placed it beside Knox's. Knox sat quietly and still. He felt like he was headed into unfamiliar territory. He had been in this exact same scenario with plenty of other guys, but this felt different. He couldn't figure out why.

Ryder cupped his left hand around the back of Knox's neck and pulled him gently closer. He brushed his lips lightly against Knox's, allowing the almost touch to linger as his other hand rested gently on Knox's knee. Ryder pulled back a little and looked into Knox's eyes. The attraction was unmistakable. He pressed his lips hard into Knox's, his tongue finding Knox's tongue with gentle precision. The kiss was unlike anything Knox had experienced before. It was gentle and rough. Passionate and hesitant. Lingering and necessary.

Ryder pushed Knox back on the bed, pulling his legs up in his lap and carefully removing his boots. Ryder then kicked his own boots off and positioned himself on his side between Knox and the wall. He unsnapped each button on Knox's shirt. Slowly, letting his warm breath drift over Knox's neck, never actually touching the skin with his lips. Knox felt his breath catch with each click of the button that Ryder unsnapped. Ryder opened Knox's shirt, revealing his furry chest. Ryder ran his fingers through the thick, brown hair as Knox moaned in ecstasy. Knox reached up to unsnap Ryder's shirt but found his hand brushed away. Ryder stared into Knox's eyes as he unsnapped his own shirt, disclosing a toned chest with a patch of fine, straight, black hair in the center. Fingers of hair patterned out to cover his nipples and extended down across his belly, disappearing into the waistband of his jeans. Knox gently touched Ryder's chest hesitantly, as if questioning whether or not he had permission. Ryder took hold of Knox's hand and guided it across his chest to show that he would allow Knox to touch anywhere he wanted.

Hands-on chests, Knox and Ryder kissed. Slow, passionate kisses, exploring and teasing each other with their tongues. Ryder broke the kiss and pushed himself back, staring at Knox's face. His hand softly caressed Knox's head, tracing his fingers along Knox's jawline, over his lips, down his chin, and along the line of his Adam's apple. Ryder continued with his forefinger, running it along the centerline of Knox's chest, pausing slightly to explore each nipple before venturing down Knox's belly, ending at the top of his belt buckle.

"Stand up," Ryder commanded.

Knox stood. Ryder joined him, facing him, moving closer until their chests touched.

"Take off your pants." Ryder continued his demands. Knox complied, slowly unbuckling his belt buckle, unbuttoning his pants, and pushing them down to his ankles. He slipped his feet out of his pants, moving the jeans to the side with his toes. Ryder had stepped back to watch, the bulge in his jeans evidence of his interest in what was happening. Knox stood before Ryder in his underwear, his erection extending up towards the waist of his black boxer briefs, the head slightly peeking out from the top.

Ryder quickly mirrored Knox's motions, his white briefs straining under the pressure of his hard-on. He moved towards Knox and pushed him back onto the bed, re-assuming the positions from before. Their faces nuzzled into each other's necks; their hands explored unhurriedly. Not being able to resist, Knox ran the palm of his hand down Ryder's smooth back, pushing his fingers under the waistband of Ryder's underwear, relishing in the feel of his firm, round, hairless ass cheeks. Knox let his middle finger wander along Ryder's crack, noticing the soft hair that lined it. Knox pushed harder into Ryder with anticipation of seeing what was inside Ryder's underwear.

Ryder started with the front of Knox. His hand rubbed lightly over the head of Knox's erection, teasing it. With a slow and definitive motion, Ryder pulled the band of Knox's underwear down and hooked it under his testicles, freeing Knox's pulsing cock. Ryder resumed the exploration with his forefinger, tracing the shaft of Knox's hard cock, starting with the head and moving down to his balls before going back up again and lightly rubbing the pad of his finger along the ridge of the glans. Knox pulled Ryder's head towards him and kissed him hard, inserting his tongue forcefully into Ryder's mouth. With the kiss, Ryder wrapped his fingers around Knox's dick, applying hardly any pressure as he moved his hand up and down. The fingers of Ryder's hand caught on the head of Knox's cock as he stroked.

Knox reached his hand inside Ryder's underwear and wrapped his hand around Ryder's cock. He repeated Ryder's technique with the underwear, exposing Ryder's erection for Knox to see. Ryder's dick was not thick, about seven inches long, perfectly symmetrical with a well-defined head and a slight curve upwards towards Ryder's belly. Ryder's thick, black pubic hair was soft to Knox's touch as he cupped Ryder's balls and massaged the base of his penis. Knox gripped Ryder's hard dick, and Ryder's hips moved in motion to his own hand stroking Knox. Ryder's strokes quickened as he felt

Knox's balls tighten. Not being able to contain himself any longer, Knox thrust his hips forward and shot his load onto his belly, covering Ryder's hand, as well. As he orgasmed, Knox's grip on Ryder's cock tightened, causing Ryder to thrust faster until he came a few minutes later. The Jizz oozed out of his dick like a volcano, covering the entirety of Knox's hand and fingers. As he came, Ryder pushed his face hard into Knox's neck, kissing just behind his ear as his breath came in jagged gasps with the force of his orgasm.

They both collapsed onto their backs. Knox reached to a compartment nearby and retrieved a packet of wet wipes. He cleaned himself, then Ryder. Once most of the cum was wiped up, Knox turned towards Ryder and kissed him softly, exploring more of his body, then resting his face on Ryder's chest. Uncommon in its restraint, yet electrifying in its raw, unspoken promise. He'd never felt such potent anticipation, even with Carl. This was something else entirely.

"This is the most uncommon hook-up I've had," Knox said softly. "It was also the most intense." Uncommon in its restraint, yet electrifying in its raw, unspoken promise. He'd never felt such potent anticipation, even with Carl. This was something else entirely.

"It was the same for me," Ryder added. "I wasn't expecting anything, then I didn't know what to expect. But it was intense. I like your body. I also like your personality. I feel like I've known you for a long time, but I really don't know much about you."

"I know." Knox reciprocated. "I feel a connection that is odd for me." And we didn't even have proper sex." They both laughed.

"Knox, I need to go soon. But I want to keep in touch. Are you okay with that? I don't know what this is, but I think it's worth exploring." Ryder said. "But I need to tell you that it is important for me to take this slow. I don't form relationships easily."

"Funny you should say that," Knox responded.

"And…" Ryder prompted.

"You said what I was going to say," Knox admitted. "I don't do relationships. At least, I didn't think I did. But I want to get to know you."

"Let's do this," Ryder suggested, "I'm going to give you my number. Text me when you feel like it. We can just see where it goes. Deal?"

"Deal." Knox agreed as he reached for his phone, unlocked it, opened the contacts app, and handed it to Ryder so that he could enter his contact info.

They chatted lightly as they got dressed. Knox learned that Ryder grew up North of Amarillo, went to UT Austin, where he studied agricultural management with a minor in environmental studies, and that he was 29 years old. Ryder learned that Knox was from California, served in the Navy, and was 38 years old. The rest they could figure out as they went. Before Ryder exited the truck, he pulled Knox close and kissed him, then hugged him tightly.

"I don't want to leave," Ryder said. "This is so different for me. I don't know what's wrong with me."

Hey, Ryder." Knox whispered in his ear. "I feel the same. It's okay. I don't know what it means either."

With one final kiss, Ryder climbed down out of Cyber Wolf and got in his own truck. He gave a wave as he backed his truck up to leave. Knox sat in the driver's seat, buckled his seat belt, engaged the motors, and began the short drive to the truck stop where he would sleep for the night. He parked the truck and put up the shades for privacy. He peed beside the truck before turning in, rinsing his mouth with mouthwash and spitting it on the ground before he climbed back in the truck for the night. As he curled up under his blanket, he could still smell Ryder on his hands. He didn't fully understand what he was feeling, but knew that he would have clarity in the coming days. He drifted off to sleep, thinking of the feeling of Ryder's hand on his chest.

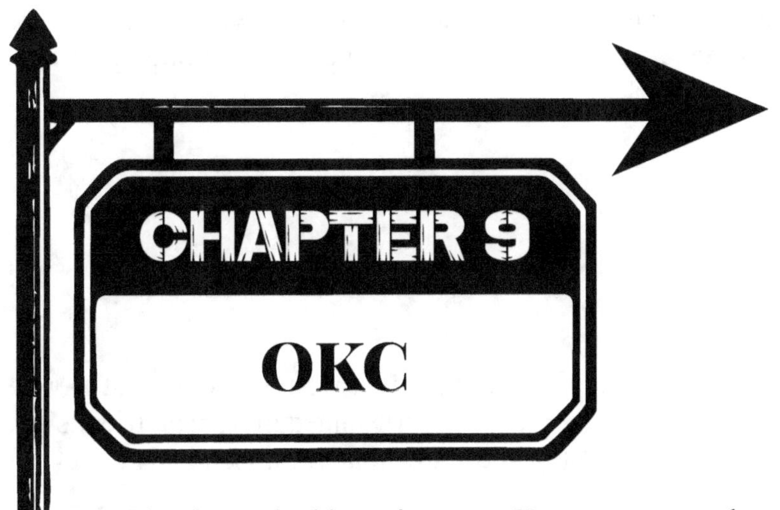

The dream had been intense. Knox sat up on the edge of the bed, disoriented and tired. He looked at his phone for the time – 2 a.m. He took a swig of water from the bottle that had been sitting in the cup holder. He tried to recall what woke him. In the dream, he had been sitting at the bar in the Western Horseman. Ricky had been standing in front of him, asking if he wanted the Ribeye or the Fillet. He couldn't decide. And Ricky kept asking, telling him it was very important for him to decide. He never ordered the fillet, so why couldn't he decide? Did he want the ribeye? Did he want the fillet? He really did not know. The bigger question was, why did this dream wake him up?

He was tired, so he got back in bed and pulled the blanket up tight under his chin, his knees curled up to his chest. Thinking about the dream made him sleepy, and he drifted off quickly. When he woke again at 7 a.m., he felt like he had gotten sufficient rest for the three-and-a-half-hour drive to Oklahoma City. Pulling on his jeans, t-shirt, and boots, he gathered his toiletries and walked to the truck stop building to shower and get some coffee, not necessarily in that order.

He stopped by the drivers' lounge to fill his travel mug with coffee on the way to the shower rooms. Other than discounted showers, one of the biggest advantages to belonging to the loyalty clubs of each truck stop brand was access to the lounge and the free coffee that came with it. As he showered, his mind drifted back to last night. What WAS that? It was intense, that was for sure. But the emotions that flooded him afterwards were new to him. He would text Ryder before he got on the road. He was making new friends on this run, and that felt good. After the shower, he stopped by the lounge to get more coffee, having finished the first mug before the shower water had gotten hot. He bought a breakfast burrito – potato, egg, and cheese - on the way out of the building and made his way to his rig to eat and text before hitting the road. When he got settled and had taken his first bite of burrito, he noticed a text from Carl.

(Carl) *hey*

(Carl) *how was ur night in TX*

Knox debated about texting Carl but knew it would be cruel not to. He also knew that, despite the conversations, Carl wanted more than friendship. And after last night, Knox was absolutely sure that he himself had no fucking idea what he wanted.

(Knox) *GM*

(Knox) *night was good.*

(Knox) *Had the best steak ever*

(Knox) *Place called Western Horsemans Club. Ever heard of it?*

(Carl) *yes*

(Carl) *my dad took me there on a road trip once*

(Carl) *years ago, but it was good*

(Knox) *How r u?*

(Carl) *good, at work.*

(Carl) *FT tonight?*

(Knox) *sure*

(Knox) *Text when u r home*

(Carl) *will do*

(Knox) *drive safe*

Knox placed his phone on the center console shelf, finished his burrito, took a few more sips of coffee, and picked up the phone to text Ryder.

(Knox) Hey, this is Knox

(Knox) Thanks for dinner last night

(Knox) really was the best steak EVER!

(Knox) my last name is Creed, btw.

Knox did not expect a response right away. He imagined that Ryder had duties at the ranch that would preclude him from having constant access to check and respond to texts. He reviewed the delivery instructions for the next destination, buckled his seat belt, checked the truck charge and other screens, and engaged the motors. He turned on his favorite playlist of music and got on I-40 East for the drive to Oklahoma City. This next delivery would take him onto Tinker Air Force Base. Being former military, Knox knew the details for accessing military bases, but wasn't entirely sure how this would play out on Tinker. Chuck's instructions simply said to go to the main gate visitor center and wait in the truck. Chuck had told him verbally that the tracker on the trailer would alert the appropriate person, who would be waiting for him there. Seemed clear enough.

Knox sang along to his favorite songs, keeping himself distracted from thoughts of Carl, Ryder, emotions, and good sex. His phone vibrated, and he glanced up at the truck's display screen to see the preview indicating a text from Ryder Garcia. His mind immediately snapped back to the previous evening. The steak, the conversation, the toffee cake, the kissing, the touching, and the intense emotions that overwhelmed him afterward. He refused to respond to texts while driving, even with the voice options the truck's interface offered. He hated the voice-to-text thing and simply refused to use it. He could, however, listen to a preview. He pressed on screen to have the AI voice read the texts to him.

(Ryder) *Good morning, Knox*

(Ryder) *dinner was my pleasure*

(Ryder) *as was dessert*

(Ryder) *Let me know how your day is when you finish your delivery*

Knox knew that Ryder was not talking about the toffee cake, which made him smile. He would respond while he was waiting for the delivery this afternoon. He turned on the music and turned up the volume, singing along with new happiness. A warmth spread through him, different from the fleeting satisfaction of a good fuck. A quiet hum that settled deep in his chest and made the flat highway feel less endless.

He briefly questioned why simply hearing from Ryder would make him smile so much, but quickly pushed it aside to focus on driving. Arriving in OKC, he took the exit for Tinker AFB and proceeded South to the main gate, which was the only option for the exit. The visitor center was immediately on the left, while the gate itself was directly ahead. There did not seem to be a place in the small parking lot of the visitor center to park the truck, and he was considering proceeding directly to the gate when he noticed that a man in the Air Force camouflage uniform seemed to be directing him to pull into the left lane and stop. Knox moved left to the far lane and drove slowly past the visitor center building. The Airman directed him to stop. Knox stopped and placed the truck in park. He rolled down his window to speak with the Airman and noticed that the guy had walked to the passenger door and was attempting to open it. Knox pressed the button to unlock the door, and the Airman climbed into the cab. The guy was slightly shorter than Knox, clearly athletic from the fit of his uniform, sandy blonde hair that seemed barely within regulations, and the unfortunate Air Force mustache. Nevertheless, he was very attractive, and Knox pushed aside the lascivious thoughts that flashed through his head. This guy was probably all of 22 years old. There was a time when Knox would have gone after this guy, but over the last few years, he had moved to a solid preference for guys closer to his own age.

"Good afternoon, sir. May I see your ID, please?" The airman asked. Knox reached for his phone with the attached wallet and extracted his driver's license. He also handed the airman the delivery paperwork. The airman's nametape on his uniform indicated his last name was Dodge, and although Knox was out of touch with Air Force ranks, he guessed that the rank on the front of his uniform was that of Sergeant or higher. So, calling him Sergeant Dodge seemed reasonable. The Sergeant handed the ID back to him, folded the paperwork, and placed it in one of the thigh pockets of his uniform. From another pocket, he pulled out another single piece of paper and his military ID.

"I'm a former Navy, and I know your rank is higher than airman, but I'd like to address you properly," Knox said.

"Tech Sergeant," Dodge said.

"Thanks, Tech Sergeant Dodge. You can call me Knox, but if you want to be more formal, my last name is Creed." Knox offered.

"Yes, Sir. Thank you, Mr. Creed. Now, if you will, please pull up to the gate and hand the Security Forces airman my ID, your ID, and this paper, please." Dodge directed.

Knox did not respond. He took the items from Dodge and engaged the motors, moving the truck forward slowly towards the gate. When he was stopped at the gate, the Security Forces airman took the IDs and paper, looked at them briefly, handed them back and motioned for him to move forward. Knox threw his own ID on the shelf and handed the other things back to Dodge.

"Please go forward until I tell you to turn," Dodge instructed. "It's not a long drive."

He drove forward, following the edge of the airfield and runway. When they reached the Southern end of the runway, Dodge told Knox to turn right, then left, then right again. They soon arrived at a set of buildings identified by typical Air Force signage in shades of brown as the *Tinker Aerospace Complex*.

"Pull around to the back of this building, and you'll see the loading dock. There are two doors. You can back up to either one." Dodge said, pointing at a large, single-floor building on the right.

Knox easily backed the truck to the loading dock door. He could see Dodge tense at the speed with which he maneuvered the truck and trailer. When he was satisfied with his positioning at the dock, he placed the truck in park and looked at Dodge.

"What now?" Knox asked.

"You can join me inside. We have a place for you to wait while we unload." Dodge answered. "Your backing skills are impressive, by the way."

"Thanks," Knox said. "Where are you from, Tech Sergeant Dodge?"

"Uh, Lincoln, Nebraska, sir," Dodge said.

"Cool. Why do you keep calling me sir?" Knox asked, thinking that it must be an Air Force thing.

"Mainly out of respect, but also because of the nature of your delivery,"

Dodge replied.

"If I asked, would you call me by my first name?" Knox inquired.

"If you ask me to, yes," Dodge said.

"Cool. Call me Knox, please." Knox requested.

"Okay, Knox." Dodge smiled. "You can call me Dillon. But please, not in front of my co-workers."

"Deal, Dillon." Knox smiled back.

They exited the truck and walked back to the loading dock. Knox and Dillon entered the pedestrian door to the right of the two roll-up doors. On entering the door, Knox looked to the left and saw a completely empty loading dock with double doors on the opposite wall. Dillon scanned his access badge on a pad next to a single door directly to the right of where they had entered. Knox followed him into a small room that reminded Knox of every military break room he had ever encountered. A series of non-matching side chairs were placed at random around the room. There was a table in the center with more chairs surrounding it. To the side was a full-sized refrigerator and a small table with a pod-style coffee maker and a well-used microwave.

"You can wait in here," Dillon said.

"Okay. How long do you anticipate it taking?" Knox asked.

"I'm thinking an hour at the most," Dillon replied.

"That's cool," Knox said as he took a seat in what he perceived to be the most comfortable of the chairs.

"Just FYSA, you can't leave this room without badge access. If you need to go to the bathroom, it the door in the corner." Dillon pointed to a door on the far wall. "Otherwise, I'll come get you when we're done."

"FYSA?" Knox questioned.

"For Your Situational Awareness," Dillon answered as he scanned his badge and exited the room.

Knox pulled his phone from his pocket and settled in. He started to text Ryder, then decided that he would wait until the evening, as agreed. There was no point in texting Carl since Carl was supposed to text him when he got off work. Slightly confused and disappointed that it was not convenient to text either man, he scrolled mindlessly through social media until Dillon entered the room an hour later.

"You're good to go," Dillon said. "I've obtained authorization for you to park overnight here on base if you like."

"What?" Knox wasn't sure what that meant. "I'll need to charge my truck, shower, eat, and those sorts of things. I usually do that at the truck stop."

"You can do those things here." Dillon continued. "There is a supercharger near the Exchange. That's where you can park your truck. The gym is across the street, and you can shower there."

"Okay, I'm in." Knox conceded, thinking it might not be such a bad thing after all. "Are you going to show me where to park? Maybe even show me around this evening?"

"Uh, sure. I will show you where to park. I live in base housing, which is nice walk from the Exchange, so I'll just ride over there with you. Do you mind hanging out here for another thirty minutes or so? I need to clear this with my flight chief." Dillon sounded both excited and nervous.

"No problem. You do what you need to do. I'll be right here." Knox smiled at him and winked, causing visible discomfort and confusion for the young Sergeant, who turned on his heels and abruptly left the room. Knox chuckled to himself at his ability to make younger guys nervous.

Twenty minutes later, Dillon re-entered the room. "I'm good to go if you're ready."

"Yep, let's do it," Knox replied, standing up and following Dillon out to the rig.

The casual conversation on the short drive enlightened Knox. Dillon was thirty years old, not in his early twenties as he had originally thought. He was the youngest of four children, worked out at the gym regularly, and seemed eager to spend time with Knox that evening. Dillon directed Knox to pull the truck around to the back of the Exchange/Commissary complex, where he would have some privacy. He also showed him the superchargers nearby. Knox had enough battery to last him through the night, so he noted the location and would charge the truck in the morning while he had breakfast. Once they had parked, Dillon seemed hesitant to get out of the truck.

"I'm going to the gym if you want to join me. You can shower after, and maybe we can have dinner together? There's a Burger King within walking distance. You're also welcome to shower at my place if you want." Dillon asked timidly.

"I wouldn't mind getting in a little cardio." Knox winked. And yes, Burger King sounds good. I'd like the company. As for the shower, are you serious about me showering at your place?"

"Yes, it's a serious offer," Dillon said. "So, I'll meet you at the gym in about an hour. It is located just down the street. Maybe a five-minute walk." Dillon pointed in the direction of the gym.

"Sounds good. I'll see you there." Knox said as Dillon hopped out of the truck and jogged off along the back side of the building.

Knox had not brought any kind of workout clothes with him since the only cardio he usually got on the road was the kind that worked best with no clothes. So, he went shopping at the Exchange, where he used the washroom, and bought a new black tank top, shorts with a 3-inch inseam, socks, running shoes, and a water bottle. He got the shoes in a dark color as well, thinking that they would not look as new. Hopefully, the walk to the fitness center would dirty them up a bit. When he got back to his truck, he changed into the new clothes and admired himself in the mirror. He might have to wear this out sometime, he thought. Tom of Finland came to mind as he turned and flexed in the mirror that was mounted on the inside of one of the compartment doors. If only the tank and shorts were leather, he thought.

Knox gathered his duffle, which held a change of clothes and his toiletries, the new water bottle, and his sunglasses. He exited the truck, made sure it was locked, and started walking in the direction that Dillon had indicated. Five minutes later, he could see the fitness center ahead and on the right. As he approached the entrance, he saw Dillon waiting for him. He had changed into tan shorts that were a few inches longer than Knox's and a bright green tank top. The shorts showed off his muscular, shaved legs, and the tank accented his smooth chest and arms. Dillon smiled as Knox approached.

"Let's put our things in the locker room, and we can talk about what we want to do," Dillon said.

"I have some things in mind, but I'm not sure the gym is the appropriate place." Knox laughed while Dillon blushed and laughed with him.

"I'm going to focus on this workout first, then we can talk about a cool-down." Dillon smiled.

"Let's do it then. What did you have in mind here? And keep in mind, you clearly do this much more than I do." Knox said.

"My plan was just to do some general arms and upper body. Nothing too heavy. I usually start out with a few minutes on the elliptical, then some stretching, then weights. Sound good?" Dillon said as they stowed their bags in a single locker. Knox had removed his water bottle and filled it at the water fountain on the way out of the locker room. The fitness center itself looked older but had been renovated in recent years. It was well-equipped with the newest machines and a well-stocked free-weight room.

They started out on elliptical machines, side-by-side. After five minutes of light cardio, each man had worked up a light glisten of sweat, which only served to accentuate Dillon's smooth skin and Knox's hairy arms. They both took small towels from the rack nearby and walked to an open area near the free weights to stretch. Knox mimicked Dillon's light stretching as they both made occasional eye contact. A few bicep curls, triceps presses, and chest flys later, Dillon seemed eager to go.

"I think I've had enough for the day. You?" Dillon addressed Knox.

"I'm good if you are, buddy." Knox agreed.

"Let's grab our things from the locker. You still okay showering at my place?" Dillon asked.

"Sure am," Knox replied.

They retrieved their bags and walked to Dillon's compact car. They stopped at the drive-thru of the Burger King nearby and ordered food. They rode in silence on the 5-minute drive to Dillon's townhome, which was part of one of the base housing complexes. The townhome itself was a modest two-bedroom, two-bath. It was basic but neatly furnished and clean. Dillon parked, got out of the car, and unlocked the door, motioning to Knox to enter first. Dillon closed and locked the door behind them, dropped his bag on the floor next to the front door, and then placed the food and drinks on the coffee table.

"Sorry, I cut the workout short. I just couldn't focus." Dillon admitted.

"What has you distracted?" Knox asked, knowing the answer.

"Uh, well, you. You had me distracted. Your shorts are revealing. And your body hair is distracting. And your face is distracting." Dillon rambled.

Knox took a fistful of Dillon's shirt in his right hand and pulled him towards him, kissing him deeply. He reached down with his left hand and firmly cupped Dillon's erection that was pushing against the front of his shorts. Dillon's cock felt smaller than Knox liked, but it was super hard. Knox himself had a semi-erection but was not yet as hard as he normally would be at this point in an encounter. Dillon kissed him back with the hunger of someone who had wanted this kind of interaction for a long time and thought that it would never come. The eagerness took Knox's cock to a state of complete erection.

Knox pulled Dillon's cock out of his shorts and stroked it lightly. Dillon groaned as he pressed further into Knox. Dillon's hand reached down to Knox's belly, lifting his shirt and running his hand through the thick fur of Knox's chest before heading back down to the waistband of Knox's shorts. He reached into Knox's shorts and firmly gripped his hard dick. He pulled on it with a force that was both pleasurable and uncomfortable. Without warning, Dillon dropped to his knees, pulling Knox's shorts down with him. On his knees, Dillon went at Knox's erect cock with a fervor that showed both inexperience and desire. Knox noticed that Dillon was pumping his own cock as he sucked Knox's. Feeling the need to get this over with, Knox pictured Carl and the way his ass milked Knox's cock. Then he thought of Ryder and what it would be like to take turns flip-flopping with him. Then he thought of kissing Ryder, and that's what made him cum. He placed his right hand on Dillon's head and pulled forward hard as he came, making sure that he swallowed it all, whether he wanted to or not. Dillon gagged but took it like a champ, continuing to pump his own cock as he came on the carpet of his living room a few minutes later, continuing to suck Knox's until it was soft.

Gasping for breath, Dillon looked up at Knox with his cum-wet lips and smiled. "That was fucking amazing!"

"Glad you liked it. "Knox smiled. "Want to shower together?"

"Yeah, that'd be cool," Dillon said.

Dillon led them upstairs and started the shower. When the water was warm, Dillon got in, and Knox followed. The shower was not big, so they had to take turns getting wet under the steam of water. Knox showed Dillon how to easily rotate their bodies while washing each other. It seemed something that Dillon had not previously done, but one that he enjoyed. Knox was sure that the shower would get him ready for a second round, but it did not. When they had finished showering and had dried themselves with the towels that Dillon had placed on the seat of the toilet, Knox dropped to his knees and started licking Dillon's balls. Dillon's dick became hard immediately. It was small enough that Knox could get his lips down to the base easily and extend his tongue to massage Dillon's scrotum. Knox circled his thumb and forefinger around the base of Dillon's penis and moved firmly up and down. Dillon came, and Knox returned the favor by swallowing it all. Dillon used his towel to wipe away any residue.

"Do you want me to get you off again?" He asked.

"Nah, that one was on me. But thanks for asking." Knox replied.

Knox wrapped the towel around him and walked down the stairs to get his clothes from his duffle. When he was fully dressed, He grabbed a burger from the bag of food, gathered his things and started for the door.

Dillon came running down the stairs, dressed in sweatpants, a t-shirt, and flip-flops.

"I can drive you back to your truck." He spoke.

"Actually, I'd like to walk. I need the fresh air, and it will clear my head. I've got a long drive tomorrow." Knox said. "Thanks for the hospitality, though." Knox pulled Dillon close again and kissed him again before he walked out the door, unwrapping the burger on his way out.

On the walk back, Knox thought about how underwhelming his orgasm had been. He had never had a challenge enjoying these casual encounters with under-experienced hook-ups. And it took thinking about Carl and Ryder to make him cum. Mainly thinking about Ryder. Thinking about Carl got him hard, but Ryder made him cum. He needed to FaceTime with Carl. And maybe Ryder.

He pulled out his phone and noticed a text from Carl.

(Carl) *I'm home. FT when you can*

That was 45 minutes ago. He initiated a FaceTime session with Carl.

"Hey," Carl said as his face appeared on the screen of Knox's phone.

"Hey," Knox said, continuing to walk to the truck.

"Where are you?" Carl asked.

"Tinker Air Force Base," Knox answered. "I'm parking on the base for the night. I'm walking back to my truck."

"Walking back from dinner?" Carl asked.

"Uh, not really," Knox said.

"Oh. I see." Carl said, the disappointment evident in his voice.

"It was just a blow job from an airman. That's all," Knox said, trying to make it seem unimportant, even though he knew Carl was disappointed. "Carl, you know what this is. It's what I do. Who I am. I made that clear."

"I know, I know," Carl said. "I just thought things might be different. You were very clear, and I just thought I might change that."

"One day, you might, but I meant it when I said I need to take things slow." Knox had reached his truck. "Listen, buddy, I have a long drive tomorrow, and I need to get some sleep. You okay?"

"Yeah, I'm okay. I'm a big boy. I'm good." Carl said. "Have a good night, my friend.

"Same to you, Carl. Sleep well." Knox responded as he disconnected the call.

He climbed into the cab of the truck and texted Ryder.

(Knox) *Hey, you up?*

(Ryder) *yes. Want to talk?*

(Knox) *Yes, please*

Ryder called immediately. No video, just a call. They talked for over an hour. They talked about everything except sex. Knox had curled up under his blanket while on the phone with Ryder. When they hung up, Knox placed his phone on the shelf and fell asleep quickly. He dreamed of being held in warm blankets like a baby and slept like one as well.

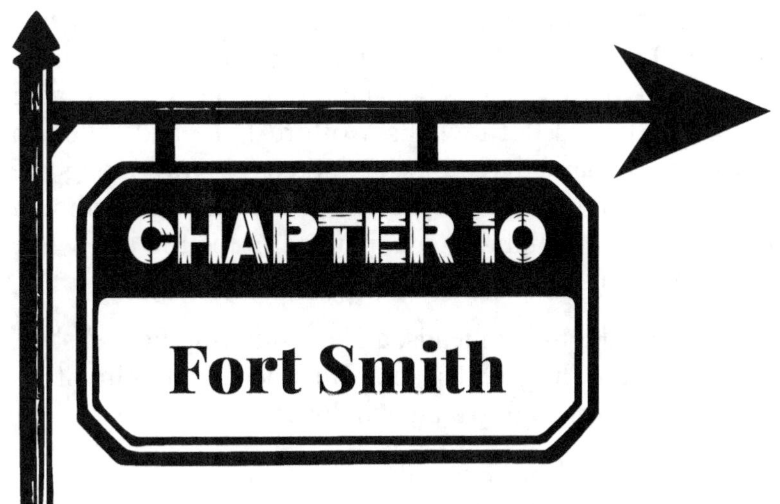

Knox woke at 6 a.m. from a very deep sleep. He did his usual stretch, got out of bed and dressed in jeans and a t-shirt. He drove his truck the short distance to the charging station and plugged it in. After buying a coffee at the shoppette nearby, he munched on trail mix for breakfast, organized the cab, and reviewed his driving plan for the day while the truck charged. It was only a three-hour drive to his next stop, just South of Fort Smith, Arkansas. Once the truck was fully charged, he exited the base and immediately entered the on-ramp for I-40 East. He turned on his audiobook and settled in for the drive.

He was an hour into his drive when he heard the text sound, and a preview appeared on his screen – it was Ryder. Knox touched the notification on the truck's info screen to hear the message.

(Ryder) Good morning!

(Ryder) know u r driving, just thinking about you.

Knox smiled. He still wasn't sure what was going on with his feelings about this guy. Their one encounter had been intense, but they hadn't really had sex. Although he frequently thought about having sex with Ryder and what that would be like. So, what was it? What was making him think about this guy so much? The conversation has been good, like old friends catching up. And when Ryder had touched him, it felt like nothing Knox had ever experienced with another guy. He needed time to process these things. Maybe a call with Ryder tonight would help.

Lost in his thoughts, the exit for Fort Smith, Arkansas, came up quickly. Knox merged onto I-540 going South towards the small town of Bonanza. 15 minutes later, he exited to take the U.S. 45 and minutes later was driving past the small town. He turned left towards Wofford Lake and followed the directions down an unmarked road that worked its way along the uninhabited South side of the lake. The road ended at a small guardhouse and a simple one-arm counter-weighted gate, painted in the red and white stripes reminiscent of pre-war military facilities.

As he approached, an older man in jeans, a blue button-up flannel shirt, and work boots stepped out of the guard shack. He touched the brim of his ball cap in greeting as Knox rolled down his window.

"Mornin'." He said in a thick Arkansas drawl.

"Good morning," Knox replied.

"You Knox?" The man asked.

"Yep," Knox said, handing his driver's license out the window, angling his arm down so that the man could reach it without climbing up.

"Looks good." The man said. "You'll see a covered area to the right. Just pull under it, and someone will tell you what to do from there."

He handed the license back to Knox and walked over to the counterweight of the gate, pushing down firmly to cause the gate arm to swing up. Knox pulled forward slowly and watched in his side mirror as the man closed the gate once the trailer had cleared the barrier. The paved road curved to the right towards the lake and continued for another half mile. The building that appeared before Knox reminded him of a warehouse that might be found at a doomsday prepper compound. A large rusty metal warehouse faced the lake. The weeds and overgrown landscape added to the abandoned look of the place. The only signs of life were three pick-up trucks and four mid-size sedans parked near a windowless door. The right end of the warehouse had a covered pull-through canopy that was open at each end. Knox could see a beautiful view of the lake through the opposite end as he pulled under the cover and placed the truck in park.

A roll-up door on the left wall opened, and two men stepped out, both wearing the same uniform as the gate guard, with only the shirts differing in color. Knox could see in his side mirror that the space beyond the roll-up door looked empty. The men approached the window, which Knox had already lowered to greet them.

"Good morning!" Once the man spoke, his accent was clearly not from Arkansas. "Knox, right? Come on out of the truck with the delivery paperwork, and we'll get started."

Knox rolled up the window and opened the door, hopping easily down from the truck, ID and paperwork in hand. Leaving the truck door open, he handed the items to the man who had spoken to him, who looked at them carefully and handed the ID back to Knox.

"This will only take about 15 minutes. You can wait by the lake if you want to stretch your legs or in the truck. Your choice." The man said.

"I think I'll take a walk," Knox said.

"Perfect. There's a small deck with a few chairs by the lake. I'll come get you when we're done." The man pointed towards the lake in front of the truck.

Knox closed the truck door and walked the short distance to the lake. The "deck" was a large wooden platform that sat on the edge of the lake. Five well-weathered plastic chairs stood in a tight circle in one corner. Knox picked a chair, turned it to face the lake, and took a seat. After sitting, he glanced back at the truck over his shoulder. Another man and a woman, also wearing jeans and flannel, had joined the other two. Knox notices them moving two large, black Pelican cases from the truck and into the warehouse. From the look of it, the cases were not heavy. Minutes later, Knox heard the distinct sound of the trailer door being closed and latched.

At the sound of boots crunching gravel, Knox stood and turned to see the man who had spoken to him approaching.

"You're good to go, Mr. Creed." The man said, handing Knox a single piece of paper. "Just pull the truck forward into the grass and circle around back to the road. Safe travels." He turned with a wave , walked back past the truck and entered the building, the roll-up door closing behind him. Knox climbed up in the cab, filed the paper in his delivery binder, and engaged the motors. He did as instructed and pulled the truck slowly through the canopy and onto the grassy area between the building and the lake, circling back to the road. As he approached the guard shack, the older gentleman from before raised the gate arm for him to pass. He headed North on the two-lane road, catching I-540 past Bonanza and merging onto I-40 East. He put on some music and exited 45 minutes later near the town of Ozark.

Directly off the highway, he parked the truck at the charging station near the Love's truck stop, connected the charging cable and walked to the Taco

Bell nearby to get some lunch. This stop would be a quiet one. Other than the small truck stop, the only things nearby seemed to be a cheap motel, a Taco Bell and a McDonalds. The town of Ozark was a few miles down the road, but Knox was not feeling social today. The drive tomorrow would be the longest of the run, and he needed to be in bed early for an early start.

He ordered a few items from the value menu and settled in to eat and respond to Ryder while the truck charged.

(Knox) Hey

(Knox) delivery done

(Knox) stopped for the day

(Knox) long day tomorrow

(Knox) having Taco Bell LOL!

Knox took a bite of a taco and chewed slowly. His phone vibrated, the screen showing an incoming call from Ryder. He swallowed quickly and touched the screen to answer, raising the phone to his ear.

"Hey, buddy!" Knox answered the call.

"Hey," Ryder said.

"Well, this has made my day," Knox admitted.

"I thought I'd take the chance since you said you are eating. How's the driving?" Ryder asked.

"It's good. Today was easy. Three-hour drive and quick delivery. Tomorrow will be long. Eight hours. I'll have to stop and charge up in Memphis." Knox said.

"You need to get to bed early tonight. No fooling around." Ryder laughed.

"There's nothing where I am, so little chance of that. Just me and anyone I can video chat with." Knox laughed, hoping Ryder would pick up on the suggestion.

"Hey, Knox, I want to throw something out there." Ryder's voice became serious, seeming to ignore Knox's previous comment. "I don't know what's going on with me, but I can't stop thinking about you. I think it might be something worth exploring. Consider spending a few days with me at the ranch on your way back West. I know this is a long shot but just think about it. No pressure. And if you want to just continue talking on the phone, that's okay too. And now I'm talking too much and not making sense, and..."

Knox cut Ryder off mid-sentence. "Ryder, Ryder. Stop talking. Listen, I don't know what's going on with me, but I'm having the same problem. And yes, I would like to spend some time with you at the ranch. Just see where this goes. I won't be able to give you a specific day until I finish the deliveries. Can I keep you updated along the way?"

Ryder sighed with relief. "Yes. Thank God you didn't shut me down. I've been so nervous to ask you. After all, we only talked and didn't really have sex, per se."

"For me, too, Ryder," Knox said. "Hey, can we FaceTime tonight? I need to do some laundry and shower, but I'm going to grab some dinner and eat in the truck and then get in bed early."

"I'd like that. What do you think about having dinner together? Say around six?" Ryder suggested.

"That would be very cool." Knox grinned.

"Excellent!" Ryder exclaimed. "I'll call you at six. Now finish your poor excuse for Mexican food and get your afternoon started."

Ryder disconnected the call, and Knox resumed eating. When he was done, he bundled up his trash and tossed it in the bin near the door before refilling his drink and walking back to the truck. He moved the truck to one of the few available parking spots and parked for the evening. He changed into sweatpants, a t-shirt, and his new running shoes and gathered his dirty laundry and toiletries into his duffle bag. He walked to the truck stop building and asked the clerk about showers and clothes-washing options. She directed him to a door at the back and told him it was on a first-come basis. The small facility had exactly one shower, one washing machine, and one clothes dryer, all of which were accessed directly from the drivers' lounge. The small lounge had a single couch flanked by a small table with four chairs and a single matching overstuffed chair. Fortunately, there was fresh coffee.

The shower was in use, but the washing machine was free. Knox tossed in two pairs of jeans, a variety of shirts, and the collection of dirty underwear and socks from the past week. He took a sheet of laundry detergent from his bag – one of the greatest inventions ever – and tossed it in with the clothes. While they washed, he waited for the shower, settling in on the couch as he scrolled mindlessly through social media, taking an occasional look at the news. Becoming quickly bored with those, he opened up his internet browser and typed in "Ryder Garcia Amarillo." The first thing that came up was Ryder's LinkedIn page. He scrolled past info that he already knew about Ryder's education. There was no information about work other than the title of "Owner/Manager" at One Horse Ranch in Fritch, Texas.

Ryder searched for One Horse Ranch, Fritch, TX. The first return was a Wikipedia page. Evidently, the ranch had a long history. Owned by the Garcia family, who were one of the largest landowners in the State of Texas. They primarily raised beef cattle and were known for sustainable ranching. The page mentioned the newest heir, Ryder Garcia, and taking the ranch into the future with innovative methods of ranch management. Knox was surprised to see Ryder's name highlighted in blue, indicating a link to a separate page. He clicked on the link, not sure at this point that he wanted to explore any further, but not being able to help himself.

Ryder Garcia, the page said, is a well-respected authority on sustainable ranching. He has published several papers on the topic and has a long list of speaking engagements. Knox didn't know what to think of this new information. Ryder had never said anything about being an important or famous person. Thinking back on the reaction of Ricky at the steakhouse, this all made sense now. Ryder wasn't just the supplier of beef to the restaurant. He was something else – a local celebrity and internationally recognized authority in the field of ranch management. A local celebrity, an internationally recognized authority. The thought both intrigued and unsettled Knox. It was a new facet to Ryder, one he hadn't anticipated, and one that made the pull he felt even more complex. This would be a definite topic of conversation over dinner tonight.

The wash finished, and Knox moved the clothes to the dryer, throwing in a dryer sheet from the supply that he kept in the bag that he had tossed into his duffle along with the laundry detergent sheets. The shower had become available, and he took his things into the shower room. He undressed and sat on the toilet, continuing to read about the Garcia family while he used the bathroom. When he was done, he tossed his phone into the side pocket of the duffle and turned on the shower.

He stood under the hot water and lathered himself well with the liquid body wash from the dispenser on the wall. He ran his hand through his wet, soapy chest hair and down to his semi-erect penis. Hi, my thoughts turned to the feeling of Ryder touching his body. If Ryder simply touching him had been that intoxicating, what must it feel like to be inside him? To have him inside him? The thought made Knox completely hard, and he softly stroked his cock at the thought. He continued to wash himself, soaping up his ass crack and letting his finger briefly enter his hole with the warm soapy water. He thought of Ryder doing the same. He would make sure that showering together was a priority if he ever made it to One Horse Ranch.

Was exploring things with Ryder a good idea now that he knew more about him and his family? Knox really wasn't sure. He would see how Ryder reacted to learning that Knox now knew more about him and his family. Putting these thoughts aside for now, Knox rinsed off, turned off the water, and dried himself with a rough towel from the stack supplied by the truck stop. He tossed the wet towel into the bin provided for used towels and pulled on clean underwear, adjusting his still-semi-erect cock before putting on the gray sweatpants and t-shirt, clean socks, and shoes from before. He gathered his things and exited the shower room. Two other drivers had joined him in the lounge; one was starting a load of laundry, and both also seemed to be waiting for the shower.

"All yours, gents," Knox said as he walked to the dryer to remove his dried clothes.

"Thanks." One of the guys said, glancing slyly at the other.

They both entered the shower room as Knox winked at them.

"More than welcome to join." One said, looking at Knox.

"Nah, thanks, though. You boys enjoy." Knox smiled, noticing the disappointment on the two men's faces as they closed the door behind them.

Knox took his time folding his clothes and placing them in the duffle. He walked back into the main store and bought a frozen dinner of Salisbury steak and mashed potatoes, a pre-packaged Cesar salad, and a two-liter bottle of diet soda. He walked back to the truck and stored the food items in his mini fridge before neatly stowing his clean laundry in the closet compartment between the driver's seat and the sleeping area. He noticed the time and felt a slight bit of happy anxiety at his upcoming call with Ryder in thirty minutes. He converted the bed to the dinette configuration and plugged in his phone to charge, placing it in the small stand that he had purchased a few months ago to make it easier to look at it while eating.

He prepared his eating area with a paper napkin and the plasticware that the clerk had given him with his food. He took out the frozen meal and started heating it in the microwave while he opened the salad and accompanying packs of croutons, shredded Parmesan, and dressing. He had everything prepared with two minutes to spare. Ryder called right at six. Knox smiled at seeing Ryder's face on the screen. Ryder was dressed in a dark gray t-shirt, and his dark back hair was still damp from what Knox assumed was a recent shower. His trimmed beard glistened with beard oil, and Knox longed to touch it.

"Hey," Ryder said.

"Hey," Knox said.

"What's for dinner?" Ryder asked.

"Salisbury steak, mashed, and a Cesar salad." Knox held up each item as if presenting a gourmet meal. "It was the best I could do without resorting to fast food. You?"

"Ah, exactly what you would expect from a rancher." Ryder held up a plate with a juicy steak, baked potato, and grilled broccoli.

"Okay, this is totally not fair." Knox laughed.

"Join me at the ranch, and I'll cook for you like this," Ryder said.

"Deal. But I think time with you will surpass the quality of the food." Knox said.

"True. But the food will be good. I promise. If it's one thing ranchers know how to do, it's eat well," Ryder teased.

"Hey, so something up front for dinner time conversation." Knox changes the subject. "I did a Google search for your name. I wasn't trying to creep on you; I just wanted to learn more before our dinner. And I learned a lot. You never mentioned that your family is one of the largest landowners in the country. And that you are a well-known authority on sustainable ranching." Knox paused to give Ryder time to respond.

Ryder looked down at his plate and finished chewing his mouthful of steak. When he looked up, there was a sadness in his eyes. "Would it have made a difference, Knox?"

"No, Ryder. No, it would not have made a difference." Knox responded.

"Knox, listen, I really felt a connection with you at the restaurant. I didn't want to ruin it by selling myself to you. I need for you to want me for who I am as a person. Okay? So, promise me that you'll let me tell you about my family and myself when we see each other."

"Deal. No need to say more. So, tell me about your day." Knox moved the conversation to a lighter topic. They ate and talked about their day. Knox told Ryder about the weird delivery, and Ryder talked about a new feed they were trying out with a small group of cattle that promised to make the beef even better. When they had finished their meals, Ryder suggested they take a bathroom break so they could clean up and Knox could get ready for bed. They agreed that Knox would initiate the next call in thirty minutes. Knox disconnected the call and quickly gathered his trash, and walked to the building to use the washroom, tossing the trash in the bin next to the door. He walked quickly back to the truck, put up the privacy shades, undressed, positioned his phone appropriately, and crawled into bed. He propped himself up on pillows and arranged the blanket just above his waist, exposing his hairy chest to the camera as he dialed Ryder.

Ryder appeared on the screen in bed, his torso exposed. Knox's cock immediately came to attention at the sight of Ryder's well-defined chest, with its light dusting of dark hair across the top and the trail of the same hair running a fine line down his flat, taught belly. Ryder's dark nipples were the perfect size, not too small and erect from being exposed.

"Okay, well, that caused a reaction in me," Ryder admitted. "You're even more attractive than I remember. Seeing your hairy chest gave me an instant boner." Ryder panned the camera down to his crotch so that Knox could see his erection, which Ryder flexed for him before taking it in his hand and softly stroking it. He moved that camera back to his face and grinned.

"Tease," Knox said, smiling, as he lowered the blanket so that Ryder could see he was having the same reaction. Knox pushed his hard cock forward with his hand and let it snap back against his belly.

"Who's the tease now?" Ryder asked.

"I really want to suck that beautiful cock of yours," Ryder said.

"I want you to suck my cock. And I want to suck yours. I also want your cock up my ass." Ryder said.

"We need to make that happen," Knox said, continuing to stroke his cock. "I'll fuck you if you promise to fuck me too."

"Deal." Ryder agreed, licking his lips and stroking his hard dick faster.

Knox stared at Ryder's face as Ryder stared back. They continued staring at each other as they stroked their dicks. Knox came first, throwing his head back as he shot his load onto his stomach and chest.

"I want you to shoot that in my mouth. And in my ass." Ryder exclaimed as he continued to stroke his cock.

"I'm going to put my hard cock anywhere you want it," Knox said as Ryder shot his own ample load.

They looked at each other in silence, and they recovered.

"I need to see you," Ryder said.

"I know." Knox agreed. "Let's make it happen.

"Goodnight, Knox. Drive safely tomorrow. Keep in touch when you can." Ryder said.

"Goodnight, Ryder. Will do." Knox said as he disconnected the call.

Knox curled up under a blanket and fell asleep with a smile on his face.

W hen 5 a.m. rolled around and the alarm sounded on his phone, Knox was in a deep sleep and resisted the notion that he had to wake up and get going. As he remained in bed, his mind churned with thoughts of the long drive ahead and of Ryder Garcia. He needed to be at the delivery point just outside Nashville by 4 p.m., so he needed to get on the road. Thoughts about Ryder would still be there when the day was done. For now, he needed to focus on the drive.

He did a quick walk-around of the truck and trailer before getting on I-40 East towards Nashville. His plan was to stop in Memphis to have lunch and charge the truck, then continue to the delivery destination, which was near Nashville International Airport. The next three days would be the most difficult part of this run, but he had planned well, and things would go smoothly as long as he focused on the plan and resisted the urge to see Ryder. He put on an audiobook and adjusted the sun visors to shield from the sun that would soon rise.

Hours later, he passed Memphis and exited to find the supercharger that was located near Wolfchase Galleria Mall. Once he had parked at the charging station, he plugged in the truck and walked across the street to get lunch. He ordered at the counter of the popular chain burrito restaurant and took a seat at an outside table under an umbrella to shade himself from the hot Tennessee sun. He took his time eating the food, not wanting to rush the remaining hour it would take to bring the truck up to a sufficient charge level. He watched people walk by and thought about the call with Ryder. In a spontaneous move that was out of character for him, he pulled out his phone to text Ryder.

(Knox) *charging truck in Memphis. Burrito for lunch.*

(Knox) *How's ur day?*

Knox took another bite of food, not expecting to hear back from Ryder but satisfied that he had initiated a conversation. It wasn't long before Ryder responded.

(Ryder) *burrito in TN, lol*

(Ryder) *We have to talk about ur food choices. jk*

(Ryder) *day is good. Busy.*

(Ryder) *how's the drive?*

(Knox) *drive was easy*

(Knox) *truck charges in 90min*

(Knox) *Just time for food and a walk*

(Knox) *btw I enjoyed our dinner together*

(Ryder) *me too*

(Ryder) *can't wait to do it in person*

(Knox) *dinner or ...?*

(Ryder) *both*

(Ryder) *don't tease. I need to work. Lol*

(Knox) *can't help it*

(Knox) *call tonight?*

(Ryder) *yes, please*

(Ryder) *family dinner will text when done*

(Knox) *cool*

Knox finished his dinner and wandered around a bookstore nearby, deciding not to explore the mall as he had planned. When his phone notified him that the rig was at 80%, he started walking back to the charging station. He unplugged the truck and settled in for the three-and-a-half-hour drive to Nashville. He continued his audiobook, attempting to divert his mind from thoughts of Ryder. He was unsuccessful.

He approached the exit for the Nashville International Airport. His directions told him to follow the signs for cargo drop-off and look for Building 47. Chuck had added a handwritten note that Building 47 was between the DHL and FedEx hangars. Knox saw the DHL hangar approaching and slowed down so that he would not miss Building 47. Turning around in this situation would be a bitch. He would basically have to circle the entire airport and deal with traffic and stoplights on the side streets. As promised, Building 47 was nestled tightly between the two large hangars. The building itself resembled a small hangar, although dwarfed by the two on either side. Knox drove the truck slowly towards the closed retractable door and stopped. A pedestrian door opened on the left front of the building, and an older gentleman in a military flight suit walked towards the truck. He motioned for Knox to get out of the rig. Knox gathered his phone, wallet, and the delivery paperwork and joined the man on the tarmac.

"Mr. Knox Creed?" The man asked.

"Yes," Knox answered, extending his ID and the paperwork.

"I'm Colonel Drake, by the way." The man offered as he looked at the paperwork and Knox's ID. He handed the ID back to Knox and continued with instructions. "We will drive your truck into the hangar and will bring it back out when finished unloading. There's a place for you to wait inside."

"What? Knox was angry. "There was never any mention of someone else driving my rig."

"I know. But it's the only way to do this delivery." Drake said.

"I need a minute." Knox said, his temper rising as he pulled out his phone and called Chuck."

"Hi, Knox," Chuck answered the call. "Is there a problem?"

"You're damn right there is, Chuck. They want to drive my rig into the hangar for the delivery. No one drives my truck except me. No one." Knox was shaking.

"Who's there with you?" Chuck asked.

"A military guy named Colonel Drake," Knox said.

"Let me talk to him, please," Chuck said firmly.

Knox passed the phone to Drake. Drake listened intently, his facial expression telling Knox that he was not happy. He passed the phone back to Knox.

"Hey, Chuck," Knox said.

"Okay, Knox. Here's what's going to happen. And you're not going to like it. You're going to pull the truck into the hangar. They will then escort you out of the hangar. You will wait outside until they are done. Then, you will need to back the truck out of the hangar. Do not talk to them. Do not engage with them. Understood?" Chuck sounded angry, as well.

"Understood." Knox acknowledged.

"Knox, I'm sorry about this. This was, shall we say, unexpected." Chuck said. "Call me as soon as you are done and can safely talk."

"Got it," Knox said and hung up.

"I don't like this, but I have no choice. So, let's get it done." Drake said with force.

Knox got back in the truck. The hangar doors retracted to each side, and Knox drove the truck into the hangar, turned it off, exited the cab, walked directly to the outside and turned to the right to wait in the small space between the two hangars. He heard the doors close as he exited but did not turn around to look. Twenty minutes later, Knox heard the hangar doors open, and a young technician that Knox had not previously seen walked around the corner and waved at Knox.

"Your truck is ready, Mr. Creed." The young man said.

Remembering Chuck's request, Knox remained silent as he walked to his truck, climbed in the cab and skillfully backed out of the hangar. Once aligned with the main road, Knox drove to the parking lot of the cargo terminal nearby and parked the truck. He called Chuck, who answered immediately.

"Okay, Chuck, the delivery is done. Now tell me what the fuck is going on." Knox said.

"Hey, Knox. Yes, this was an unfortunate and unforeseen development. Basically, a matter of ownership of goods. The original owner sold them before the delivery. When this happens, we usually cancel the delivery.

This time, however, the parties involved have sufficient power to direct the delivery. I told them that your truck did not belong to us and we could not guarantee the delivery unless you parked the truck. Our contract with you states that the truck cannot be moved during delivery. So, what happened was the only way to make it work. Thanks for complying." Chuck explained.

"It's okay, it just threw me off. I mean, it's my rig we're talking about. I worked hard for it, and for them just to assume that I would hand it over is just…well, it's just rude." Knox ranted. His voice trembled with a rare, raw anger. The rig wasn't just metal and motors; it was a testament to years of struggle, a tangible piece of the freedom he'd fought for. To have it assumed, handled, invaded, felt like a personal affront.

"I totally agree, Knox. You did the right thing calling me. If anything like this ever happens again, do the same thing. Call me first." Chuck reassured him. "I know you've had a long day, so get some rest."

Chuck hung up, and Knox navigated the truck out of the airport complex and back onto I-40 East. It took him thirty minutes to reach the Pilot truck stop in Lebanon, Tennessee, where he would spend the night. His route tomorrow would take him to Asheville, North Carolina, across the Blue Ridge Mountains and steep grades that would drain the batteries. He would power up in the morning while getting breakfast and top off in Knoxville before the push across the pass. But for now, he needed some rest. And he wanted to get settled before talking to Ryder.

Knox parked the truck and gathered his things so that he could shower. He walked to the main building of the large truck stop, reserved a shower with the checkout clerk, and walked to the driver's lounge and shower area. As the warm water ran over his body, he realized how tired he was. The long drive, combined with the drama at the delivery, had taken it out of him. He dried himself with the towel, got dressed, and purchased a sandwich from the restaurant before walking to his truck. As he was finishing his dinner, his phone notified him of a text. The preview showed that it was from Ryder. He felt a warm sensation wash over him at seeing Ryder's name on the screen.

(Ryder) just finished dinner with fam

(Ryder) I can talk in 5

(Ryder) may I call?

(Knox) just finishing dinner myself

(Knox) gimme 10

Ryder acknowledged Knox's last text with a thumb's up emoji.

Knox quickly finished his sandwich, washed it down with diet soda, and cleaned up his trash. It was only a few minutes before his phone vibrated with the incoming call from Ryder.

"Hey, buddy!" Knox answered the phone enthusiastically.

"Hey, Knox! How was your day?" Ryder was excited to talk to him.

"It was crazy. I had this Colonel tell me that they had to drive my truck into the delivery area. I said NO WAY! And caused all sorts of problems. I had to call the company and get them to talk to them. But it all worked out. How was your dinner?" Knox realized how nice it was to be able to tell someone about this day.

"That IS crazy! That is so rude to demand to drive YOUR truck. The family dinner was good. I have a really great family. You will meet them when you come to the ranch. I hope that doesn't scare you off from visiting." Ryder approached this last piece of information hesitantly.

"As long as most of my time is with you, it shouldn't be a problem," Knox responded.

"Cool," Ryder said. "Listen, Knox, I still can't stop thinking about you. Do you mind if we don't talk for a couple of days? Just so I can sort things out in my mind."

"I think that's a good idea, Ryder. I'm having the same challenge, and I need to think things through. I can text you when I'm on my way back West. I'll know then when I might arrive at the ranch." Knox was relieved that Ryder was feeling the same as him.

"You know, Knox, even if this is about sex, your visit to the ranch could just be about that. There are so many things I want to do for you. And with you. So, we can approach it that way if it helps." Ryder extended this to Knox to ease the tension.

"Yep." Knox agreed. "So, what kind of things?"

"Oh, so we're doing that now?" Ryder laughed. "Okay, well, the first thing I'm going to do is kiss you. Then I'm going to make you watch me undress and touch myself. You won't be allowed to touch me. Then I'm going to undress you and explore your body, inch by inch, kissing every part. When I've satisfied myself with that, I'm going to turn you over and fuck you softly while pulling your head back with my arm and kissing you. I'm going to shoot my load far up into you and let it sit there while if fuck you some more. If you make it that far without cumming yourself, then you can do the same to me. How does that sound for a start?

Knox was silent. He had been stroking his hard cock while Ryder talked and had emptied his balls after Ryder's last statement. His hand and belly were sticky with his jizz.

"You just made me cum." Knox said breathlessly.

"That was the point." Ryder laughed. "Now it's my turn. Tell me what you're going to do to me."

"Well," Knox started, "First, I'm going to kiss you. Then I'm going to unbutton my jeans and let my hard cock hang out. You're going to stroke it with your hand while we kiss. I'm going to slowly unbutton your jeans and pull them down just enough for me to flip you over and fuck you. I'm going to fuck you hard and fast. The load I drop in you will be legendary. It will be so much that it will be dripping out of your hole for a week. And if you make it through that without cumming, I'm going to flip you on your back and suck you off till you fill my mouth."

Silence from Ryder then sounds that let Knox know the thoughts of getting fucked had made him cum.

"Wow. I can't wait. I have so much more that I want to do. Promise you'll fuck me like that." Ryder said.

"I promise," Knox said.

"How many deliveries do you have left?" Ryder suddenly changed the subject.

"Two. Asheville and Goldsboro. Then I'm done." Knox said.

"Okay. Text me the morning after Goldsboro, and let me know your plans." Ryder suggested.

"Will do. Have a good night, Ryder.

"Have a good night, Knox."

Knox pressed the screen to disconnect the call and took a napkin left over from his dinner to clean himself. He took a few minutes to get things ready for the next day before climbing into bed. As he drifted off, he thought of the many things he and Ryder would do together.

noxvplugged in the truck after a restful night. His exhaustion from the stress of the previous day and the calming mutual masturbation with Ryder had combined for a good night's sleep. While the truck charged, he settled into a booth in the truck stop restaurant to have a proper breakfast. The waitress delivered fresh coffee with a smile and kept his cup full while he ate fried eggs, bacon, hashbrowns, and pancakes. When his belly was full, he paid for the meal and walked back out to his rig to get the next leg of the trip started.

Knox put on some music and started down I-40 East with a clear mind. The three-hour drive to Knoxville, Tennessee, was uneventful. He exited the highway just before Knoxville at Northshore Drive and pulled the truck up to one of the charging columns, blocking off several other parking spaces in the large parking lot. While the truck was charging, he walked across the parking lot to Five Guys Burgers to have lunch. After ordering his burger and fries, he filled his drink cup, scooped some unshelled peanuts into a small paper tray, and sat at a table to wait for his number to be called. As he was enjoying his peanuts, a very attractive older gentleman walked in the door and glanced around as he made his way to the register. He made eye contact with Knox, and the man winked, taking Knox by surprise. The seating area was filling up quickly, and the man walked up to Knox's table, drink and peanuts in hand, and looked Knox directly in the eyes.

"Mind if I join you? The place is filling up quickly." The man asked with a thick southern drawl.

"Don't mind," Knox answered, intrigued by the forward request.

"Joe." The man said, extending a hand.

"Knox," Knox replied, shaking Joe's hand.

"Knox in Knoxville." Joe chuckled.

"Yep, just thinking that." Knox laughed.

"You from around here?" Joe asked, seeming to know the answer.

"Nah, California. Just passing through." Knox answered.

"Nice. I'm here for business. Staying at the hotel next door." Joe offered.

"Where's home?" Knox asked, thinking that the guy seemed nice and company during lunch was not a bad thing.

"Memphis," Joe said.

"I was just in Memphis," Knox said as he heard his number called. He rose from his seat, walked to the counter, and returned with a brown paper bag full of fries and the burger wrapped in foil at the bottom. He proceeded to unpack the bag, munching on fries and offering some to Joe, who refused.

"How long you here for?" Joe asked.

"Couple of hours. I drive a rig. Electric. It's charging." Knox said while chewing his burger.

"Electric? I didn't know they made those?" Joe admitted.

"Yep. It's pretty cool." Knox said while shoving fries in his mouth.

Joe's number was called, and he stood up, returning seconds later with his bag of food. He tore the bag open and spread it out to create a makeshift plate for his burger and fries. They ate in silence until Knox had finished his burger and most of the fries. Joe ate quickly and finished soon after Knox.

"I'd really like to see that rig if you're up to it," Joe asked.

"No problem. I like to show it off." Knox winked.

They threw their trash in the bin and exited the establishment, walking the short distance to Knox's truck. Knox opened the door and motioned for Joe to climb in. As he scaled the running board with ease, Knox noticed how fit Joe was. His tight dress pants and golf shirt gave hints of a well-toned physique underneath. Joe had to be at least 15 years older than Knox, and Knox found himself getting semi-aroused at the thought of an encounter with this older man.

When they were both inside the cab, Knox proceeded with his usual tour, pointing out all the features, including the conversion of the dinette to the bed. As Knox was demonstrating this feature, He found himself face-to-face with Joe, who leaned in and kissed Knox, running his hand along Knox's crotch to feel the now full-on erection.

"My hotel is across the parking lot. I need to get fucked. You up for that?" Joe whispered in Knox's ear.

"Yes. Let's go." Knox responded, exiting the truck quickly and locking it after Joe had exited as well. They walked over to the hotel and took the elevator up to Joe's room. When they were in the room, Joe wasted no time getting himself and Knox undressed.

"Listen, here's what I need," Joe said. "Fuck me hard and fast. If you do it hard, I'll cum while you're in me. Then you can leave. Got it?" Joe's body was trimmed and toned. His white chest hair fit well with his rugged handsomeness.

"I'm all in, buddy," Knox said as he shoved Joe back on the bed and grabbed his ankles, which he placed on his own shoulders. "Lube?"

Joe squirted some lube in his hand from the bottle on the nightstand and stroked Knox's hard cock, getting it slick and ready. He then started fingering his hole while Knox pushed into him. Joe kept his finger inserted as Knox pushed his cock in alongside it. When Knox was fully in, Joe removed his finger and placed his hand by his side on the bed, letting Knox do his thing. Knox gripped tighter on Joe's ankles for leverage, pushing hard into him with each thrust. Knox fuck him hard and fast, as requested. Joe stroked his own cock as Knox pillaged his hole. Joe came quickly, shooting thick white liquid on his chest. Knox pulled out and quickly pumped his own cock, thinking that he might not be able to finish this time, then thinking of Carl, then Ryder, and finally cumming on Joe's softening cock and balls. His orgasm was mediocre, at best. Another quick release, another fleeting connection. The quick release he once craved now felt hollow, a pale imitation of the connection he yearned for, a void only Ryder seemed capable of filling. This wasn't working anymore. Joe relaxed his legs and spread out on the bed.

"Thanks. That's just what I needed. Make sure the door closes on your way out." He said.

Knox walked to the bathroom and quickly washed his dick with a wet washcloth before getting dressed and leaving the room. He walked back to his truck with his mind turning. Why didn't he enjoy that like he should? That was the perfect quick daytime fuck that he loved. Sex with strangers. No commitment. But this had hardly been worth it. He unplugged the truck and peed in his portable urinal before getting back on the road.

The drive to Asheville was tedious. Managing the batteries on mountain passes was always something that Knox approached with careful planning. He adjusted his speed and power appropriately to maximize the regenerative braking and safely navigate the curves and slopes.

The delivery instructions for Asheville were strange. He was to enter the Biltmore Estate and follow signs for deliveries. The note provided by Chuck said that there would be a warehouse on the backside of the property and that it would be obvious because it was the only warehouse there. Knox got off the highway and carefully navigated the narrow streets to get to the entrance to the estate. He checked in with the guardhouse, where cars of tourists were lined up to gain access. Following the signs for deliveries, he could see the massive house in the distance. The road wound around for several miles before Knox saw the warehouse. It was partially hidden in the trees, but clearly the only warehouse in the immediate area.

Knox pulled up the only door that he could see and placed the truck in park. He waited for a few minutes, expecting someone to come out to greet him as with the other deliveries. When it was apparent that that would not happen, he left the truck and walked to the door. There was no signage to indicate any instructions, so he opened the door and stepped into the space. Inside, an older woman sat at an older steel desk. The desk reminded Knox of government office furniture from decades ago. The room was sparsely furnished with a side chair and a credenza with a coffee maker and a basket of snacks. A door on the far wall, Knox assumed, must lead into the warehouse.

"Good morning!" the woman said, in an accent that sounded more neutral than North Carolina. "You must be Knox?"

"Yes, Ma'am," Knox said as he handed her his ID and the paperwork.

"Thank you very much. I'm Sue," she said.

"Where should I pull the truck?" Knox asked.

"Right, right, you're going to pull it around back. There's a roll-up door there. If you can back it up to that, it would be perfect." Sue instructed, smiling and handing him back his ID.

"Thanks," Knox said. "Should I wait in the truck or come inside?"

"Oh, I didn't think about that. This will take about an hour. If you don't mind walking back around the building, you can wait in here with me. I'll make some coffee." Sue said

"That would be great. I'd love a cup of coffee. I'll be back in just a few minutes." Knox gave Sue a smile and a wink, which made her blush.

He followed the paved drive to the back of the warehouse, backed the truck up to the roll-up door, and walked around the building to the front. The two doors were the only access to the building. Back in the office, Sue had a pot of coffee waiting. She poured some for Knox into a porcelain teacup that she retrieved from the credenza, placing it on a matching saucer before handing it to Knox. She motioned for him to sit in the side chair, which he now noticed had a small table tucked between it and the wall. He carefully placed the full cup of coffee on the table before he sat.

"I just love seeing a big, burly man with a fancy cup of coffee." She laughed.

"I'm just happy if the coffee's good." He laughed with her, taking a sip. "And this is delicious."

"Thank you, Knox. I get it from the estate coffee shop. They do a good job roasting the beans." Sue said with satisfaction.

"You don't sound like you're from here," Knox said.

"I'm not. I grew up in California. Barstow. But I've been here for about twenty years now." Sue said.

"I live in Barstow!" Knox said with excitement.

"I guess that makes sense since that's where BarsTech is headquartered. But I never thought about it til now. It's nice to meet you, Knox." Sue said, turning away from Knox and getting back to whatever work she was doing on her computer. "It won't be long. Help yourself if you need more coffee."

"Thanks," Knox said as he drained the small cup and walked to the coffee pot to get more. He sipped the good coffee and checked his phone for texts. Nothing. Still exploring his emotions, he decided to text Carl.

(Knox) hey

(Knox) how r u

No reply, but Carl was probably still at work. Knox sipped more coffee and scrolled through the news and social media.

(Carl) Hi Knox

(Carl) I'm good. u?

(Knox) I'm good

(Knox) Delivery in Asheville, NC

(Carl) Long text coming…give me a minute

(Carl) listen, Knox, I thought we had something, but I guess we didn't. I met someone last night, and I think there's something there. Don't want you to think there's still something. I know the text is not best for this, but I need to get this out. If you are ever in my area again, please text me. I hope we can be friends.

(Knox) No problem, Carl. Want nothing but happiness for you

(Knox) We will always be friends

(Knox) I hope we can have a drink and catch up when I'm in your area

(Carl) thanks, I'd like that

(Carl) btw you have no idea how important you are to what you deliver

The last text was strange to Knox. What did Carl mean by that? He would have to mention it to Ryder. But then he remembered that he wasn't going to talk to Ryder for a few days. And that made him kinda sad. As he drained the cup of coffee. Sue's desk phone rang. She picked up the receiver without saying anything and then hung it up a few seconds later.

"Your truck is ready, Knox. They said they left the paperwork on your door. Not sure what that means, but come see me if it's not there." Sue stood and took the empty cup from him, placing it on the credenza.

"Thanks, Sue. Have a good afternoon." Knox said as he walked out the door.

He walked around the outside of the building and found the single piece of paper folded in half and wedged neatly in the crack where the door joined the body of the truck. He pulled it out, opened the door, and climbed in the cab, stowing the paper in the binder before he started the truck. He engaged the motors and drove back along the road that had brought him to the delivery site. It took almost an hour to get off the estate. Knox found it difficult to navigate around the distracted tourists. Once he was securely on I-40 East, he drove another thirty miles to the Love's truck stop in West Marion, North Carolina.

Knox parked his truck, which had maintained a 60% charge, and walked to the main building to scope out the drivers' lounge and shower situation. The drivers' lounge had been recently remodeled and was nicely furnished with comfortable chairs, a large TV, and a coffee station. A door off the lounge led to five shower rooms. There were four other drivers in the room. Knox took a seat in one of the chairs to plan out his evening as well as tomorrow's drive. It would be his last delivery for this run. Then, he would need to figure a few things out. But until then, he was still on the clock, so to speak.

One of the drivers, seated with his back to Knox, turned and took a look at Knox, then stood and walked over. The guy was maybe in his mid-twenties, with blond hair cut in a style similar to Knox's and a slim runner's build. He had an attractive face and a nice smile.

"Are you Knox Creed?" The guy asked.

"Yep, who're you?" Knox responded, looking back down at his phone, then back up at the guy.

"Kyle. Kyle Tanner. That's your EV? The dark gray one?" Kyle pointed out the window towards the lot.

"Yes, that's mine. Have you ever seen one up close?" Knox chided.

"No. I've always wanted to." Kyle said.

"We can take a look later if you want." Knox offered, thinking that he was just being nice to the kid. He didn't get any other vibe from him. "I'm just going to get some dinner, then we can take a look."

"Where are you going for dinner?" Kyle asked.

"I saw a Waffle House. So, probably there. They don't have those in California." Knox said.

"Mind if I join you?" Kyle asked. "I know this is intrusive. Sorry."

"Actually, not at all. I'd like the company." I need to go back to the truck. Meet you out front in ten minutes?" Knox mentioned.

"Great. See you then." Kyle turned and gathered his things, and left the lounge.

Knox walked back to his truck, made sure things were presentable for a tour, and walked back to the building where Kyle was waiting. They walked the short distance to the Waffle House and sat at a booth adjacent to the service counter. Knox ordered a pecan waffle with a side of sausage. Kyle ordered an omelet. They chatted over dinner, and Knox learned that Kyle was a new driver. He lived in Idaho, where he grew up, and was driving a truck that was owned by his company. He was 26 and liked the job so far. Although he admitted to Knox that he got lonely. Knox assured him that he would eventually find ways to deal with that.

They laughed and shared stories. Kyle was fascinated by Knox's experience and kept wanting to hear more. Knox was delighted to be able to share his knowledge and experience with a young trucker. When they got to the truck, Knox did as usual and allowed Kyle to enter the cab first. Kyle looked around in awe at the extensive amenities that were no doubt better than his own truck.

"You own this?" Kyle asked.

"Yep." Knox smiled.

"This a goal for me, for sure," Kyle commented.

"I was where you are once. I worked hard, and now it's paying off." Knox said as he moved closer to Kyle. "I know what it's like to get lonely on the road. I can help with that if you're up for it?"

Kyle moved in and hugged Knox, nuzzling his face in Knox's neck. Knox wasn't expecting this but went with it anyway, hugging him back and pulling him closer. This guy was starving for physical contact. Kyle pulled back and clumsily kissed Knox. Knox knew immediately that his experience was limited. Knox could help with that. He pushed Kyle away gently, keeping his hand on Kyle's shoulder.

Let me show you how this works." Knox said, pointing at the bed that was folded up against the wall. He lowered the table and then lowered the bed. He pushed Kyle down gently to sit on the bed, then told him to lay down. Knox got on top of Kyle and kissed him. Kyle kissed back with an urgency that was distracting for Knox.

"Kyle, slow down," Knox said.

"Okay. Sorry." Kyle said as he resumed kissing Knox, easing into it and taking his time.

Knox raised himself up and took off his own shirt. He placed Kyle's hands on his chest, where Kyle ran his hands through Knox's thick chest hair. Knox could feel the strength of Kyle's erection. Knox reached down and unbuttoned Kyle's shirt, spreading the fabric to each side to reveal an athletic, hairless chest. Knox played with Kyle's nipples, which made him moan. Kyle's hand continued to explore Knox's torso. Knox pushed himself back, unbuckled Kyle's belt and unbuttoned his pants. Knox gripped the waistband of Kyle's pants and underwear together and pulled them down, releasing a hard cock that was narrow and long. Kyle's dick had a nice shape and was straight as an arrow. Knox leaned in and flicked the head with his tongue. Then he took the whole thing in his mouth and gave it one slow up and down before getting off the bed and removing his own pants. He removed Kyle's boots and completely removed his pants, letting them fall to the floor. Knox stood with his erect cock just inches from Kyle's face. Kyle gripped it with his hand and explored its length and girth before tasting it with his mouth. Kyle's warm tongue felt good as it caressed Knox's cock. Not wanting to delay it any longer, Knox took a packet of lube from the shelf and tore off the top with his teeth. He drizzled some on Kyle's cock and the rest on his own hand, which reached back to wet his hole.

Knox straddled Kyle and slid Kyle's long cock along his crack. With gentle pressure, he allowed Kyle to enter him. Kyle's thin dick felt nice up Knox's ass. Knox rocked on Kyle, letting his hard cock slide in and out with ease. Knox stroked his own dick in the process. Kyle's hand explored Knox's body, his hips, his chest, and his balls, and eventually brushed Knox's hand away so he could play with his cock.

Kyle stroked Knox's cock with urgency as Kyle reached orgasm. When Kyle came, his body shook all over, his head tilted forward, and his grip on Knox's cock was severely tight. Knox fucked Kyle's tight fist quickly, eventually coming on Kyle's stomach. It was not the most intense orgasm, but Knox enjoyed helping Kyle get off. Knox leaned forward and put his full weight on Kyle.

"How was that?" Knox asked, kissing Kyle's neck.

"Fucking amazing," Kyle said. "Can you fuck me if we wait a few minutes? I've never been fucked, and I want to know what it feels like."

"Sure," Knox said. "I need a few minutes."

Knox pulled himself off Kyle's softening dick and used some wet wipes nearby to clean himself. Throwing them to Kyle to do the same. Knox sat on the bed, and Kyle moved over to cuddle in tight to Knox, holding him, needing the physical connection. They chatted for a few minutes about trucker things when Kyle made the next move and started kissing Knox's nipples.

"Can I explore your body?" Kyle asked.

"Yes. Enjoy." Knox laughed and smiled as he laced his fingers behind his head and relaxed back on the bed.

Kyle started at Knox's head and discovered every inch of Knox's body. His eagerness was amusing to Knox, who let him have his fun. When Knox was hard again, he turned Kyle onto his back and spread his legs. Knox grabbed another packet of lube and gently played with Kyle's hole. Kyle's expressions indicated that he enjoyed the sensation. Knox lubed up his own cock and placed the head against Kyle's sphincter.

I'm going to apply pressure. When I say so, try to squeeze the head of my dick with your hole. Understand?" Knox instructed.

"Yes. Go slow, please."

"I will now squeeze," Knox said as he could feel the tightness increase around the tip of his penis. "Now release." Kyle released, and Knox slowly slid his thick cock into Kyle's warm, wet hole.

Kyle gasped but took it in, pushing himself even farther onto Knox's cock as he got used to the feeling. Knox remained still, letting Kyle find his way with the new sensations. Knox playfully rubbed Kyle's rock-hard dick as Kyle's hips moved to find new ways to stimulate his hole with Knox's cock. Eventually, Knox started thrusting. Kyle's eagerness grew as he got closer to cumming. Kyle gripped his own cock, but Knox pushed his hand away and started pumping it for him. Kyle came on Knox's hand. Knox leaned in and licked up some of the jizz, looking at Kyle as he did so. Knox pumped for a few minutes more, finding it difficult to reach orgasm. He pictured Ryder on the bed beneath him, running his hand along Ryder's chest, Ryder touching his chest and Ryder's beautiful face. Knox closed his eyes and continued to thrust into Kyle, thinking about Ryder, whispering his name over and over. He eventually emptied his load inside Kyle. Kyle took

Knox's face in his hands and pulled him closer. Knox collapsed on Kyle, his head turned to the side of Kyle's chest, his eyes closed.

"Ryder," Knox whispered again.

"What?" Kyle asked. "Who's Ryder?"

Knox pushed off Kyle and sat up on the bed. "Nobody, just a fantasy."

Disoriented, Knox cleaned himself and offered Kyle to join him in the showers.

"No sex, just some human contact," Knox said.

"I'd like that," Kyle said.

Knox gathered his bag for the shower, and they stopped by Kyle's truck for him to get his things. There was no one in the drivers' lounge when they got there, and they were able to slip into a shower room together without notice, not that anyone would have cared anyway. They showered together, washing each other, talking. Kyle got hard again, and Knox sucked him off in the shower. It was a gift for the young trucker. Knox had no interest in doing anything else. They dried off and got dressed. Kyle asked for Knox's number, which Knox refused.

"Not how I work, Kyle. If we see each other again, we can talk. Okay?"

"Okay. This was nice. Thanks for teaching me. I'll never forget this." Kyle said.

"No problem. Be safe out there." Knox said as he exited the shower room to walk back to his truck.

As he shouldered his duffle, his phone vibrated with an incoming call. It was Chuck. That's odd, Knox thought.

"Hello," Knox answered the call.

"Knox, where are you?" Chuck asked, his voice panicked.

"Just finished showering. Just outside Asheville, North Carolina. Why?" Knox asked.

"We got a notice that the trailer lock is being manipulated. Are you close to the truck?" Chuck said hurriedly.

"Yes. Walking there now. I can see the truck, but no one is around it." Knox said.

"Okay, we're looking at the video now. Stay with me on the phone while you walk to the truck." Chuck requested.

Knox walked towards the truck, being vigilant for anyone who might be hiding behind one of the other trucks parked nearby. He did not notice any movement."

"Okay, it looks like a single person tried to pick the lock. Which is stupid because it's a digital lock, and anyone that would know what they were after would also know that there are cameras." Chuck said.

"Anything I need to do?" Knox asked.

"Just walk to the back of the trailer and get a visual of the lock, please," Chuck asked.

"Approaching it now," Knox said as he walked around the back of the trailer and looked at the digital lock. "It looks like scratch marks on the lock itself, Chuck."

"So, most likely just a random thief seeing the short trailer and fancy truck as a target of opportunity," Chuck replied.

"Probably. Anything I need to be worried about?" Knox asked.

"No. The lock is almost impossible to pick without advanced cyber-hacking skills. And the cameras track anyone who tries. Thanks for responding so quickly. We have not had this happen before, so it threw of off a bit. But that's why we have the cameras." Chuck continued.

"Chuck, is there anything I need to know about my cargo?" Knox asked, already knowing the answer.

"No, Knox. Just that it's very valuable. Which you already know." Chuck said. "You've got one more delivery. It's the largest one and will probably take several hours. Just get that done, and you're good to make your way back at your leisure. Got any plans for the trip home?"

"Just going to stop to visit with a friend in Texas," Knox said.

"Got it. Safe travels, Knox. We appreciate you more than you know." Chuck said before disconnecting the call.

Knox had a restless night. He could not fall asleep and then woke up, often thinking about what was in the trailer and the potential of someone wanting to steal it. His mind also turned frequently to thoughts about Ryder. The absence of contact with him for a single day was more painful than Knox wanted to admit. When it was time to get on the road the next morning, he was still tired. And confused.

CHAPTER 13

Goldsboro

Knox topped up the truck to 80% while he got coffee and a breakfast sandwich to go. Knowing that this last delivery might take a few hours, he would stop again in the Raleigh-Durham area to top up the charge before continuing to the delivery destination on Seymour Johnson Air Force Base in Goldsboro. The drive should be easy, as he drove the relatively flat roads across the Piedmont region of North Carolina. He was in the mood for some tunes, so he put on one of his favorite playlists and hit the road, going east on I-40.

The drive was pleasant, and he felt a sense of pride as he passed the Volvo Truck North America Headquarters in Greensboro. They had three models displayed in front of the large building, one of which was a VNR Electric in Sparkle Jade. Identical to Cyber Wolf, except in color. It was a beautiful truck, but he preferred the stealthy look of his dark gray metallic.

He drove past Durham and the Research Triangle Park area, deciding to stop once he had navigated the heavy traffic that he was experiencing on that section of road. He drove past Raleigh and exited the highway at an area called Cleveland. The truck had maintained a 40% charge, and he could make it to the delivery with that, but having it topped up would make it easier to find a place to stop for the night. And he wanted some lunch.

He pulled up to the charger, shut down the truck, and plugged it in. The charger was adjacent to a North Carolina Barbeque restaurant. He had heard about the unusual pulled pork with vinegar-based sauce and decided to give that a try. As he stood at the counter, trying to decide what to order, he noticed that most customers were ordering a sandwich, which seemed to consist of pulled pork with coleslaw on a hamburger bun. He ordered a sandwich combo, which came with shoestring fries and a version of fried cornbread called "hushpuppies." He mentioned to the young girl and the counter that this was his first time eating North Carolina barbeque, and she said people like to sprinkle pepper vinegar on it, which seemed to be on every table with the other condiments. The sandwich was amazing. Knox had never had anything like it. He ate the hushpuppies but abandoned the fries to order another sandwich, which he savored before ordering two more to go. He also ordered a bag of the hushpuppies on the recommendation of another customer who had noticed him tucking into the sandwiches and surmised that it might be his first time. According to this older, truly southern lady, the hushpuppies were a great snack when cold. And evidently, he should try dipping the cold ones in ketchup. What a strange place this is, Knox thought.

With a very full belly and bag of food for the road, Knox walked across the parking lot to the truck, which had reached 90% by the time it took him to eat. He placed the bag of food in the fridge and verified his destination on his map app before getting back on I-40 East and quickly taking the Hwy 70 by-pass towards Goldsboro. He anticipated the drive to take just over an hour.

As he took the exit onto North Berkeley Blvd, he thought about how similar the area looked to the base in Oklahoma. This thought reminded him of his encounter with Dillon. The inexperienced Tech Sergeant had been one of Knox's most amusing and underwhelming hook-ups. Knox wondered if he might have a similar opportunity here. He approached the visitor center, which was located just before and to the right of the main gate to the Air Force base. He pulled the truck into the small parking lot, blocking in the cars that were already parked there, and placed the truck in park. Two minutes later, someone knocked on the driver's door panel. Knox rolled down the window to see a very short female airman looking up at him.

"Good morning! Are you Mr. Creed?" She said.

"Yes," Knox replied.

"Great. I'm Airman First Class Stanton." She greeted him. "Do you mind if I join you in the truck? I'll ride with you to the delivery area."

"Sure," Knox said, pressing the door unlock button as Airman Stanton walked around the front of the truck to the passenger side. His hopes for another Tinker scenario vanished as he realized that she would be his primary contact for the delivery.

She opened the door, for her height, was surprisingly agile, climbing into the cab.

"May I see your ID and paperwork, please?" Stanton said.

Knox handed her his driver's license and the paperwork, which he had ready before she had knocked on the door. She looked at the paperwork and the ID, folded the paperwork, shoved it into a packet in her uniform, and handed the license back to Knox.

"Okay, let's go. Please proceed out of the parking lot and to the gate." She instructed.

Knox drove the truck slowly forward, allowing the blocked cars to back out of their parking spaces. He stopped at the gate and rolled down the window, allowing the security forces' airman to climb up on the running board. The tall male gate guard noticed Stanton, gave her a brief hand signal and jumped down with a "You're good to go." Knox pressed the accelerator gently and moved the truck forward.

Stanton directed him through several turns as they wound their way around to the far side of the runway. Just past the TACAN, which Stanton informed Knox stood for Tactical Air Navigation System, there was a small building situated far from any other structure. Stanton told Knox to pull to the back of the side of, and parallel to the building. Knox complied, moving the truck forward until she told him to stop, then placing it in park and shutting it down.

"I guess you know that this might take a few hours. Do you want to wait here, or would you like me to get you a ride to the Exchange, where you can walk around?" Stanton offered.

"I'm good to wait here. I have food." Knox said, holding up his bag of sandwiches and hushpuppies."

Stanton laughed. "I'm from Colorado, and I don't like the barbeque here. But the locals have a distinct love for it. Do you like it?"

"It's the most amazing thing I've ever eaten." Knox laughed with her. I had two sandwiches for lunch and got two to go!"

"Good for you." She said. "I'm glad someone likes it. Follow me, and I'll get you settled.

As Knox followed her inside, a team of military and civilian personnel had already started erecting a large tent at the back of the trailer. There were two military box trucks backed up to the tent, perpendicular to the trailer. They must be transferring the cargo, he thought. They entered the building into a hallway with an interior glass window to the right. The door next to the window led to a small room with several generic chairs and a small table.

"You can wait in here," Stanton said. The restroom is down the hall on the left. There is a breakroom across the hall from the restroom. There is coffee in there and maybe some snacks. Help yourself to whatever is in there. I'll check in with you every thirty minutes."

"Sounds good. I'm an expert at entertaining myself. So, no worries." Knox chuckled.

Stanton laughed and smiled as she left the room. Knox pulled a chair up to the table, placed his bag of food there, and his phone next to it. He walked down the hallway to use the restroom and explored the breakroom after peeing. There was a cheap pod coffee machine with generic pods and a collection of donated coffee mugs. A few cereal bars and a bowl of individually wrapped chocolates completed the inventory on the counter. He opened the fridge and found a collection of sauce packets dominating one of the shelves. He rifled through them to find ketchup packets and took three to try with his hushpuppies. He walked back to the front room, settled into his chair, and picked up his phone to text Ryder. Remembering their agreement, he opened a social media app instead, briefly pondering why not being allowed to text Ryder made him sad. Distracted by social media, he opened the bag of food, pulled out a hushpuppy, tore off the corner of a ketchup packet, and squeezed a dollop onto the tip of the fried cornbread. Turns out this weird concoction is more delicious than one would think. By the fourth piece, he realized that he would need to slow down with the eating and pace himself for the long wait.

The next two hours passed uneventfully. By the time Stanton came to tell him the delivery had been completed, he had finished the hushpuppies and the two sandwiches.

"Your truck is ready," Stanton said, peeking her head in the doorway without entering the room.

"Thanks." Knox gathered his things and followed her out of the building.

"I have obtained authorization for you to overnight on base if you are interested in doing that. Might be better than any of the truck stops nearby." Stanton informed him.

"That would be good. Thanks." Knox was grateful for the option. "Can I park near the fitness center so I can shower?"

"Yes, that's what I was thinking. It's a bit of a walk if you want to go to the Exchange or get food, but only about ten minutes. There's a sandwich shop at the Exchange, but we're a small base, so there's not much else for food unless you go off base." Stanton seemed to be apologizing for the inconvenience of parking being unbalanced with the limited choices of food.

"I'm not picky about dinner tonight. So, I'll be fine. Thanks, though." Knox reassured her.

"Good. I'll ride with you to the place where you can park. Then, I'll give you an overview of where things are.

Knox drove the rig to the parking lot near the fitness center with Stanton in the passenger seat. Once they had parked, she walked with him into the fitness center and explained the arrangement to the attendant. The attendant was a non-military government employee who greeted Knox with a friendly handshake.

"Welcome, Mr. Creed. I'm Brandon. I'll show you where things are, and then you can come and go as you please." The attendant smiled at Knox, his dark, close-cut hair and trim physique typical of someone who spends a lot of time at the gym.

"Thanks, Brandon." Knox smiled back, their eyes meeting in a way that made Knox think there might be more to Brandon showing him around than Stanton suspected.

"Well, I'll leave you to it, then," Stanton said as he turned and walked out the door.

"Are you interested in working out or just showering?" Brandon asked.

"Mainly just showering. I need to get on the road early tomorrow, and I need to get dinner. So, no to working out." Knox replied. "Well, at least not the kind of workout that might happen in the gym." Knox laughed and winked at Brandon.

"You'd be surprised at the variety of workouts you can do here." Brandon winked back.

"I might be interested in hearing more about that," Knox said, looking Brandon directly in the eyes to see if he could read whether this guy was actually coming on to him. He suspected that he was. Knox would eventually make a move. What's the worst that could happen? He gets kicked off base and must spend the night at a truck stop?

"Let's start with the locker room, then. That's where all the good equipment is." Brandon laughed again.

Knox followed Brandon down a wide hallway to the entrance to the Men's locker room on the right. There was a room to the left with cardio equipment and a larger space directly ahead with a basketball court, free weights, and other equipment. The locker room was large, with several rows of lockers and a shower corridor to the back with eight shower stalls. A bank of toilet stalls and urinals balanced the counter of sinks to the left. Brandon moved quickly through the space, mentioning the obvious use of things as he went. As they walked back to the exit of the locker room, Brandon stopped in front of a closed door. The sign read "O-6/GS-15/SES and above. Key available at the desk."

"This," Brandon said, "Is the high-ranking officer and civilian private shower. It's a single-person use, and we hand out the key at the desk. You can use this if you want. Would you like to see it?"

"Yes, thanks," Knox said.

"I'll grab the key from the front. Be right back." Brandon said as he turned and jogged off to get the key. He returned less than a minute later and unlocked the door, motioning for Knox to enter.

Knox walked through the door, and Brandon followed, allowing the door to close and lock behind him. The room was like a large, private bathroom. A sink counter to the right, situated next to a toilet, and a large shower stall at the far end. A wood bench stood to the left.

"There are towels provided." Brandon pointed to a stack of towels on one end of the long bench. "And shower gel, shampoo, and conditioner are in the dispensers on the wall in the shower."

"What time do you get off work?" Knox asked casually.

"Uh, seven. The gym is open 24/7, but you must have a government ID to scan for entry after that. This shower room is only available before 7 p.m." Brandon responded, looking at Knox as if he knew what was coming next.

"I'll come back just before seven then. To shower." Knox stated. "I'm going to get dinner first. Can you point me towards the Exchange?"

"Sure." Brandon opened the door and walked out of the shower room and towards the exit of the building. He pointed to the left. "Just follow this sidewalk. It's about ten minutes."

"Thanks," Knox said, knowing Brandon was expecting something to happen then and enjoying the tease of making him wait. "I'll see you at seven. When you get off. To shower."

Knox walked to the Exchange and bought a sub sandwich and a large diet soda, which he took back with him to the truck and enjoyed in private. He finished his sandwich and packed his duffle with things that he might need in the shower, including two packets of lube. He changed into the workout clothes that he had bought at Tinker so that he would fit in better at the gym. At a quarter to seven, he shouldered his duffle bag and walked the short distance to the fitness center. Brandon smiled brightly when he saw Knox. He had the key to the shower room ready and handed it to Knox.

"Let me know if you need anything?" Brandon offered.

"Thanks. Do you mind checking on me when you get off work? Knox asked.

"Uh, sure," Brandon said, locking eyes with Knox to make sure he understood. Then he winked.

Knox winked back, turned, and walked towards the shower room. He unlocked and opened the door, threw his bag on the bench, and left it there while he went to the main bathroom area to take a shit. When he returned to the private room, he engaged the security lock on the door before it closed, ensuring that anyone from the outside would be allowed to enter. He started the shower and removed his clothes. When the water was hot, he stepped in and quickly washed and rinsed himself well. He heard the door open and the security lock disengage and then re-engage after the door closed completely. He pulled the shower curtain back completely, standing naked in front of Brandon as the water continued to cascade over his hairy chest, running in rivulets down his stomach and off the end of his semi-erect penis in the appearance of a strong stream of urine.

Brandon stared, licking his lips, his left hand massaging the growing bulge in his pants.

"Your body… just, wow," Brandon said. "It's even better than I imagined."

"Join me," Knox commanded.

Brandon quickly stripped and stepped into the large shower with Knox. Brandon was shorter than Knox. His body was lean, firm, and cut. The definition in his abs and chest was clearly visible through the layer of black hair that covered his chest and belly. His skin was creamy white, indicating that he stayed out of the sun or used sunscreen. Knox found the contrast of white skin and black hair attractive. Brandon's dick was seven inches and average girth, with a fat mushroom head that now pulsed with his full erection.

Brandon stepped forward, his body coming into full contact with Knox's. Their erect cocks were pressing against each other as each man's hands reached around to grasp the other's butt cheeks. The water from the showerhead covered both of them, making their hairy bodies slick. Brandon's right middle finger ventured to Knox's ass crack and started slowly massaging Knox's hairy hole. Having found a suitable target, Brandon forcefully turned Knox away from him, pushing away on his upper back. Knox bent forward, his hands supporting himself on the tile of the shower wall. Brandon squatted behind Knox, his toned thighs showing clear muscle definition through the black hair on his white legs. He split Knox's ass cheeks with his fingers and pressed his face firmly into the hairy crevice. Knox released a gasp of breath as Brandon's tongue found his hole. Brandon drew a circle with his tongue, flicking and probing in the moist orifice. Knox pushed against Brandon's face, grinding his hips in pleasure.

Brandon stood, placing his hard cock pointing up in Knox's crack, moving it up and down as the hair on Knox's ass created friction. Brandon reached up with his right hand and grabbed Knox's hair, pulling his head back, teasing his hole but not entering him. Knox reached over and turned off the water. He turned back to Brandon, pulling him in and kissing him, tasting his own musk in Brandon's mouth.

"I've got lube on the counter. I want you to fuck me." Knox said.

Knox stepped out of the shower and reached for one of the two packets of lube on the counter by the sink. He tore off the corner and squeezed it all into his hand. He reached around and lubed up his own hole quickly, then reached out and did the same with Brandon's ready cock. Knox placed one foot up on the bench and his hands on the wall. He arched his back and pushed his ass out, an invitation for Brandon to continue. Brandon took his own dick in his right hand and guided the big head to Knox's hole. When in position, he moved both hands to Knox's hips and applied light pressure forward. Knox pushed back hard, forcing Brandon's oversized head inside him. The sensation was intensely painful and then immediately pleasurable.

Brandon started thrusting, moving his hips from side to side and in circles as he went in and out. This was not his first time, Knox thought. He reached under Knox's raised leg and firmly gripped his throbbing cock. He stroked Knox's cock downward as if milking it. Slower as he approached the head, then quicker as he went towards the base. The ridges of his fingers rippled across the head of Knox's cock with each stroke. As Brandon's thrusts became faster, so did the strokes on Knox's dick. Brandon came inside Knox with several hard thrusts, collapsing on Knox's back. Brandon's hand released Knox's cock, and Knox placed his raised foot on the floor, turning so that he was sitting on the bench.

"Give me a minute, and I'll suck you off," Brandon said.

"I have a better idea," Knox said as he reached for the other packet of lube.

Knox rapidly opened the packet and smeared the contents in Brandon's ass, pulling him back to sitting on Knox's hard dick. Knox's cock entered Brandon with resistance. His hole was tight and warm. Brandon gasped and tried to pull forward, but Knox held him in place. Brandon quickly settled onto Knox's crotch and started rocking back and forth. This position usually made Knox cum quickly, but this time he was different. The sensation was amazing. Brandon's hole was tight and hot. Knox could feel the hairs in Brandon's crack brushing against his dick as it moved in and out. Knox reached around to rub the hair on Brandon's chest, which reminded him of Ryder's.

Ryder's face came into Knox's mind, and he fucked Brandon thinking he was fucking Ryder. He ran his hands along Brandon's legs, his eyes closed. The hair on Brandon's legs felt like Ryder's.

"Ryder." He whispered quietly as he came inside Brandon's hole. The sound, unbidden and raw, hung in the humid air. It was undeniable now: Ryder wasn't just a possibility; he was becoming a constant, an inescapable presence in Knox's thoughts, even in the most intimate moments with another man.

"Did you say something?" Brandon asked as he stood and moved to the shower, turning on the water and motioning for Knox to join him. Knox hesitated a moment, then entered the shower, not answering Brandon's query. They kissed lightly while they lathered up their bodies and rinsed off. They dried themselves with the towels on the end of the bench and started getting dressed.

"That was hot," Brandon said. "Your hole is perfect. And your body is gorgeous. But I have to tell you, I haven't been fucked in a long time. I consider myself a top, so that took me by surprise."

"You seemed to like it," Knox said casually, staring at Brandon and daring him to deny it.

"I did. A lot." Brandon admitted. "I'm not sure what that means."

"It means you like what you like with certain guys. That's all it means." Knox said. "I used to be the same way as you. Now, I just do what I like. I don't feel like bottoming with every guy I hook up with. Just when it feels right. Like with you. And you ate my ass like a champ. Clearly not your first time." They both laughed at this last comment.

"Well, your ass is very edible." Brandon smiled.

When they were dressed, Brandon led the way out of the building, which was quiet.

"Thanks for letting me use the private shower," Knox said.

"Thank you for sharing. Have a safe trip back to your home." Brandon turned and walked to his car.

Knox climbed in the cab, got undressed and crawled under the covers. He turned on the TV, selected an action movie to watch, and arranged a bag of popcorn and a cup of diet soda from the sandwich shop on the shelf beside the bed. The hero in the movie reminded him of Ryder, and he resisted the urge to text him. He drifted off to sleep before the movie ended, holding his pillow tight and imagining that he was spooning Ryder.

The morning came with an urgency to get on the road. Knox moved the truck to the charging station and plugged it in. He walked the ten minutes to the shoppette to get bad coffee and a breakfast sandwich, which he ate on the walk back to the truck. The truck needed only a short period to charge to a level to get on the road, and Knox used the time to plan his route. The truck's app had a feature that allowed him to find charging stations along a route to maximize drive time, and he projected he could be in Amarillo in two days if he took time only to charge the truck and take naps. He would text Ryder with an update when he got to his charge stop.

Knox selected a new audiobook and left the Air Force base, making his way west to link up to I-40. The four-hour drive to the truck stop in West Marion went quickly. He parked the truck at the charger, plugged it in, and walked to the main building to use the restroom and grab a snack. He expected that he might see Kyle and would deal with that if it happened. After using the restroom, Knox bought two bottles of water, three bags of beef jerky, and several small bags of nuts. Back in the truck, he stretched out on the bed to take a quick nap, setting the alarm on his phone to avoid sleeping more than an hour.

Forty-five minutes later, Knox woke without the alarm, turned the alarm off, and texted Ryder.

(Knox) Hey

(Knox) I'm on my way back west

(Knox) chat?

Knox prepared to leave, not expecting to hear back from Ryder so quickly.

(Ryder) Hey

(Ryder) Yes, to chat. I'll call in ten minutes.

Knox smiled. He got in the driver's seat, buckled his seat belt, and got back on the road. A few minutes later, the screen on the truck notified him of an incoming call. He pressed the screen to talk to Ryder.

"Hey, Ryder." Knox opened the call.

"Knox. It's so good to hear your voice. The past two days have been difficult." Ryder admitted.

"I know, buddy. I know." Knox agreed.

"I'm not used to dealing with this kind of thing. New stuff. For both of us, I think." Ryder said.

"Agree. Let's just acknowledge that we feel the same and be good with that. Sound good?" Knox suggested.

"Totally," Ryder said. "So, what's your ETA?"

"Sometimes, day after tomorrow," Knox said.

"Okay. When you get closer to Amarillo, I'll text directions to the ranch. Maps won't get you to the right place." Ryder said.

"Got it. I'll text along the way." Knox offered.

"I'd like that," Ryder responded. "Hey, Knox..."

"Yes?" Knox said.

"I'm really looking forward to seeing you," Ryder responded.

"Me too, buddy, me too." Knox smiled to himself at Ryder's admission.

"Get here safely, Knox," Ryder said, his voice betraying his need to see Knox.

"I will, Ryder. I will." Knox reassured him.

Knox pressed a button on the steering wheel to disconnect the call and resumed listening to his audiobook. His next planned stop was in 5 hours. He trusted the solar panels would help get him there. If the batteries got too low, he would find a closer charging station. The sun was bright and would help the solar panels extend the range. Knox also focused on maximizing the regenerative braking when he could, particularly on the downward slopes of the mountain pass. When he rolled into the charging station outside Nashville, the battery level was down to under 5%, which was uncomfortably low for Knox.

After plugging in the truck, Knox found a place nearby to use the restroom and got back in the cab for a short nap. He texted Ryder before setting his alarm and falling asleep.

(Knox) Nashville to charge and nap

(Knox) having beef jerky and nuts, lol

(Knox) getting more excited to see you

He fell asleep quickly and was slightly disoriented when his alarm sounded ninety minutes later. He sat up on the bed, grabbed a bottle of water, and gathered his thoughts. He walked to a nearby convenience store to use the restroom and get some coffee. He was happy to see that Ryder had texted back.

(Ryder) beef jerky and nuts, lol

(Ryder) I've got some jerky and nuts for you

(Ryder) VERY excited to see you

(Ryder) be safe

Knox felt a warm feeling wash over him as he read Ryder's texts. He allowed himself to enjoy the emotion and smiled at the thought that he would see Ryder soon. He got back on the road and settled in with his audiobook for the next five hours to Little Rock, Arkansas. The drive was uneventful, and Knox was able to maintain his focus on safely navigating the flat, dark highway. He arrived in Little Rock just after 2 a.m. He was feeling like he needed more than an hour of sleep, so he plugged in the truck and set an alarm for three hours. When the alarm woke him, he felt rested and ready for another five hours of driving. He put on some music and got on I-40 West towards Oklahoma City.

Knox arrived in OKC four and a half hours later. As he passed Tinker Air Force Base, he thought about the underwhelming sex with Dillon. He now realized why it had been so lackluster as he forgot about Dillon and thought about Ryder. He pulled into a supercharger station and hooked up the truck. He was not able to sleep while the truck charged, opting for watching TV instead. With the truck at 99%, he got back on the road, his next stop - Amarillo.

Three and a half hours later, he approached Amarillo. On the east side of the city, he stopped to add some charge to the batteries and to text Ryder.

(Knox) just outside Amarillo

(Knox) topping up the rig

(Knox) directions?

The response from Ryder arrived quickly.

(Ryder) You're close!

(Ryder) take the 335 Loop North and get on 136 North

(Ryder) Go about thirty miles and take a right on County Road A

(Ryder) Take a left on County Road C

(Ryder) you will see the entrance to One Horse Ranch on the left.

(Ryder) you can't miss the gate

(Knox) got it.

(Knox) see u soon!

Knox got back on the road and pushed the speed limit in his excitement to get to the ranch. Thirty minutes later, he was on County Road C. A few miles after turning onto the two-lane road, Knox saw a structure on the left. Two huge, pink granite columns stood on the side of the road. The columns were joined by a high arch of weathered steel. Attached to the upper section of the steel arch were the words One Horse Ranch. The height and width of the gate were large enough to accommodate the rig. Knox looked in his mirrors to make sure there were no other approaching vehicles and paused before pulling through the gate. He wasn't capable of sorting through the emotions that flooded him. So, he pushed them down and pulled through the gate.

Knox could see the paved drive stretching out ahead of him in the early afternoon sun. He moved forward slowly and drove for about a mile when the road curved to the left and started on a very slight downward slope. As he rounded the curve, he saw the ranch house before him. The first thing he noticed was the view beyond the roof of the massive, one-story structure. The North Texas landscape reached far into the distance. Large sections of flat pastureland were sliced by undulating hills, low cliffs, and shallow canyons. Shades of muted greens and browns were enhanced by the orange and yellow light provided by the setting sun. Immediately beyond the long dwelling was a small lake, appearing to be attached to the house itself. Knox slowed to a roll, taking it all in and determining where he might park the rig.

Knox took in the house as he rolled slowly forward. The house was huge. At the center was a portico that was wide and tall enough for him to pull the truck under. Access was provided by a wide circular drive that intersected the portico. A matching length of pavement veered to the right and wound around to the back of the house and what must be garages and parking areas. The wings of the house stretched out to either side. There appeared to be an absence of windows on the front of the building. Knox could see a large amount of glass under the portico and a series of walled courtyards on either wing, but otherwise, no windows that would look out to the front drive. The thick, square columns that supported the portico were of the same pink granite as the gate. Light brown brick, timber beams, and cream-colored stone accented the top and base of each column. The rest of the house was a graceful combination of the same materials. Knox decided to proceed with boldness as he pulled the rig under the portico. When he had placed the truck in park, he looked forward and noticed several other buildings near the house that he had not seen before. A large stable building and a barn were connected to the house by a large patch of grass and a narrow, paved driveway. The outbuildings were constructed of the same materials as the house.

Knox hopped down out of the truck and walked around the front to approach the door, preparing himself for ringing the doorbell and seeing Ryder. As he rounded the front of the truck, he saw him. Ryder was standing in the shadow of the front door, leaning casually against the brick wall, his arms crossed, smiling.

"I enjoyed watching you pull in," Ryder said, uncrossing his arms and walking towards Knox.

"This is some place," Knox said.

"Family home," Ryder said as if there was absolutely nothing special about it.

Knox moved forward quickly, wrapped his arms around Ryder and pulled him close.

"I've been driving for two days, haven't showered, and haven't had much sleep. And I am so happy to see you." Knox whispered in Ryder's ear.

They kissed gently at first, exploring each other's mouths as if they had never met. Then, the kiss became more passionate as the memories of each other surfaced. Knox took Ryder's head in both hands as Ryder's arms reached around Knox's waist and pulled him close. The two men tightened their hold on each other as if they might be torn apart and never allowed to see each other again. Ryder pulled his face away from Knox's and buried it in the crevice of Knox's neck.

"I was afraid you might not come." He admitted as tears welled up in his eyes. "I was preparing myself for not seeing you again."

Knox pulled Ryder's head up, regaining his hold on each side, his thumbs gently wiping at Ryder's tears. "Ryder, I'm here. Like I said, I would be. Just you and me. I needed to see you just as much as you needed to see me. Understand?"

"Yes, I understand." Ryder smiled and wiped at his own face. "I'm really looking forward to getting to know you, Knox Creed."

"Me too, with you, Ryder. Me too." Knox reassured him, not fully understanding why he meant that but knowing that he did.

"Why don't you come in and shower. Then I can show you around before we have dinner." Ryder offered.

"Sounds good," Knox said as he followed Ryder into the house.

Ryder led the way through the massive double doors, turned right down a long hallway, and stopped before a large door at the end. Knox did not pay attention to anything as they walked. His focus was only on Ryder and the feel of their hands touching as Ryder pulled him along. Ryder opened the door and entered a large foyer, a living room with two facing sofas was directly in front of them. The floor-to-ceiling windows beyond the living room looked out over the lake and the landscape that Knox had noticed on his approach.

Ryder guided Knox through the living room and turned left into a bedroom. The king-sized bed was situated against a half wall, with the bed itself facing another set of windows that shared the view of the living room. The bed was made of timber and iron, the four posts extending almost to the ceiling. The décor in the rest of the room was eclectic. Two leather chairs flanked a stone fireplace, with an odd collection of side tables, credenzas, and rugs that covered the wide plank wood floors. On the opposite side of the wall behind the bed was one of several rows of built-in closet cabinets. Ryder led Knox through these on the way to the shower. A few of the closet doors were glass, and Knox could see an impressive display of cowboy hats, boots, and other accessories.

They reached the bathroom, with a large copper soaking tub, a long counter with two sinks, a separate toilet room, and the prime feature of the bathroom – the shower. The shower sat in the very center of the large space. A complete glass cube, with the pipes for the showerhead rising from the floor and floating against the glass wall.

"Soap and stuff is on the teak stool in the shower. Towels are on the rack here by the door." Ryder pointed to the free-standing wooden rack that stood next to the glass cube.

"Join me," Knox said.

"What? Ryder responded.

"Join me. I don't want to wait another second to explore your body." Knox repeated himself.

"Gladly, Knox. I know you're tired, but I want to touch you so badly." Ryder admitted as he started taking off his clothes, letting them drop to the floor in random piles.

"Knox undressed quickly, leaving his clothes on the floor, as well. Naked and aroused, the two men entered the large glass cube. Ryder started the water, and Knox noticed that there were two showerheads on opposite sides of the shower. The water got warm quickly, and Ryder gently moved Knox under the crossing streams of water. Their erections reminded them of the mutual attraction that each man had been suppressing for the past week. Knox moved towards Ryder, pulled him close, and started kissing his face. Knox's kisses were soft, attentive, and teasing. Ryder tilted his head back, pushing his crotch forward so that his hard cock pressed against Knox's and between their bellies.

Ryder reached over to the teak stool and pumped a large amount of sandalwood body wash into his palm. He stared at Knox's chest and worked the lather through Knox's thick fur, moving up to his shoulders, down his arms, and into the creases on each side of Knox's testicles. Knox gathered some of the bodywash and performed a similar motion for Ryder. The two men continued exploring and kissing, their hands moving slowly and deliberately. Occasionally, they would break from the kissing to nuzzle into each other, enjoying the simple presence of the other.

Knox reached a soapy hand down to Ryder's cock and started to stroke it lightly. Ryder firmly pulled his hand away.

"Not yet," Ryder whispered through the sound of the falling water. "We're going to rinse off, dry off, get dressed, and then I'm going to show you around before dinner. After dinner, we're going to come back to my bed, and I'm going to make love to you all night long. Understand." Ryder pulled back and looked directly into Knox's eyes, smiling.

"I understand that you're a tease." Knox smiled back. "But, yes, I understand. You're going to keep me horny for several hours and then tease me some more. I like it. Besides, I've been wanting to make love to you for over a week now, so another few hours won't kill me. At least, I don't think it will." Knox laughed as Ryder continued to rub Knox's chest.

"Good boy," Ryder said, which made Knox blush. He was usually the one who said that line, but he kinda liked it being said to him.

They rinsed and toweled off, and Ryder handed Knox a robe to wear to his truck to get his clothes.

"Is there anyone else in the house that I should know about?" Knox asked.

"Not really. The chef is in the kitchen, and the other staff have all left for the evening." Ryder answered.

"Chef? Staff?" Knox said.

"Listen, Knox, it's a large house and a working ranch. We have a staff, a chef, a ranch manager, and other people who work for us. I will tell you all about ranch operations tomorrow. For now, it's just us. My parents will be home tomorrow evening. They have a suite like mine at the other end of the house. You and I can have as much or as little privacy as we want." Ryder explained.

"Okay, Ryder, okay. I'm good with that. It's just a very different world than I live in." Knox said.

"I've learned the hard way that it's a very different world than most people live in, Knox. I've come to terms with that. If you want to be here with me now, you need to do that as well. Can you do that?" Ryder asked. It was a world of unseen hands and effortless luxury, so far removed from the meticulous self-sufficiency of his own life, it felt almost alien. But Ryder was here, and that was everything.

"Ryder, if I'm with you, I feel like I can do anything. So yes, I'll be okay. Just tell me if I'm making a fool of myself around anyone." Knox said.

"Deal. But just be yourself. Promise me that." Ryder requested.

"I will, Ryder. I promise."

Knox walked in the robe to his truck and gathered his things. He returned to the bathroom and got dressed, not seeing Ryder. The clothes he had left on the floor were gone, and his phone, wallet, and belt were sitting on the counter next to one sink. His boots had been moved to the floor by the counter. As he walked out of the bathroom, Ryder entered from the living room.

"I was just checking on dinner," Ryder said as he walked up to Knox and put his arms around his waist, pulling him close. "I can't believe you're here. You are more beautiful than I remember."

"I was just thinking the same thing," Knox said. "When I saw you getting undressed, I couldn't believe how much more attractive you are than I remember from the truck and the FaceTime call. I'm also happy I'm here. Being around you seems comfortable. And I'm not gonna lie, that makes me a little uncomfortable."

"I know, Knox, I'm experiencing the same thing. Let's just roll with it and see where this goes. Deal?" Ryder suggested.

"Deal." Knox agreed.

Ryder led Knox out of the bedroom to show him around the house. The hallways to Ryder's bedroom also contained two guest suites, a library, a theater room, and a billiards room. The area off the front entrance comprised the main living areas, a great room that centered around a massive stone fireplace, and a large kitchen with enough counter space and commercial appliances to cook for many ranch hands. The dining room featured a table that sat twenty guests comfortably. The other wing of the house held Ryder's parent's suite and three other guest rooms. Knox learned that each guest room had a private courtyard. There were two guest rooms with private terraces that faced the lake. The extensive terrace off the great room also presented a swimming pool and vast entertaining areas. By the time they sat down to dinner, Knox was overwhelmed with the wealth that would provide such a life.

Ryder ended the tour in a small room off the kitchen that had been set up as a private dining room. The room itself had no windows and was absent of furniture except for the table set for two and the credenza that was topped with a chocolate cake under a glass dome, along with a stack of plates and a tray of silverware. The table was set with white linens, a bud vase with a single purple Gerbera daisy and a bottle of wine with two glasses. Ryder motioned for Knox to sit, then walked over to him, placed a hand on his shoulder, leaned in and gave Knox a slow, lingering kiss on the lips, his tongue slipping slightly between Knox's lips before retreating. He took the bottle of wine to the credenza, opened a drawer and retrieved a wine key, which he used to open the wine. He poured generous amounts into the two glasses.

Knox usually preferred beer but was not unfamiliar with wine. He had attended several wine tastings over the years and knew what he liked, as well as what characteristics might be considered positive traits for both reds and whites. Ryder sat down opposite Knox and lifted his glass.

"Here's to something new for both of us." He toasted.

"Agreed." Knox lifted his glass and touched it to Ryder's with a clink.

Knox took a tentative sip of the wine. It was luxurious, rich, velvety and delicious. He recognized that it was not a cheap bottle. He took another long draw from the glass, savoring the feel of it in his mouth.

"I don't drink a lot of wine, but this is a really good one," Knox said, immediately realizing how stupid he sounded.

"It's one of my favorites," Ryder said. "I can get you a beer if you want."

"No. This is really good." Knox replied. "And I need to expand my horizons with what I drink with dinner." Knox smiled.

"Speaking of dinner, I need to let Felix know that we're ready," Ryder said as he stood, walking around to Knox and kissing him again, this time letting his tongue and lips linger longer than before.

"You're such a tease," Knox said, grabbing Ryder's wrist and forcing his hand down to feel how hard he had become. Ryder did not reply, simply pulling Knox's hand back to his own crotch, where he had a similar reaction. Ryder left the room and returned seconds later.

"Dinner is on the way. By the way, my erection has not gone down since the shower. So, the first time tonight might be quick." Ryder said.

"Good thing we have all night to do it several times." Knox winked as the door opened, and Felix entered with a rolling cart. The cart was topped with two silver domes. Knox could not remember what those things were called. A cloche, maybe? He would try to remember to look that up later. Felix was an older gentleman, possibly in his sixties, with silver hair, a clean-shaven face, and clearly of Mexican descent. He placed each plate, with dome intact, in front of Ryder and Knox. He lifted the domes with grace, exposing ribeye steaks, grilled asparagus, and twice-baked potatoes. Felix carefully placed small ramekins of various condiments on the table, along with a basket of warm rolls and softened butter sprinkled with coarse sea salt.

"Will there be anything else, Mr. Ryder?" Felix asked.

"No, Felix. Thank you. This looks delicious." Ryder responded.

"Dessert is on the sideboard. Just leave things here when you're done, and I will clean up in the morning. I'll be heading home now if that's okay." Felix said.

"Thank you, Felix. Have a good night. I'll take care of breakfast in the morning, so don't worry about coming to the house until the afternoon." Ryder instructed.

Felix nodded and left the room.

"He's been with my family for thirty years," Ryder said, picking up his fork and steak knife and cutting into the juicy steak. "He lives in a house on the ranch that we provide. We treat our staff well. They have good benefits and a solid retirement plan. All we ask is loyalty to the family and that they do a good job."

"That's very kind of your family," Knox said. "And this steak looks delicious!"

The steak was delicious. Knox and Ryder chatted while they ate. Knox learned that Ryder is an only child. There had been a sister, but she died shortly after birth, and his parents never tried for another. He is the sole heir to the ranch. His parents are progressive thinkers and accept him being gay. Ryder already knew that Knox was an only child. Knox told Ryder about his parents and that he was not as close to them as Ryder was to his own. They discussed political views that were similar to theirs and talked about foods they liked and disliked. Knox ate pretty much anything, while Ryder was more picky, disliking things that had "squishy" textures, like marshmallows and soft vegetables. Ryder likes to cook and did not quite understand Knox's method of putting things together in the kitchen. Knox just told him that he would have to experience it at some point. They laughed and smiled over the chocolate cake that Felix had left on the credenza.

When they were done eating, Ryder started clearing the plates and placing them on the rolling cart that Felix had left in the corner.

"I thought Felix said to leave things." Knox pointed out.

"He did. But I don't like not doing my part. Felix is getting older, and it's a lot of work for him. He would happily clean up in here and not complain, but I like to help him when I can. Sometimes, he lets me cook with him. I'm just going to load things onto the cart and roll it into the kitchen for him." Ryder responded.

"Yet another thing to like about you," Knox said as he helped Ryder clean up.

When the cart had been loaded and moved to the kitchen, Ryder walked to the bar in the great room and got another bottle of wine and two clean glasses. He opened the wine and partially re-inserted the cork before they walked back to the bedroom. After entering the bedroom, Ryder placed the bottle of wine and the two glasses on the bar in the living room and casually walked to the bedroom. Knox followed him. Ryder walked to the bed, removed the throw pillows and pulled back the duvet and sheets. He turned towards Knox, who remained a few feet away and made eye contact. Ryder kicked off his boots. Knox mirrored him. Ryder started unsnapping his own shirt. Knox did the same. Standing facing each other, they maintained eye contact. When Ryder's shirt dropped to the floor, Knox broke the look by gazing at Ryder's torso. Ryder had a perfect body. His well-defined chest was covered at the top with dark hair that tapered to a single line running down his belly. Knox knew he would never tire of having access to this hair pattern and Ryder's body. He felt intense attraction towards Ryder at seeing him shirtless, wearing just his jeans and socks. Knox removed his shirt and got the same reaction from Ryder.

Both men simultaneously unbuckled their belts. Pulling them out of the belt loops and letting them drop to the floor with their shirts and boots. They continued the process with their jeans and socks, eventually standing in front of each other, wearing only their underwear. For Knox, this was a pair of dark green boxer briefs, and for Ryder, it was a well-fitting pair of generic white briefs. Both of their underwear strained at the erections pushing forward. Ryder walked towards Knox and dropped to his knees. He softly kissed Knox's furry belly as he hooked one finger into the waistband of the underwear and pulled down slightly to expose the head of Knox's hard cock. Ryder used his tongue to lick the underside of the head, causing Knox's penis to flex and jump with the sensation. Ryder teased it, running his tongue around the ridge, slowly placing his lips over the entire head and pulling up slowly.

Ryder placed a finger from his other hand in the waistband and pulled Knox's underwear to his ankles. Knox quickly stepped out of the underwear and pushed them aside with his left foot. Ryder placed both hands on Knox's hairy butt cheeks and took his dick fully into his mouth, pushing forward until he could feel the head pulse against the back of his throat. Knox moaned and ran his hands through Ryder's dark hair. Knox allowed Ryder to play with his penis for a few minutes before grasping his shoulders and pulling him up. They looked into each other's eyes. Without touching him, Knox knelt and considered Ryder's bulge. He extended his tongue and traced the erection through the white underwear. Ryder placed his hands on Knox's shoulders, his grip tightening as Knox teased him. Knox reached behind Ryder and inserted his hands into the waistband of Ryder's underwear. Knox pulled the underwear down to rest at the lower edge of Ryder's round, hairless ass. Knox massaged Ryder's butt cheeks and slowly moved his hands forward to pull the underwear completely down. Ryder's hard cock caught in the fabric and popped up, slapping against his belly. Knox caught it in his mouth, taking the entire length in on the downswing.

He slowly pulled his mouth back, pausing when his lips reached the head, his tongue rubbing the underside. Ryder pulled Knox to his feet, bringing him close in a tight embrace, his head resting on Knox's shoulder as their cocks rubbed together.

They kissed softly, unhurriedly, enjoying the sensations and knowing they had all night to make this last. Ryder led Knox over to the bed and climbed in under the sheets, patting the bed beside him to let Knox know to join him. Knox got into bed and turned to face Ryder. Ryder pulled him close, their bodies, dicks, and legs intertwined. They continued to kiss softly, their hands exploring their bodies, gently caressing and venturing along every inch of skin.

Ryder pushed Knox onto his back and straddled him, feeling the pressure of Knox's ample cock on the space under his balls. Ryder took a moment to enjoy Knox's chest, running his hands and fingers through the hair. Ryder filled his right palm with lube from the pump bottle on the right nightstand and reached his hand between his legs from the front. He distributed the lube along his ass crack, getting Knox's erection wet at the same time. He pulled his hand back and rubbed the remaining lube onto his own cock. He grabbed Knox's hands in his own and forced them above Knox's head on the pillow, leaning forward to continue kissing him. With his hands pinned against the pillow, Knox moved his hips in circles, trying to find the right position to enter Ryder. Ryder assisted by moving his hips forward and backward until the tip of Knox's cock rested against his hole. Ryder's sphincter quivered at the sensation of Knox pushing against it. With a firm push, Ryder allowed Knox to enter him. His back arched, and he took in a sharp breath as Knox's thick cock opened him up. Their kissing became more passionate.

Ryder moved his lips to Knox's left ear and nibbled the earlobe.

"I don't know how long I will last," Ryder said.

"Don't hold out. We can go as many rounds as we need to tonight," Knox whispered in Ryder's ear, the sensation of Ryder's attention bringing him closer to orgasm.

Ryder continued riding Knox. Their hips moved in a syncopated rhythm. Knox reached between them and encircled Ryder's trembling cock with his fingers. Just as Knox was reaching orgasm, Ryder came in Knox's hand. The sensation of Ryder's warm jizz spreading between his fingers made Knox thrust faster. He tried to hold out, but the sensation of Ryder's softening dick in his hand quickened Knox's arrival. He unloaded in Ryder, continuing to pump until his dick and balls were empty. Ryder kept rocking his hips, even after Knox had finished. Now that they were both satisfied, Ryder collapsed on top of Knox, releasing his hands and running his own hands down Knox's flanks to enjoy the hair along his thighs, then back up to his chest. Ryder rolled off to the side, letting Knox's softening cock free itself from his cum-soaked hole. Ryder nestled his face on Knox's chest as Knox softly played with Ryder's hair.

"I've been wanting that so badly, Knox. And it was better than I thought it would be." Ryder admitted.

"Me too, Ryder. Me too." Knox responded.

"Do you want to sit in the hot tub? Maybe have a little more wine?" Ryder asked.

"That sounds nice. Let me use the bathroom, and I'll put on some clothes." Knox said.

"No need to put on clothes. There's a private hot tub on the terrace outside the bedroom here." Ryder smiled at him in the dark, leaning over to give him a quick kiss on the lips. "I'll get the wine and meet you outside."

Knox went to the bathroom and peed, thinking how surreal this all was. When he got back to the bedroom, one of the glass doors to the terrace was partially open. Knox walked over, naked, and went outside into the warm Texas night. To the left, in a secluded alcove, Ryder stood, also naked, beside a sunken hot tub that was softly lighted. The landscaping was designed to provide complete privacy from the other terraces, as well as anyone walking by, while still providing a view of the lake. As Knox approached, Ryder was facing away from him, opening the wine. He was struck by the perfect silhouette of Ryder's physique. Ryder had exquisite proportions. His ass was firm and tight, round but not too big. His legs were muscular, and his torso trimmed to a perfect V from his shoulders. Knox's loins stirred, his dick starting to react. He would need to pace himself. He also wanted to get to know Ryder more. He had an unfamiliar urge to allow his time with Ryder to be about more than just sex.

Ryder stepped into the hot tub and lowered his body so that his shoulders were below the surface of the water. Knox joined him. Ryder had placed the two wine glasses on the edge of the stone rim of the hot tub. He handed one to Knox, raised it to the air in toast, and took a sip. Knox did the same. Their legs touched under the water, and they casually rubbed their legs together. Ryder's free hand found Knox's thigh and rested there.

"Knox, that was really good for me. I'm going to just be completely open with you about my emotions. I know it might not be easy for you to do the same, so I just want you to know that there is no pressure and no expectation for you to do the same. Okay?" Ryder looked at Knox seriously.

"Okay," Knox replied, a look of fear and uncertainty on his face.

"I don't know what this is, and I'm struggling to understand my feelings when I'm with you. I mean, I've only known you for five minutes, for fuck's sake. But when I'm with you, like just now in the bed, it's different from any other guy I've been with." Ryder continued. "I'm just saying that I don't know what it means, but it is different enough for me to take notice."

Ryder and Knox were both quiet. Each took sips of the wine, looking down at the water. Ryder's free hand remained on Knox's leg. Knox placed his free hand on top of Ryder's and looked over at him.

"Ryder, emotions like these are difficult for me. So please be patient with me. But... I feel exactly like you. It IS different. And that must mean something. I want to see where this goes. But I need a promise from you." Knox's voice was firm.

"Anything, Knox." Ryder agreed.

"Don't string me along. If you start to feel differently at any point, just tell me. Don't hurt me by letting me think things are what they are not." Knox said with a serious tone.

"Deal. I expect the same from you." Ryder agreed.

Knox moved to straddle Ryder. He placed his hands on the back of Ryder's neck and kissed him, feeling Ryder's response between his legs.

"I need to get some sleep when we get back to the bed. But when we wake up, I want to ride you like you rode me. Sound good?" Knox asked.

"Yes, Knox. That sounds perfect." Ryder agreed.

They enjoyed the hot tub and the wine before going back into the bedroom and getting into the bed. Knox fell asleep quickly, with Ryder curled up on his chest. He woke a few hours later, in the dark, slightly disoriented and very horny. Ryder had turned his back to Knox and was pressed tightly up against him. Knox's hand ventured down to Ryder's ass and lightly rubbed Ryder's smooth ass cheeks. Knox's finger wandered to the crack of Ryder's ass, fingering the hair there and probing to feel the moist hole where he had dropped his load earlier. Ryder stirred and turned to face Knox.

"You ready for another round, big guy?" Ryder said softly.

"Yes," Knox responded, moving Ryder's wrist to his crotch to let him feel how ready he was.

"Yep, I'd say you're ready," Ryder said, taking Knox's hand and putting it on his own erection. "Me too."

Knox pushed Ryder to his back and stretched out on top of him. He took some lube and rubbed a small amount between Ryder's thighs, inserting his own dick between them for some teasing frottage before he rode Ryder's cock. Ryder groaned as the head of Knox's penis rubbed his taint, remembering what it was like to have his thick dick up his hole. Knox pushed up with his hands, with the agility of a gymnast, and positioned his knees on either side of Ryder. Getting more lube, he wet his hole and Ryder's hard, throbbing cock. Knox didn't tease this time. He wanted this, and he wanted it now. Using his right hand, he positioned the head of Ryder's cock at the entrance to his hole and lowered himself onto it. The feeling of Ryder's cock inside of him was better than he could have imagined. It was as if it were designed to perfectly fit him. Knox grabbed Ryder's shoulders with both hands and rocked his hips back and forth slowly. Knox's hands wandered along Ryder's torso, exploring and enjoying as he milked Ryder's cock. Ryder matched Knox's rhythm, his hands on Knox's hips to guide the motion.

Knox leaned forward and kissed Ryder, their tongues exploring more of what was now familiar territory. Ryder removed his right hand from Knox's hip and reached under his balls. The tips of his fingers felt where his cock was sliding in and out of Knox's ass. Ryder curled his fingers to trace a line up along the crease in Knox's tightening scrotum and up his cock. At the head, Ryder made a circle with his thumb and forefinger and applied pressure just below the ridge of the head. He moved the loop of his fingers up and down the head of Knox's cock. The feel of Knox's cock in his hand brought Ryder close. He held out as long as possible, using all his willpower to enjoy the sensation as his cock built towards eruption. Not being able to hold it any longer, he thrust upward and held it there while he let go in Knox's hole. Knox ground down to get as much of Ryder in him as possible. Ryder maintained his hold on Knox's dick. Knox kept moving his hips after Ryder's orgasm. The feeling of Ryder's hand around his cock was intoxicating. Ryder placed both hands on Knox's chest, running his fingers through the hair and finding the nipples. Ryder pinched and flicked, then rubbed his fingers across them, letting the ridges of his whole hand ripple across Knox's erect nipples. The sensation overwhelmed Knox with ecstasy, and within minutes, his cum arched from his penis and landed in blobs and streaks across Ryder's chest and belly. A small amount hit Ryder's chin as his tongue extended across his bottom lip and caught it before it dripped to join the amount on his chest. As he was cumming, Knox looked down at Ryder, at his beautiful face and the dark hair across the top of his chest. Knox's own cum hitting that dark hair expounded the pleasure of his orgasm. He leaned forward, his face resting in the wet of Ryder's chest. Ryder's softening cock escaped Knox's ass. Breathing hard, Knox kissed Ryder's nipple, then his neck, moving himself up to kiss him fully on the mouth.

Knox slid to the side of Ryder, put his arm under Ryder's neck and pulled him close, hugging him tightly. Ryder reciprocated, wrapping his arms around Knox and pulling him in.

"Thank you," Knox whispered.

"I know," Ryder responded.

They both fell asleep quickly.

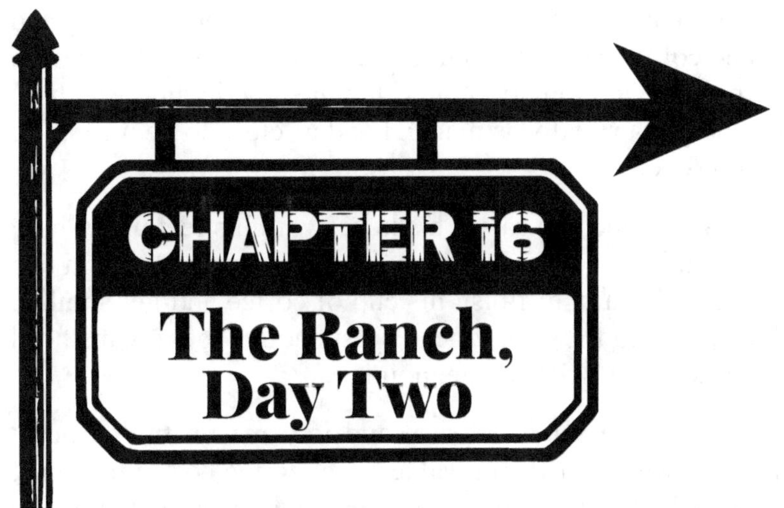

When Knox woke, he was alone in the bed. He stared at the ceiling, taking a moment to process where he was and what had happened the previous evening. As he recalled the diner, fucking Ryder, the hot tub, and Ryder fucking him, a smile appeared on his face. He was experiencing a sense of contentment that was both unfamiliar and comfortable. He could get used to this. But what did that mean? At this moment, he did not care. He was committed to simply enjoying his time with Ryder. The early morning sun was filtering through the large glass doors that led to the terrace. Knox sat up in bed, thinking that Ryder must have good coffee and where he might find it. He looked out over the lake and noticed Ryder on the terrace. He was naked, on a yoga mat, face down in a pose that Ryder thought might be a child's pose. Ryder rose to his feet, one leg in front of the other, his hands extended above his head. Knox watched as Ryder continued with his flow, moving gracefully from position to position. The beauty that Knox had seen in Ryder's body when he was standing by the hot tub was amplified. Knox had never seen such beauty in another man. Knox also found that he had an erection. Would it be rude to interrupt his yoga practice by walking out there and sticking his dick in Ryder's ass? He thought it might be, but it still might happen at some point. The thought made Knox chuckle.

The faint smell of coffee wafted into the room. Knox leaped out of bed and walked to the living room area. On the bar, a fresh pot of coffee had just finished brewing. The coffee maker was a Ratio Eight. Knox had heard about these but did not know anyone who had dropped the $900 on what some would consider a machine that did the same thing as a Mr. Coffee and was one-twentieth of the price. Knox took a glass, double-walled mug from the shelf above the bar and poured himself a cup. He walked back to the bedroom and stood at the glass door. He took a sip from the mug and watched Ryder. The coffee was amazing, rivaling the quality of brew from his Gaggia. To Knox, the combination of coffee this good while watching Ryder in his morning yoga ritual was magical and as close to heaven as he ever thought he would be.

Ryder finished his routine and sat on his knees with his feet under him, facing the lake, his hands resting lightly on his thighs. He remained in this position long enough for Knox to finish his cup of coffee and get another. When he rose, he walked to the door, opened just enough to stick his head in, and gave Knox a lingering kiss on the mouth.

"Mmm, coffee. Get me a cup, please, and join me on the terrace." Ryder smiled at Knox, who turned and walked back to the coffee machine. Seconds later, Knox joined Ryder on the terrace. Ryder was seated on the stone ledge that overlooked the lake. Knox walked to him, handing him his coffee before taking a seat beside him. They sat silently for a few minutes while Ryder took his first few sips.

"Good coffee," Knox commented. "I've heard of the Ratio Eight but never seen one. It's almost as good as my Gaggia."

"Life is too short for bad coffee," Ryder said. "And you have a Gaggia? You are full of surprises, Mr. Creed."

"Speaking of surprises," Knox continued. "Yoga?"

"Yep. Got into it a few years ago. It helps me clear my mind and maintain a healthy body. You ever tried it?" Ryder asked.

"Once. It was not a good experience." Knox admitted.

"Hmm, maybe it was with the wrong teacher." Ryder mused.

"Maybe," Knox said. "But I'm open to it."

Knox, I like coming out here in the morning because it helps me process my thoughts. And my thoughts are all about you right now. I've spent one night with you. And it was amazing. And the encounter in your truck was amazing. And the phone calls were amazing. Dinner was amazing. You're amazing." Ryder went on. "It's all happening so quickly."

Knox was expecting this. He thought he knew where this went. He was wrong.

Ryder continued. "Knox, this is something special. I'm smart enough to know when something is good and needs to be explored. So, I've made the decision to be honest with you. You can take that how you want. The truth is, Knox, I'm falling in love with you."

Ryder was silent, letting Knox process what he had said.

Knox looked at Ryder. He placed his mug to his side and then took Ryder's mug from his hand and did the same. He leaned in and kissed Ryder. Long, slow, and reassuring. He took Ryder's head in his hands and touched his forehead to Ryder's.

"Thank you, Ryder. I think that's what I'm feeling, too. I just need more time to process it. Are you okay with that?" Knox said very softly. Love. The word felt immense, terrifying, a raw, exposed nerve he'd meticulously guarded for decades. It was a leap, a plunge into uncharted emotional depths he wasn't sure he was ready for, but desperately wanted to take.

"Yes, Knox. I just need you to know what's going through my mind and in my heart. Take as much time as you need." Ryder reached up a hand and caressed Knox's face, moving their lips together for another slow kiss.

"I want some breakfast," Ryder said matter-of-factly.

"Me too. What are my choices?" Knox asked.

"Right now, your only choice is to sit here," Ryder said as he moved to his knees, kneeling on the grass below the ledge where they were sitting. He placed his hands on Knox's knees and spread his legs. Knox had developed a raging erection with the feel of Ryder's hands on his legs. Ryder ignored the erection. He stared at Knox's face as his hands slid up to Knox's nipples, which he playfully pinched. In the movement of reaching his hands forward, his chest hair brushed lightly against Knox's hard cock, sending shivers through Knox's entire body. Ryder moved his hands down Knox's hairy belly, taking his time to explore the patterns in the hair. As his hands reached Knox's crotch, they circumvented the persistent and erect penis and traced lines along the side and down under his balls.

Ryder extended his forefingers under Knox's testicles and applied pressure there, pulling his fingers forward until the skin of the scrotum stretched on the tips. Ryder turned his palms to face Knox's thighs, running his hands flatly down to the inner knee and down to Knox's ankles. He wrapped his fingers around Knox's ankles, squeezed tightly, and on loosening his grip, let them glide gently across the top of Knox's feet. When he reached the toes, Ryder encircled each big toe with his thumb and forefinger, grasping firmly.

Ryder moved his mouth to the head of Knox's erect dick and placed it lightly in his mouth. When Ryder applied pressure with his mouth to Knox's cock, he simultaneously slid the entire thing into his throat while pulling firmly on Knox's big toes. Ryder maintained this pressure on Knox's toes while he slowly sucked his cock. The sensation was unlike anything Knox had experienced. The orgasm arrived quickly and was intense. Ryder swallowed it all, then licked everything that dripped out. He attended to Knox's cock with focus, exploring every vein, every crease, every line until it was soft and clean.

"Okay, now we can have breakfast," Ryder said, kissing Knox lightly on the forehead as he stood up. Knox stood and followed Ryder to the bedroom. He approached Ryder and wrapped his arms around him from behind, kissing the back of his neck.

"Thank you. That was amazing." Knox whispered in his ear.

Ryder leaned back into Knox and turned his head back and to the side. "I enjoyed doing it. I love your cock."

Ryder took Knox's hand and walked to the closet area. He opened a cabinet door, pulled out a drawer and took out two pairs of shorts. Both are dark gray, three-inch inseam, and designed for running. He threw one at Knox and slipped the other pair on himself. Knox put on the shorts and followed Ryder, who had left the closet and was headed to the living room and the door to the hallway.

"What do you usually like for breakfast?" Ryder asked as they walked to the kitchen.

"Whatever is available. You?" Knox asked.

"Same. If Felix has something prepared, I'll eat that. Otherwise, I just grab whatever is available. However, today, I feel like making you an omelet. Want to do it together?" Ryder continued.

"Yes, please." Knox smiled. "But just so you know, I'm sort of an ad hoc cook. I just take whatever is available and make it work. I can also follow directions." They both laughed.

"Cool. Let's figure it out together then." Ryder said, rifling through the refrigerator.

Ryder took out six eggs, a small bag of pre-shredded cheddar cheese, a carton of cream, and a variety of vegetables. Mushrooms, cherry tomatoes, an onion, and slices of cooked bacon from a previous meal made for a good start. Ryder proceeded to break the eggs into a bowl, added a splash of cream and whisked forcefully as he instructed Knox to chop up the other ingredients. They stood side by side, hips touching as they silently worked.

"I think I'll do a frittata rather than an omelet," Ryder said, pausing to preheat the oven.

"I've never made a frittata, but I'm game," Knox said, looking at Ryder, who smiled back at him, leaned in and kissed him firmly on the lips. Ryder let his mouth linger on Knox's, enjoying the taste of coffee and the sensation of the casual affection.

"Keep that up, and we'll never make it to breakfast." Knox laughed.

"I just can't help myself!" Ryder exclaimed, laughing with Knox.

"I know. We've got all day. And tomorrow, if you're feeling it." Knox offered.

"Right now, I'm feeling I want to get as much of you as I can," Ryder said as he tumbled the chopped veggies, cheese, and bacon into the eggs and cream.

He slid the bowl towards Knox, who stirred the mixture slowly, while Ryder got a skillet from the cabinet. Ryder placed the skillet on the gas cooktop to preheat and started fresh cups of coffee for them both. The machine in the main kitchen was a popular brand that was built into the cabinetry with the rest of the appliances. With a single touch, it made decent Americanos. Ryder took the egg mixture and poured it slowly into the heated pan, moving it around with a spatula as he reduced the heat. Knox pressed himself to Ryder's back and wrapped his arms around Ryder's waist, gently kissing his neck as Ryder stirred the eggs.

"You're distracting me," Ryder said softly. "And I love it."

Knox continued his affection as Ryder continued cooking. Ryder turned off the gas and moved the pan to the oven, closing the oven door and turning to face Knox. Ryder pulled Knox close and kissed him.

"I was thinking that we might go in the pool for a swim after breakfast, then I want to show you around the ranch. My parents will be here this afternoon and will expect us to join them for dinner. Are you okay with that plan?" Ryder asked.

"Yes, are your parents expecting me to be here?" Knox wanted to know.

"Yes, I told them about you. I have never had a guy stay overnight, so they are curious." Ryder replied.

"I see," Knox said as he looked at the oven's glass door. "How do we know when this is ready?"

"It puffs up like it is now." Ryder smiled, using an oven mitt to remove the pan from the hot oven and place it on a trivet sitting on the counter. He turned off the oven and took two plates from the cabinet, placing them side-by-side to the right of the frittata, using a spatula to place a generous portion on each before getting two forks from a drawer nearby.

"Let's eat outside. It's a beautiful day," Ryder suggested, handing Knox a plate.

They walked to a shaded area of the expansive terrace and sat at a small table to eat their breakfast. They were mostly silent, simply enjoying the company of each other. When they were done, Ryder gathered up their plates, and Knox followed him inside as he placed all the dirty dishes in the sink, rinsing them to make it easier for Felix to clean up. They walked back to the bedroom, and Ryder took two short-inseam jammers from a drawer, tossing one at Knox.

"Felix might arrive soon, so no skinny dipping today." He smiled as he removed his other shorts and slipped on the swimsuit. Knox stared, marveling at the level of attraction he felt for this man. Knox took off his own shorts and pulled on the stretchy swimsuit. It was not something he would normally wear, and he found it very comfortable. He looked up to see Ryder staring back at him.

"What?" Knox chided.

"The best thing about these," Ryder pointed to his own swimsuit, "Is that I can be constantly teased by seeing the outline of your magnificent penis."

Knox looked at Ryder's crotch and noticed his erection evident against the material of the suit. "Yep, that's gonna be hard to ignore." He stepped towards Ryder and traced the erection with a single finger before pulling back. "Now, let's go for a swim." He winked at Ryder.

They used the door from the bedroom to access Ryder's private terrace, which hid a gate amongst the potted landscaping that led to a walkway along the grass and the lake edge. It was a short walk to the main terrace and the swimming pool. Ryder dove in without waiting for Knox. When he surfaced, his wet hair plastered against his toned chest glistened in the mid-morning sun. Knox enjoyed this view for a moment before jumping in. The water was cool but not cold and felt refreshing. Knox and Ryder splashed around playfully, their bodies occasionally intertwining as they moved in the water. Ryder swam a few laps while Knox settled against the edge nearest the house, admiring the views of both the lake and Ryder.

Ryder suggested that they dry off and get dressed. He wanted to show Knox one of his favorite places on the ranch. Knox walked up the steps to exit the pool and grabbed a towel from a nearby chair. His body hair was slick from the water and glowed in the light of the sun. Ryder seemed incapacitated as he stared at Knox. He looked as if he wanted to say something, then seemed to center himself as he walked up the steps to join Knox.

"You okay?" Knox asked, sensing a change in Ryder's demeanor.

"Yes. Just can't believe you're here. And sorting through things in my mind. It's all good, Knox." Ryder said.

"I need to charge my truck." Knox changed the subject. "You said you have a charger?"

"Yes, in the barn. We'll get that plugged in before heading out." Ryder said.

They walked back to the bedroom, mostly dry by the time they got there. They dressed in silence, each putting on jeans, boots, and snap-up short-sleeve shirts. Ryder placed a ball cap on his head and did the same with Knox. They laughed as Knox made a comment about Ryder dressing him. Ryder instructed Knox to pull his truck into the barn. Knox started the truck and drove it towards the barn where Ryder had opened a large roll-up door. Knox had an eerie sense of déjà vu as he pulled the truck into the barn, thinking that it seemed like many of the deliveries he had just completed. Ryder's truck sat in the barn, plugged into one of three Level 2 chargers. Ryder had the truck connected before Knox could exit. It would take several hours to charge with the slower charger.

Ryder motioned Knox to the far end of the large barn where four black Polaris Ranger XP Kinetics sat side-by-side, each plugged into its own conduit. Ryder unplugged the one closest to them and climbed into the driver's seat, motioning for Knox to join him. Ryder drove the small vehicle out of the barn and joined a dirt path that wound along the edge of the lake. Along the way, Ryder told Knox about the ranch, which was just over 900 acres and was evidently one of many that the Garcia family owned. Ryder told him that his two uncles had their own ranches, and the family jointly owned a lot of land. When Knox questioned how much land, Ryder's response was vague, just saying that it was several hundred thousand acres or so. They continued the drive quietly, enjoying the scenery and the beauty of the sun shining on the lake. Without thinking, Knox's hand would occasionally wander over to Ryder's thigh and rest lightly there. Each time, Ryder would look at him and smile.

The path eventually turned away from the lake and meandered through low trees and underbrush before turning back to the lake. Ryder drove the capable vehicle through seemingly impassable overgrowth, eventually emerging onto a small private beach. The view of the lake and the ranch house barely visible in the distance was breathtaking.

"This is my favorite place," Ryder commented, gazing out towards the water. "I come here to think and be by myself. I wanted to share it with you today."

"Thank you," Knox replied. "Thank you for sharing it with me."

Ryder turned his head to look at Knox. "Knox, I'm in love with you. I'm sorry. I know that might make you uncomfortable. I can't help it." A single tear ran down Ryder's face.

Knox touched Ryder's face and wiped the tear with his thumb. "I love you too, Ryder."

Knox leaned towards Ryder and kissed him gently. His emotions were confusing, and he felt he had nothing to lose at this point. Ryder extended his hand to Knox's crotch and felt the evidence of Knox's love for him. He slowly unbuckled Knox's belt and unbuttoned his jeans, reaching in and releasing Knox's hard cock. Ryder quickly unbuckled his own belt, unbuttoned his jeans, and pushed them to his ankles, kicking his boots off at the same time in the tight space. Knox pushed his jeans to his knees. Ryder straddled Knox, his yoga practice coming in handy in the tight compartment of the small vehicle. He spat generously into his palm and spread the saliva on his hole. He positioned himself on Knox's dick and pushed firmly to force it into him. The friction from the minimal amount of spit felt both rough and pleasurable. Rather than moving up and down, Ryder rotated his hips in tight circles, working the base of Knox's hard-on while dry stroking his own dick. He pushed back on Knox's chest with his right hand while the fingers of his left hand moved from his cock to Knox's mouth. Ryder inserted four fingers into Knox's wet mouth. Knox sucked on Ryder's fingers, getting them sloppy wet. Ryder re-gained his grip on his cock with his now-wet fingers and stroked quickly, his hips picking up speed. Ryder pushed back harder on Knox's chest, his back arching as he shot an ample load of jizz onto Knox's shirt. The force of his orgasm caused his pelvis to push forward, increasing the sensation for Knox's inserted penis. Knox continued moving his hips in small thrusts but was unable to control his arrival much longer. His hands reached up to grab the canopy of the open vehicle as he came, his hips thrusting up and pushing Ryder's head into the roof.

Ryder's fingers, wet with cum, found Knox's mouth and probed there before they kissed once more. Knox softly caressed Ryder's face. Ryder leaned forward and rested his head on Knox's for a moment before unfolding himself and regaining his seat. Knox buttoned up his jeans as Ryder got dressed.

They drove back in silence, Knox's hand resting on Ryder's leg as Ryder's hand rested on top of Knox's.

CHAPTER 17
The Ranch, Family Dinner

When they got back to the house, Felix had arrived and was working busily in the kitchen. Ryder and Knox made their way directly to Ryder's bedroom to shower and get dressed for dinner.

They showered together, enjoying the casualness of being with each other without the expectation of sexual release. While they were drying off, Knox's thoughts turned to the pending dinner and meeting Ryder's parents. Considering their earlier declarations of love, he felt the pressure of making a good impression, regardless of where this path with Ryder went.

"Ryder, I don't really have anything nicer to wear than what you've seen me in," Knox admitted.

"So, Knox, I did something, and I hope it doesn't make you angry," Ryder said, looking down at the floor before walking to one of the closets.

Ryder pulled out a box and handed it to Knox. "I had boots delivered for you," Ryder said.

Knox opened the box to see a new pair of ostrich skin boots in medium brown. The upper of the boots was dark green with an elaborate pattern stitched in gold thread.

"I, uh, I don't know what to say." Knox stammered. "Thank you."

"That's not all." Ryder continued reaching into the closet and showing Knox a new Ariat long-sleeve snap-up shirt in dark green. "I thought the color would accent your eyes."

"I love it," Knox said quietly.

"Oh wait, there's more," Ryder said sheepishly. "I know this is a lot. Just let me do it, then we can talk."

Ryder opened a drawer and handed Knox a bolo tie. The clasp was a beautiful green pixie turquoise attached to dark brown leather cords. Without hesitating, Ryder walked to another cabinet and handed Knox a brand-new felt cowboy hat. The hat was black and very expensive. Knox guessed that the items Ryder had handed him must have cost several thousand dollars. Knox stood naked, holding the items. A tear escaped his eye, and he turned away quickly and walked to the bed, placing the things carefully on the duvet. He did not remember the last time he had cried. He also could not remember the last time someone had taken care of him without wanting something in return.

Ryder joined him, also still naked, and walked up to Knox, turning him to face him.

"Let me take care of you, Knox. What's the harm in that? Please let me take care of you tonight." Ryder said, pulling Knox close.

"Okay," Knox said, sobbing softly on Ryder's shoulder. "No one takes care of me. I've always taken care of myself. It feels good. Too good."

"You deserve this. Can you just let it happen tonight, and we can check in later?" Ryder asked. "If you really don't want me to do these things after tonight, I'll stop. But right now, I need to take care of you. For me. Understand?" Ryder pulled Knox to face him, softly caressing his face.

"I understand. And yes, for tonight." Knox said as Ryder kissed him.

"Good. Now get dressed, you sexy beast. I didn't get you jeans. The ones you have fit you so well." Ryder teased Knox and slapped his bare ass.

They laughed and joked as they got dressed. Ryder wore a similar shirt in royal blue, his boots alligator, and his bolo stone, a beautiful lapis set in silver. Ryder had changed his belt. The buckle was a larger letter G in gold against a silver background.

"Oh, I almost forgot," Ryder said, walking to a closet drawer and handing Knox a belt buckle. It was like Ryder's, but with the letter C instead of the G. Knox changed out the buckle, re-threading it through the belt loops on his jeans. When fully dressed, they stood side-by-side in front of a full-length mirror in the dressing area of the closet. Knox wrapped his hand around Ryder's waist and let it slide down to rest on Ryder's butt cheek, which felt firm under his hand. Knox felt a stirring in his groin, which he tried to ignore.

"We look like we're getting ready to film a high-end porn." Knox laughed.

"Now you're giving me after-dinner ideas." Ryder winked.

"Easy, tiger." Knox laughed. "Keep it in your pants til after dinner. I'm just worried about concealing my erection for the evening. I can't even glance at you without it happening."

"I know, Knoxman, I have the same challenge," Ryder admitted.

"Knoxman?" Knox said.

"I honestly have no idea where the fuck that came from!" Ryder laughed.

"I kinda like it," Knox said. "I'm the Knoxman!" He laughed and strutted around the room, kicking his boots out, his hands on his hips with his elbows sticking out. They both laughed hysterically.

"Okay, Knoxman, let's go to dinner. We're having cocktails on the terrace. Just be yourself. They're going to love you." Ryder said as he walked out the door to his private terrace.

They followed the path to the terrace. The setting sun provided a stunning picture of the lake. When they arrived at the main terrace, Ryder's parents were talking with Felix, going over the meal for the evening. Ryder approached his parents while Knox hung back. Ryder greeted both parents with hugs, asking about their trip and generally catching up. Ryder stepped back and motioned for Knox to approach.

"Mom, Dad, this is Knox Creed," Ryder said. "Knox, these are my parents, Maria and Antonio."

"Pleased to meet you." Knox extended a hand to shake Antonio's.

"Call me Tony, please." Ryder's father said.

"Pleased to meet you, Tony." Knox corrected.

Knox extended his hand to Maria, as well, who stretched her arms wide and embraced Knox. "I like to give hugs." She spoke.

Knox hugged her back tightly, feeling the genuine and warm welcome in her embrace. Maria pulled back, keeping her arms on Knox's shoulders. "You are a gorgeous man!" She said, "Ryder, you did not mention how handsome he is." She smiled and winked at her son.

Knox blushed.

"Thank you." He said.

"Let me get you a drink." Tony said, "I drink old fashioneds, and I make a pretty good one. That okay?"

"It's his favorite drink," Ryder said before Knox could respond.

"Excellent," Tony responded. I'll be right back."

Tony walked back to the house, passing Felix, who was carrying a large wooden board laden with an extensive charcuterie of cured beef, cheeses, crostini, fruits, nuts, and various condiments.

"The beef and cheeses are from the Garcia farms," Felix said, smiling at Knox and placing the board on a table before returning to the house.

Ryder stepped forward and assembled a piece of bread with cheese, meat, and a dollop of spicy mustard. He handed it to Knox, who popped the entire thing in his mouth. It was delicious, and he was still chewing when Tony arrived with a round wooden tray containing three old fashioneds and a martini that looked to be cranberry. Knox took the drink from Tony and smiled while he finished chewing.

"Thanks," Knox said as he took a sip. "This is hands down the best old-fashioned I've ever had."

"You're gaining points, Knox. Antonio makes his own simple syrup, and the whiskey is from the family distillery in Dallas." Maria smiled at Knox, her hand resting gently on his arm.

Knox was halfway through his second drink when Felix called them in for dinner. Knox, Ryder, and Tony removed their hats and hung them neatly on hooks provided on the wall between the living room and the large dining room. The table had been set to accommodate four place settings at one end of the long table, two facing two, to allow for conversation. They sat down, and Felix immediately delivered a basket of warm homemade corn tortillas and bowls of soup. The soup was a corn chowder that Knox found particularly delicious. As he ate, he noticed that Ryder favored his mother in the face and had his father's build. For a man in his sixties, Tony was fit and incredibly handsome. He had dark hair, like Ryder and kind, brown eyes. Maria was stunningly beautiful, with dark flowing hair and facial features that unmistakably told the heritage she shared with Ryder.

Felix cleared the soup bowls and returned soon after with a large wooden board of grilled meats. Quarters of chicken, sausages, and large chunks of beef tenderloin mingled together in the presentation. He placed it down and told them that the sausages were a mix of rabbit and snake, which he had made himself. Maria's facial expression made it clear that she would leave the sausages to Tony, Ryder, and Knox. Felix disappeared and returned with a bowl of roasted potatoes and a platter of what looked like sautéed greens.

Tony passed the side items to Maria, who took out small portions. Tony used his fork to spear a piece of chicken and place it on Maria's plate. Maria, in turn, dished out sides onto Tony's plate. Knox noticed the way they cared for each other. This is where Ryder got this trait. It gave Knox a feeling of belonging. A belonging he hadn't realized he craved. A warmth that both comforted and, in its unfamiliarity, subtly unnerved him. It was a lot to take in. One that made him feel special and a little uncomfortable. Would he be able to reciprocate this for Ryder? It wasn't something that he was used to doing outside the bedroom.

The dinner conversation was pleasant. Maria asked most of the questions, getting to know Knox. He was honest with her about his childhood and his career. Ryder talked a lot to his dad about Knox's truck. Tony was impressed that Knox had taken on such an ambitious adventure by driving an electric rig across the country. Tony had many questions about range, charging, and the general capabilities of the truck. When Ryder mentioned that Knox's contract was with BarsTech Industries, Tony was quiet. It was evident that he knew the company, and this gave Knox a moment of pause. How would this rancher know about BarsTech?

Tony and Maria were clearly supportive of Ryder and his transformations to the ranch. Tony even admitted that their cash flow was better than it ever had been since Ryder had taken over management of the ranch. And this gave him and Maria more time to travel and enjoy an early retirement.

Felix checked back with them occasionally and eventually cleared the table, offering coffee, which Knox happily accepted. Dessert was a cake made from a local cactus fruit. The taste was new to Knox, and he liked it immensely, cleaning his plate and politely refusing a second helping. After the meal was finished, the four of them moved to the leather sofas in the great room. Maria and Tony sat next to each other, their hands always casually touching some part of each other. They were clearly still in love with one another after almost forty years of marriage. Knox sat on one end of the other sofa, and Ryder sat directly next to him, his hand resting on Knox's thigh. Knox noticed a look of approval from Maria. They all chatted for a short time before Tony and Maria excused themselves to go to bed, using the excuse that they were tired from traveling. Knox rose, and Tony gave him a big hug while saying good night. Maria did the same, hugging him tightly before hugging Ryder and saying goodnight with a kiss on the cheek.

When they had left, Ryder and Knox retrieved their hats and walked through the house to Ryder's suite. Ryder stowed their hats on the shelf in the closet. They kicked off their boots, and Ryder put those away, as well. Knox started to unsnap his shirt.

"Let me," Ryder said. "Undressing you is one of the things I like best about being with you."

Knox stood still while Ryder undressed him. Knox reciprocated, fully allowing himself to enjoy the non-sexual intimacy of the simple actions. When they stood before each other in only underwear and socks, Ryder removed his own underwear and socks while Knox did the same. They both had partial erections. Ryder placed his hands on Knox's chest, running his hands through the thick hair. This brought Ryder's erection to full bloom.

"Let's get in bed and talk," Knox suggested. "I want to hold you before we make love."

Knox surprised himself at the words he was using.

They got into bed, facing each other. Knox grabbed Ryder's hand and brought it to his lips, kissing the fingers.

"Do you think your parents liked me?" Knox asked nervously.

"Like you? They loved you!" Ryder said. "I've never seen my dad that comfortable with someone he's just met. And my mom… she looked at you like she looks at me!"

"I really like them," Knox said. "They were so kind and welcoming to me."

"So, what's the problem?" Ryder asked.

"There's no problem. Well not really." Knox continued. "I'm just jumping into this headfirst, and I don't really know where it's all going. We expressed our love for each other this afternoon, and that's something I never saw myself doing. But I mean what I say. I am falling in love with you, Ryder. And that scares the living shit out of me."

"I still don't see the problem," Ryder said, kissing Knox on the forehead.

"Okay. I'm just going to do this. If you hurt me, you hurt me. I don't know how else to do this, Ryder." Knox was baring himself to Ryder.

"I'm not going to hurt you, Knox. Are you going to hurt me?" Ryder asked.

"No, I'm going to try not to. I promise I'm going to try harder than I've ever tried at anything." Knox said, wrapping his arm around Ryder and pulling him close. They held each other like someone was trying to rip them apart against their will.

They made slow love that night. They took turns with each other, not speaking. They enjoyed each other's bodies, exploring and testing new sensations. The familiarity from the previous day only exacerbated by the recently expressed love for each other. When they were content from the intense orgasms, they fell asleep in each other's arms. As he drifted off, Knox once again experienced the wash of contentment that had confused him the previous night. This time, he welcomed the emotion, allowing it to consume him. What would a life with Ryder look like? Would he miss his freedom? Would he continue driving? Yes, he could not give that up. But how would that work when he had the opportunity to hook up? One thing he knew as he fell asleep – he was going to give it a try.

Knox woke to see Ryder finishing his morning yoga routine on the terrace. He found some comfort in this dynamic of waking up and watching Ryder's body go through the fluid movements. Knox was going to get out of bed and get coffee when Ryder stood from his final pose and came back into the bedroom. Ryder jumped on the bed, standing above Knox before flopping down next to him. Ryder planted a big, wet kiss on Knox's cheek.

"I need coffee," Knox said, laughing as he pushed Ryder off.

"Me too," Ryder said. "Give me a proper kiss, and I'll get it for us."

Knox pushed Ryder back, straddling him, grinding his hips down into Ryder's as he held Ryder's hands above his head and inserted his tongue into Ryder's mouth, kissing him deeply. As Ryder moaned and pushed back up and into him, Knox rolled off and positioned himself flat on the bed, his hands by his side.

"No more until you get me coffee." He said, trying to keep his face serious.

Ryder tried to give Knox affection, but was denied. Knox rolled away from Ryder, moving around the bed as Ryder teased him. Eventually, Ryder got out of bed and walked to the living room.

"You owe me!" He said over his shoulder as he walked away.

"You'll get it. After you bring me coffee." Knox shouted after him, laughing heartily.

Ryder arrived a while later with a tray topped with two steaming mugs of coffee and a plate with two homemade biscuits. Melted cheddar cheese oozed from the center of each warm biscuit.

"Where did these come from?" Knox asked, sitting up in bed and taking a mug of coffee.

"Felix brought them by," Ryder said casually.

"You're going to have to teach me how all this works. I mean, I'm not complaining." Knox said with a mouth full of biscuits and cheese.

"Fair enough," Ryder responded. "While the coffee was brewing, I used the house phone, the one hanging on the wall near the coffee machine, to call the kitchen. When Felix answered, I asked if he had prepared anything this morning. He said he would bring something down. He arrived at the door a few moments later with the tray and biscuits. I added the coffee, and here we are."

"And if Felix had not answered?" Knox asked, winking at Ryder.

"You would be eating a pre-packaged protein bar. So be grateful." Ryder poked Knox in the side and laughed. The reaction caused some of Knox's coffee to splash out and land on his chest.

"Sorry," Ryder said as he placed his own mug of coffee on his nightstand and leaned over and sucked the warm coffee from Knox's chest hair. His lips brushed Knox's right nipple, and Knox took in a deep breath, placing his coffee carefully on the nightstand. Knox's erection appeared quickly, and Ryder took notice. Ryder reached his hand under the covers and lightly caressed Knox's cock and balls with a single finger.

"Your choice this morning, Knoxman. What'll it be? I'll do anything you want. Anything." Ryder whispered in Knox's ear, continuing his attention down below.

"I'm going to turn on my stomach, and you're going to fuck me from behind. Make it slow." Knox's voice was breathless as he whispered the words in Ryder's ear. "With each thrust in, make it hard. I want to feel you all the way inside me."

Ryder pulled back to allow Knox to roll over. His own cock was now hard and pulsing with anticipation. When Knox was on his belly, Ryder ran his fingers through Knox's hair and traced a line down his back until he reached his crack. At the feeling of Ryder's finger near his hole, Knox arched his back and pushed his butt up. Ryder pushed it back down with his palm, continuing his teasing by running a hand down Knox's leg and back up to his testicles, tickling the hair there with his fingertips.

Ryder rolled on top of Knox, letting his knees fall to either side. He reached down and pushed his cock between Knox's thighs, letting it sit there, teasing him. Ryder kissed Knox's back, moving to the back of his neck, his ear lobes, his shoulders, and then back to the center of his torso. Ryder grabbed the lube from the nightstand and slowly lubed up his own cock. He then took his time getting Knox's hole ready. Applying a little lube, teasing it with his fingertip, stoking with multiple fingers, more lube, then inserting a finger slowly. Knox made noises that moved between low moans and sharp intakes of breath that sounded like pleas for Ryder to fuck him.

Ryder moved the tip of his hard penis to Knox's crack and let it sit there, teasing Knox's hole. Knox pushed back, trying to make it enter. Ryder pushed him down each time.

"Shhh, Knoxman. Be patient." Ryder whispered each time as he continued to kiss Knox's back.

Ryder hooked his arms under Knox's armpits with a firm grip and slowly and deliberately entered Knox. Knox sighed with relief once Ryder was inside him. As Knox had requested, Ryder pulled out slowly and thrust in hard, moving with intention and purpose.

"Fuck, that feels good," Knox said, his face buried in the sheets.

"For me, too, my love," Ryder said.

Ryder released one arm and moved it along Knox's flank, inserting his hand between Knox and the sheet. His fingertips touched the head of Knox's cock. He teased it for a few minutes and pulled his hand back, reaching between their bodies to get some lube on his fingertips. He re-inserted his hand to feel Knox's head. His slick fingertips rubbed the underside of his cock, feeling it twitch and move. Ryder released his other arm and wrapped it under Knox's neck, pulling his head back as his thrusts became quicker and harder. Knox writhed under him.

"Do you want it? Tell me you want it." Ryder said

"I want it. Unload in me, Ryder. Give me your juice. Give it to me hard." Knox responded as he came on the sheets under him.

Ryder thrust faster, harder, longer, biting into Knox's shoulder. Ryder continued to thrust, pushing more cum out of Knox's spent penis. Ryder slowed his strokes, wanting to make the approach to orgasm last as long as possible. When he could feel it approaching, he slowed almost to a stop, allowing it to build. He slid his hands to grip the top of Knox's shoulders and raised himself slightly, pulling Knox back into him as hard as he could with the final thrust when he could hold it no longer. As he came, his body trembled. He collapsed on Knox, kissing at the toothmarks he had left on Knox's skin. Knox was breathing hard and wriggled to turn over. Ryder started to roll off, but Knox held him firmly in place as he turned, needing to remain under him. They held each other in that position until Ryder broke the silence.

"That was the most intense orgasm I've ever had," Ryder said, kissing Knox on the face as he spoke. "Did you enjoy it? Is that what you wanted?"

"It was perfect, Ryder. You're perfect." Knox reassured him.

"Let's shower. I want to show you around today." Ryder said.

They showered in their typical manner, washing each other as they talked about what they would do today. Ryder wanted to show Knox some of his favorite places in the small town of Fritch. They would have dinner again with Tony and Maria.

"Ryder," Knox said as they got dressed.

"Yes, Knox," Ryder answered, turning to give Knox his full attention.

"I have to take the trailer back," Knox said sadly.

"I know. We should discuss that. It's doesn't make sense to ignore it. What are you thinking?" Ryder asked.

"I think I should drive back tomorrow, drop off the trailer, and go to my house to check on things. It will take me a few days to get things done." Knox paused. "And then I need for you to come to my place. You need to know more about my life. Right now, all we know is what we have here. You need to see where I live, how I live. It's important."

"I know. Let me think about this. Can we pick this up later? I just need to let it turn in my mind for a bit." Ryder said, moving close to Knox. "But, Knox, you need to know this…I'm committed to this. Whatever that looks like. Okay?" It meant laying himself bare, trusting someone else with pieces of himself he hadn't known existed. This was a deeper commitment than any contract, any haul. And he was all in.

"Okay," Knox said. He kissed Ryder, then hugged him tightly. Knox was learning that Ryder was thoughtful with important decisions. He did not have knee-jerk reactions. He likes to allow things to incubate in his head. Knox considered this a good quality and knew that he needed to be patient while Ryder processed his thoughts.

Once they were dressed, they walked to the barn and disconnected Knox's truck, which was fully charged. Ryder disconnected his own truck, and they headed off toward the small downtown area of Fritch. Twenty minutes later, they were driving through the small town. As they drove along Broadway Street, Ryder pointed out a small diner on the right. The sign said the place was called Chris's Kitchen.

"We'll come back there and have lunch," Ryder said. "But first, I want to show you something else."

He continued along Broadway, eventually turning right on Lakeview Drive. Lakeview meandered past several small housing developments before opening to the grassy plains on the shore of a large lake. The signs that Knox could see said they were in the Harbor Bay Recreation Area. Ryder parked the truck and looked out over the lake.

"This is Lake Meredith." He spoke. "The Canadian River feeds it, and most of the town's drinking water comes from here. So, it's important that we keep it clean. My family invests in the community by making sure the water is drinkable for the 2000 residents here."

Knox looked out at the undulating hills and small cliffs around the edge of the lake. He could see people boating and riding jet skis. There was a small beach to the left where people were swimming and sunbathing. It was not the most beautiful lake that he had seen, but there was a feeling of community and peace about it. They got out of the truck and walked to the edge of the water. A slight breeze moved Knox's hair and felt cool on his skin.

"Thank you for sharing this with me." He looked over at Ryder, who smiled at him and moved closer so that their arms touched.

"Let's get some lunch," Ryder said and headed back to the truck.

They drove back into town, and Ryder parked the truck on the street near the diner they had passed. When they entered the diner, it was apparent that everyone in the place knew Ryder. Knox could not keep track of the introductions and names. When they finally sat down at a booth, Knox admitted to Ryder that he would not remember most of these people. Ryder laughed and reassured him that he would, over time. The menu was simple.

Basic sandwiches and soups were enhanced with a variety of typical Mexican food, as well as things like fried cheese curds and chicken fingers. Ryder told Knox that everything was made in-house by the family that owns the restaurant. According to Ryder, the best thing not on the menu was the meatloaf sandwich with fries.

A pretty woman about Ryder's age approached the table with two glasses of sweet tea. She and Ryder chatted for a few minutes, and Knox learned that her name was Lisa, and they graduated high school together. Her family owned the diner, and she and Ryder had once dated. The admission of such to Knox made them both laugh.

Knox was looking over the menu when Lisa arrived with two plates. Each had a meatloaf sandwich on white bread alongside a mound of French fries covered in white gravy. She sat the plates down on the table and walked away.

"I get the same thing here each time, and Lisa brought the same for you because she knows that you need to try it." Ryder laughed. "Welcome to small-town Texas, Knoxman."

They both laughed, and Knox was happy that it worked this way because the sandwich and gravy fries were unexpectedly better than any diner food he had experienced on the road. As they ate, Maria texted Ryder and asked him to stop by a local florist and pick up flowers for the dinner table. Knox was touched by the way Ryder's family operated. It was so different from the family that he had grown up with. His father and mother had always been pleasant with one another, but there was never any resemblance to the love that he saw with Ryder's family. Even now, he would go for months without talking to his parents. They would call him if they needed anything, and he would call them simply to make sure they were still alive.

They finished eating and left without paying. According to Ryder, many businesses in town simply billed his family at the end of each month for anything they purchased, including meals and services. It was an odd concept for Knox, who lived in a world where things were generally paid in advance.

The flower shop was a block over from the diner. Ryder and Knox walked there, with Ryder touching the brim of his hat in greeting to most people they passed on the way. The florist, Jenny, was a childhood friend of Tony, Ryder's father. She had a beautiful arrangement of wildflowers ready for them. She was delighted to meet Knox, letting him know that she had already heard all about him. Ryder said this was one of the more distressing things about living in a small town – everybody knew your business unless you worked very hard to keep them from knowing. Knox did not like this. It made him uncomfortable that he was already being known around town as Ryder's new man. He expressed this to Ryder, whose expression turned serious as he apologized to Knox. He said he would talk with his parents to make sure that the information was better controlled. He also told Knox that the reason the news was spreading so quickly was that everyone was happy for him to have found someone so strikingly good-looking. Knox admitted that the flattery worked.

They arrived back at the house with two hours to kill before they were to meet Tony and Maria for drinks and dinner. Knox and Ryder went to the bedroom to relax before the evening meal. Knox found his clothes from the first day washed and neatly folded on the bed.

"This is a nice surprise," Knox said, not remembering the last time that someone had done his laundry for him.

"Yes, Janet, our housekeeper, generally takes care of things like that. That's why I told you not to worry about it. But I do know how to do my own laundry. I don't want you to think I'm completely helpless." Ryder joked as he faced Knox and pulled him into a close embrace.

"I would never think of you as helpless." Knox chuckled.

"Knox, I still owe you an answer about visiting in Barstow. Can we talk about that now?" Ryder asked, his voice turning serious.

"Yes, I'd like that. We need to get that out of the way." Knox replied as he moved to one of the leather chairs by the fireplace.

Ryder joined him, taking a seat in the other chair.

"I'm going to come see you in Bartow. You are right. I need to know more about your life. You know about mine, but I don't know about yours. I just know you." Ryder started the conversation.

"That makes me happy," Knox said as he waited for Ryder to continue.

"When you get back to Barstow, let me know when I can come out. I can be out there the same day or the next." Ryder said.

"It's more than a day's drive," Knox said. "Will you fly?"

"Yes, we use a private jet shared service, so I'll use that," Ryder said, smiling at Knox. "I know that doesn't surprise you."

"It doesn't," Knox said, laughing with Ryder. "The airport in Barstow is not far from my house."

"Knox, I'm not going to plan a return. We can figure it out after I've been there a few days. Is that okay?" Ryder asked hesitantly.

"More than okay, Ry," Knox said, trying out a new nickname to see if Ryder reacted.

"So, it's Knoxman and Ry now?" Ryder said as they both laughed.

As they got dressed for dinner, Knox found himself content with the dynamic that he and Ryder were developing. Their actions around each other seemed natural and well-seasoned. It did not feel at all like they had only known each other for two weeks. In addition to the new shirt and boots that Ryder had bought for Knox previously, he had evidently bought more than just those items. He opened a closet door and allowed Knox to pick what he wanted to wear. Knox was briefly overwhelmed. Not just by the kindness and care that Ryder was showing him but also by having so many things to choose from.

"Can you just pick something for me?" Knox said.

"Of course, I like to dress you. So, if you're okay with me picking your clothes, I'm happy to do it." Ryder smiled. This clearly makes him very happy, Knox thought.

They got dressed Ryder in jeans, boots, a button-up short-sleeve shirt in bright colors, and a straw cowboy hat. Knox wore what Ryder handed him, which consisted of new boots, new jeans, a new straw cowboy hat, and a black short-sleeved snap-up shirt with dark gray piping along the sleeves and pockets. Standing in front of the mirror, Ryder snapped a picture of them together.

"We look like a power couple going to a social event." He said happily.

"I don't know what that means, but it makes you happy, so I'm happy. Text me that pic, please." Knox requested.

They walked outside to the terrace and joined Tony and Maria, who had drinks ready for all of them. Knox enjoyed Tony's old-fashioned, and the one tonight did not disappoint him. According to Maria, Tony was experimenting with making flavored simple syrups, and tonight's variety was apple-infused with cinnamon and cardamom. Knox found it delicious and refreshing. He told Tony that he would like to learn how to make simple syrups, and Tony agreed to show him. The bond that was developing between them was noticeable to Ryder, who kept glancing at his mom and smiling. Felix attended to a large charcoal grill laden with think ribeye steaks, asparagus wrapped in bacon, onion halves, and slices of other veggies. The smell of the charred meat and vegetables made Knox's mouth water.

The conversations with Tony and Maria were pleasant. They treated Knox like family, and the discussions involved getting to know him and learning what his intentions were with Ryder. Ryder attempted to interject on behalf of Knox, but Knox stopped him and told Tony and Maria that he was in love with Ryder, that he didn't know how it was going to work, and that he was committed to finding a way. Maria and Ryder were emotional at Knox's response, and their eyes welled with tears of happiness. Tony smiled at Knox and told him that he was a welcome member of their family since he could see how happy Ryder had been over the past week. When dinner was done, Ryder told his parents that Knox had a long drive tomorrow and they would be going to bed early. Knox said goodbyes to Tony and Maria and let them know that he would see them soon.

Ryder and Knox walked back to their room along the lake, each quietly dreading Knox's impending departure. They arrived back at the bedroom, undressed, brushed their teeth, took care of other nighttime routines and got into bed together. Knox turned to face Ryder, gently touching him. Ryder leaned in and kissed Kno softly, lingering, then settled back on the pillow.

"I don't want you to leave tomorrow," Ryder said. "I know that's selfish, but it's how I feel."

"I don't want to leave either, but I have my life and responsibilities back in Barstow," Knox said. "We will figure this out, Ryder. Things will be clearer by the time you get to Barstow. I promise."

"I know." Ryder agreed. "It just hurts to think of not being around you for even a day."

"I feel the same, Ry," Knox said, smiling at the use of the new nickname.

"Are you okay if we just cuddle tonight? I just want to enjoy being with you." Ryder requested.

"Of course," Knox replied softly.

Ryder turned away from Knox and backed up tightly to him, taking the position of little spoon. Knox wrapped his arms around Ryder and kissed him softly on the neck.

"I love you, Ryder Garcia." He whispered in Ryder's ear. He meant these words that he never expected himself to say to another man.

"I love you, too, Knox Creed," Ryder said through tears mixed with joy and sadness.

They fell asleep in each other's arms and rested peacefully through the night.

When Knox woke, Ryder was cuddled up next to him. Knox caressed Ryder's body, moving his other hand down to his own erect cock. Knox stroked Ryder's soft dick, which quickly became hard. Ryder's eyes flickered open as he moaned at being woken by the sensation.

"No yoga this morning?" Knox asked.

"No, I stayed in bed for this," Ryder said as he rolled over on top of Knox, grabbed the lube, wet his hole and slid Knox's hard-on inside him.

"Ahhh, that's what I needed this morning," Ryder said, grinding his hips and stroking his own dick.

"Fuck, it feels so good to be inside you," Knox said, happy with how quickly Ryder had responded to his needs.

Ryder leaned down to kiss Knox, and they made quick, passionate love. After Knox came, Ryder continued to pump his own dick while Knox played with his nipples. When he came, it hit Knox in the face, which made them both laugh. Knox realized that he could get used to a life with this man.

"Let's shower and get you ready to go. As much as I hate it, I know it must happen." Ryder said as he got out of bed and headed towards the shower.

Knox followed him, and they did their usual shower routine, washing each other and having conversations about coffee and breakfast.

"I can't believe you got me to shower without coffee first," Knox said.

"I'll make you some as soon as we get out." Ryder smiled and kissed him.

While Knox was getting dressed and gathering his things, Ryder made coffee for both of them, walking back into the bathroom with the coffee and two donuts.

"Sorry, no fresh biscuits today," Ryder said.

"Not that high maintenance." Knox said, taking a donut and shoving the entire thing into his mouth, followed by a swig of coffee." You forget that I'm still a trucker." He winked at Ryder.

"Keep talking like that, and I'm going to have another go," Ryder said.

"Nope, you're going to wait until next week," Knox replied, smiling.

"Tease," Ryder said.

"Yep," Knox responded.

When they were dressed, they walked out to the Cyber Wolf. Knox got things settled inside and did a cursory walk-around to make sure everything looked good.

"I don't like long goodbyes, so I'm just going to leave. We will communicate while I'm on the road." Knox said, stepping forward and wrapping his arms around Ryder.

"Be safe, Knox," Ryder said, kissing him and giving him a final squeeze before letting him go.

Knox climbed in the truck, engaged the motors, and pulled out of the barn. He slowly drove along the road leading away from the house. As he approached the large granite columns that marked the exit of the ranch, he noticed motion in his side mirror. It was Ryder's truck, speeding towards him at a dangerous pace. Knox stopped the truck and placed it in park, quickly opening the door and climbing down to the ground to see what was going on. Ryder skidded up next to him, placed the truck in park, and got out of the truck, leaving the driver's door open. He rushed up to Knox, grabbed his head in his hands, and kissed him. Knox embraced Ryder, kissing him deeply.

"I just needed to hold you one more time," Ryder said.

"This makes me so happy. That someone needs me and wants me so much that they would race after me for one more kiss." Knox said, holding onto Ryder tightly.

"I love you, Knoxman," Ryder said.

"I love you, Ry," Knox said.

As they hugged, Knox reached down and cupped Ryder's crotch with affection. "I'll see you soon."

Ryder grinned widely. "Text me when you stop to charge."

"Will do," Knox promised as he got back in the truck. Ryder remained parked at the gate, waving at Knox until he was out of sight.

Knox was soon on Highway 136 going South. Within the hour, he had joined up with the 335 loops and was trucking along on I-40 West. During the four-hour drive to Albuquerque, he rotated between an audiobook and music, actively keeping thoughts of Ryder out of his mind. He felt a sense of peace and contentment about where things were going, and he did not want to let those feelings fade by overthinking things. But the quiet hum of the truck was almost drowned out by the louder thrum in his chest. A constant, insistent pull back towards the man he'd left behind. A pull he knew he'd have to actively manage lest it consume him. Or maybe... he just needed to let it.

By the time he stopped at the supercharger in Albuquerque, he was hungry and walked to a chain restaurant that seemed to be the only option for food near the charger. When he was seated and had ordered a soup and sandwich combo, he pulled out his phone to text Ryder.

(Knox) hey babe

(Knox) stopping in ABQ to charge

(Knox)   having some lunch

(Knox) I wish it was the diner, haha

(Knox) I miss you already

Knox ate slowly, trying to kill time while waiting 2 hours for the truck to charge to 100%. It did not take long to get a reply from Ryder.

(Ryder) I've spoiled you

(Ryder) no other food will be the same, lol

(Ryder) I miss you, too

(Ryder) badly

(Ryder) what's for lunch

(Knox) soup/salad

(Knox) chain restaurant

(Knox) next stop, Holbrook

(Knox) might need to take a nap there

(Ryder) rest when you can

(Ryder) text when you stop again

(Ryder) no matter what time

(Knox) will do

By the time Knox had finished his lunch, the truck was close to reaching max charge. He got back on I-40 West towards Holbrook, allowing himself some time to think about Ryder and this past week. He realized that somewhere deep within him, this was what he had been searching for. All the guys at all the truck stops over the years. It was all just searching for something. There was one thought that bothered Knox. Right now, Ryder was enough. But what happens if that fades? Would Ryder be open to including others? Knox made the decision to have that conversation with Ryder when he came to Barstow. He knew that it might end things, but it needed to be discussed. Knox refused to enter this relationship with false expectations and deceptions. If he was right about Ryder, it would be okay, and they would figure it out.

The last hour of the drive to Holbrook was tenuous. Construction, combined with the changing road grade, took the truck to an uncomfortably low battery level. When Knox pulled up to the charger, the battery level was below 10%. The solar panels had helped, but they would only do so much and worked best when he could be stationary for a long period in the sun. He had been told by BarsTech that the solar panels were truly for emergencies. They would provide minimal assistance while driving, but were intended to charge the batteries to a low level in an emergency. So, basically, if he were stranded, he could sit tight for 24 hours and have enough charge to get to the next charger.

Instead of getting food in Holbrook, he found a place to properly use the restroom and returned to the truck to nap while it charged. He texted briefly with Ryder to let him know what was going on and quickly fell asleep. When he woke two hours later, he was briefly disoriented, thinking that he was back at the ranch as he reached for Ryder, only to find he wasn't there. He walked to the nearby convenience store, used the bathroom, and got some bad coffee for the road.

The drive to Kingman was easy and uneventful. As he approached, he decided that he should call Carl. Using the voice function, he had the truck call Carl's number.

"Knox?" Carl answered the phone.

"Hey, Carl. How are you doing?" Knox needed to be kind but also wanted to get to the point.

"I'm good. It's good to hear from you. Are you in Kingman?" Carl asked.

"I will be in about an hour. I know it's super late, but I was hoping we could meet. And talk. Just talk." Knox also needed to make it clear that he was not asking for a hook-up.

"Yeah, I'd like that. Where will you be, and I'll meet you there?" Carl offered.

"Thanks, buddy. I'm going to top up the truck at the supercharger by the Route 66 Arch. I'll be there in thirty minutes." Knox said.

"Cool. I'll be there." Carl said. "Hey, Knox."

"Yes, Carl."

"I'm really looking forward to seeing you."

"Me too, Carl."

Knox worried about seeing Carl and what he might expect. But Knox owed him an explanation. Carl was waiting when Knox pulled up to the charger. Knox plugged in the truck, and Carl joined him in the truck. Knox quickly converted the bed back to the dinette so they could talk properly. Knox quickly texted Ryder where he was and that he would call him when he got back on the road, but it might be late.

"Are you hungry? I brought burritos and coffee." Carl held up a bag as he sat down in the truck.

"I could eat," Knox replied. "Thanks, Carl, you're so kind. You didn't deserve the way I dismissed you. I'm sorry about that. I want to tell you what's been going on with me."

"It's all good, Knox," Carl said. "I've met someone, and it's pretty serious. He wasn't too happy about me seeing you tonight, though."

"I'm happy for you, Carl. I've met someone, too." Knox continued. "When I met you, I was searching for something, and I did not know what that was. You were so good to me, so good FOR me. But it wasn't it. I wanted it to be, but it wasn't."

"I know, Knox, I thought it was the same. But it wasn't. I know that now. But at the time, it hurt." Carl admitted.

"I'm sorry I caused that. And I'm glad we found what we were looking for." Knox said.

They finished eating, and Carl stood to leave. He placed his hand firmly on Knox's upper arm and pulled him in, kissing him. Knox let him kiss him, recognizing it for what it was – a goodbye kiss. As Carl drove off, Knox unplugged the truck and got back on the road, thankful for the coffee as well as the closure that he felt with Carl. He pressed the voice button on the steering wheel and called Ryder.

"Hey!" Ryder sounded like he had been asleep.

"Hey, Ry," Knox said, the emotion evident in his voice.

"Are you back on the road?" Ryder's voice sounded more awake.

"Yes. I had to see someone in Kingman. I want to tell you about it." Knox waited for Ryder to respond. Ryder was quiet for a few minutes.

"Okay. I'm not going to assume anything. Just tell me." Worry consumed Ryder's tone.

"When I was passing through Kingman before I met you, I hooked up with this guy named Carl. The sex was good. It seemed like it was more than just sex. Then he drove to meet me in Flagstaff after my delivery there. And we had a threesome with another guy. He thought it was more than it was. And I sort of led him on for a few days. I'm embarrassed to tell you this." Knox paused.

"It's okay, Knox. Did you hook up with him tonight?" Ryder asked, his voice getting angry.

"What? No. Of course not." Knox realized he should have disclosed this upfront. "I just needed to apologize and tell him that I've met someone. The last time I talked to him, we left it as an option if every I was passing through his area. I needed to tell him that it would never happen."

"Okay. Thanks for telling me." Ryder sounded relieved. "What was his reaction?"

"He has met someone and thinks it's serious, so he was okay," Knox said.

"Hey, Ryder, did you really think I would hook up with guys on the drive home?" Knox asked.

"Not really, but the way you were telling the story, I just didn't know," Ryder admitted.

"I won't do that to you. I'm all in with you, Ryder. Promise." Knox reassured him.

"I need you all in me." Ryder laughed, trying to lighten the mood.

"Same, Ry, I miss you so badly. And it hasn't even been a full day." Knox said.

"Don't worry, Knoxman, I'll see you soon. You say when, and I'm there." Ryder said.

"I've got three hours to Barstow. I'm going to turn in the trailer, go home, and sleep. I'll text when I get home and then when I wake up, and we can talk about timing. Sound good?" Knox suggested.

"Yes, sounds good. And Knox, I love you." Ryder said so softly that Knox could barely hear him.

"I love you, too, Ryder." Knox reciprocated.

They disconnected the call, and Knox focused on the drive, allowing the warm feelings to wash over him. The remainder of the drive went by quickly. Knox had decided to go directly to BarsTech and turn in the trailer, giving himself one less thing to worry about over the coming week. It was just after 6 a.m. when he pulled up to the security gate, and Janet had just started her shift. Knox rolled down his window as Janet stepped up on the running board.

"Hey, Knox. How was your haul?" Janet asked as Knox handed her his ID.

"It was good. Easy." Knox replied. Janet handed him back the ID.

"Any idea when the next one is?" Janet continued.

"Nope. Hoping to talk to Chuck today about that today." Knox said.

"Good luck, Knox. I hope you see you soon." Janet hopped down off the running board and pressed the screen of her digital pad to open the gate.

Knox drove down the familiar road to the BarsTech buildings. The roll-up door raised as he approached, and he drove the truck to the line at the far end. Chuck was waiting for him as he got out of the truck.

"Welcome back, Knox. Another successful run. Thank you." Chuck greeted him. "Join me in the lounge. We need to talk about the next one."

Knox followed Chuck into the lounge, made himself a cup of coffee, which he badly needed, and joined Chuck in one of the comfy club chairs.

"How are things, Chuck?" Knox asked, taking a sip of the excellent coffee.

"Things are good. Looks like you took a short vacation before returning the trailer. Did you have fun?" Chuck knew exactly where the trailer had always been during the deliveries and after.

"Well, it wasn't planned. I met someone, Chuck. I'm not a hundred percent yet, but I think he might be the one." It felt good to tell someone about Ryder.

"That's great, Knox. I must say I'm a little jealous." Chuck laughed, and Knox accepted the teasing.

"So, what's next for me? I need at least a week or two." Knox stated.

"I've got a new haul coming up. It's different from the rest. I won't have all the details until next week, but it might mean being gone for over a month. Are you good with that?" Chuck seemed hesitant to tell Knox even the small amount of information that he had already shared.

"Sounds ominous," Knox said.

"Well, it's not going to be an easy one like this last one. I'm not going to say more until I have all the details. I'll text you next week, and we can set up a time to meet. This one will require briefing before you pick up the trailer." Chuck said.

"Sounds good, Chuck. Let me know." Knox was tired and ready to go.

Chuck checked his phone as Knox drained the last sip of coffee from the cup.

"Your truck is ready. I think they even washed it for you." Chuck smiled at Knox.

"Seriously? That would be so great! I'm tired, and I just want to sleep." Knox admitted as he followed Chuck back to the loading area.

Sure enough, Cyber Wolf was sparkling clean, the floor still damp from the pressure washers they had used. The trailer was also clean and had been disconnected and moved away from the truck. As soon as Knox climbed up in the truck, Chuck turned and walked back into the building. Knox engaged the motors and moved the truck forward and out of the building as the door rolled up quickly to allow the exit. He did not remember the drive home. He parked the truck in his driveway and retrieved the plug from the garage. He plugged the truck into the level one charger and went into his home. He threw his duffle on the floor, undressed, and crawled into bed. His phone still in his hand, he texted Ryder.

(Knox) home

(Knox) dropped off trailer

(Knox) so tired

(Knox) going to sleep will text when I wake.

(Knox) love u

Knox dropped the phone on the bed and immediately fell asleep. He awoke five hours later. It was mid-afternoon, and he was once again disoriented. He was holding a pillow and realized quickly that it was not Ryder. This constant expectation that Ryder would be next to him as he slept was the most difficult thing in his situation with Ryder. He picked up his phone and noticed that Ryder had texted him back.

(Ryder) get some rest, my prince

(Ryder) love u

Knox smiled. His heart was warm that someone loved him deeply enough to call him his prince. He got out of bed, gently stroking his semi-erect cock to enjoy the sensation, and walked to the shower, where he peed while the water got hot. After he had washed and dried himself, he walked to the kitchen to find something to eat. There was a frozen meal of Salisbury steak in the freezer, and he put that in the microwave. While it was heating, he texted Ryder.

(Knox) Just woke

(Knox) showered

(Knox) making some food

(Knox) naked

The microwave beeped, and Knox removed the plastic tray, peeling back the clear cover, and the steam slightly burned his fingers. He got a fork from the drawer, placed the hot meal on a paper plate so that he could hold it, and walked to the front window. He stood there, naked, eating his food, admiring his truck, when he heard his phone ring. He walked quickly to the kitchen where he had left it on the counter, sliding the screen to answer the call, then pressing the speaker button.

"Hey," Knox answered the call from Ryder.

"Hey. Did you get some rest?" Ryder asked.

"Yes. I just woke up confused. I was holding my pillow and got sad when I realized it wasn't you." Knox took a mouthful of food.

"I did the same. I miss you, Knox." Ryder confessed.

"When can you come here?" Knox asked.

"I can be there tomorrow. Or possibly today…I'll have to check to see if a pilot is available." Ryder sounded excited.

"Let's make it tomorrow. As much as I would love you have you in my bed tonight, I need to get the truck and house settled." Knox said.

"Okay. This is exciting. I'll get a car at the airport. Wait, I don't know your address. Text me your address." Ryder was getting very excited.

"I'll drop a pin when we get off the phone," Knox said.

"Knox, I love you. I know I keep saying that. And you don't have to always say it back. Okay? I just say it because I need to." Ryder rambled.

"Ryder, Ryder, slow down. I love you, too." Knox smiled at Ryder's excitement and nervousness and at his own excitement.

Knox spent the day stocking up on groceries and other items that might make Ryder's visit more comfortable. The 'stang was happy to be driven, and Knox was excited to show it to Ryder. In the back of his mind, he worried that his simple life would change the way Ryder felt about their developing relationship. He had to keep reminding himself that he was going to ride this wave of happiness until it ended, whenever that was and whatever that meant.

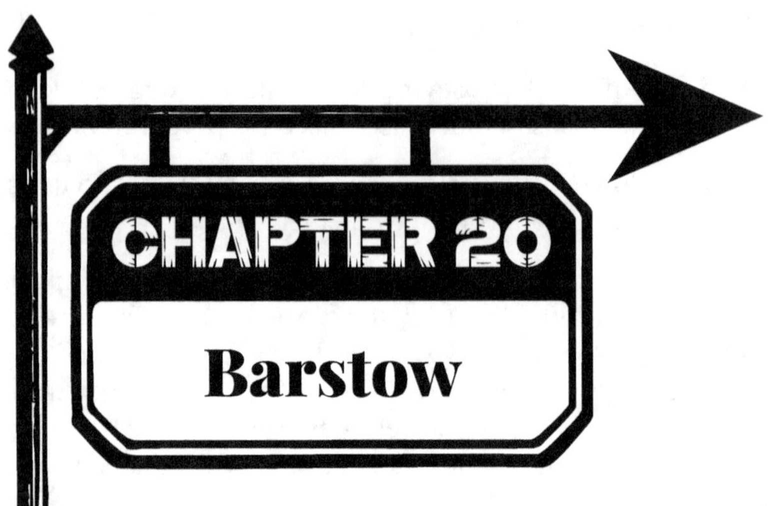

Knox woke at 7 a.m. without an alarm. He had been in bed early and had needed the sleep. He felt rested and was not as disoriented as he had been the last morning. He clutched the pillow he had been holding tightly, knowing that Ryder would be in his arms in just a few hours. He got out of bed and slowly stroked his semi-erect penis on the way to the bathroom. He told it to be patient because it would be getting a lot of attention very soon. It seemed to listen as it reduced in size and allowed him to pee. After shaking off the residual drops of urine, he walked naked to the kitchen to make himself some oatmeal.

After he put the water on the stove to boil, he opened the fresh container of whole oats and thought about any changes to his routine that he would need to make for Ryder. He came to the decision that he would not change anything. If this was going to work, he needed to be himself, just as Ryder had done with his life. He scooped the appropriate amount of oats into the boiling water and stirred it slowly, his thoughts cataloging the vast differences between his life and Ryder's. Ryder lived a life that expected certain things to be done for him. It was a life of excess masquerading as the life of a common rancher. Yet Tony and Maria had seemingly instilled in him a culture of humility and ability. Ryder was very capable and doing things on his own if he needed to. But what happened if he didn't get his way? What would happen if he had to do without all those luxuries for a longer period? These were questions that Knox would see answered over time.

Knox turned off the burner and poured the thick oats into a bowl, adding a generous portion of unsalted butter and a heavy pinch of coarse sea salt. This was his favorite breakfast. He had not told Ryder about it at the ranch because others had joked about the odd combination. He would, however, introduce it to Ryder this week, for better or worse. He walked to the window in the living room and stood naked with his bowl of oats in his hand. He slowly ate his oats while gazing out at his truck. He still could not believe where his life had taken him. He owned his own truck. And not just any truck, but the very best truck money could buy. He owned his own house and had a great job that he absolutely loved. And to top it all off, he had found someone who loved him for who he was as a person. Was it all too good to be true? At the moment, he didn't care. He was going to live for the now. He had once heard a song with the lyrics, "The one thing in life that is certain is death. So, I'm going to live." He didn't remember the artist, but those lines had become very poignant to him over the last week. He had decided to live his life to the fullest, and if that meant giving himself fully to Ryder, then that's what he would do.

He finished the oatmeal and took the bowl to the kitchen, rinsing it in the sink before placing it in the dishwasher along with the spoon and the cooking pot. He had bought ingredients to make food for Ryder that evening, and he did a quick inventory to make sure he had not forgotten anything. He walked to the bathroom to shower, placing his phone on the counter by the sink. He turned on the water to get warm and grabbed a towel from the cupboard, hanging it on the hook by the shower door. Just as he was stepping into the shower, his phone made a sound, indicating a new text message. He looked at the screen and saw that it was Ryder. He quickly turned off the water and picked up his phone.

(Ryder) on the plane

(Ryder) ETA 11

(Ryder) so excited

(Knox) me too

(Knox) just getting into shower

(Ryder) tease

(Knox) yep

(Ryder) can't wait to hold you

(Knox) same

(Knox) text when you land

(Knox) love u

(Know) see, I said it first lol

(Ryder) love u Knoxman

Knox hung up with a big, beautiful smile on his face. He decided to trim his beard before showering. He attached the guard to the rechargeable trimmer and cut the shaggy beard down to a neat half-inch. He then applied a small amount of lather to his upper cheeks and neck and used a standard razor to shape it up for a nice, clean look. He started the shower back up and stepped in. He washed his hair, rinsed it, and applied a generous amount of a matching sandalwood and patchouli conditioner that he had picked up at the grocery store yesterday. Letting the conditioner sit in his hair, he lathered up his body with a shower gel that was the final piece of the matching scent of the shampoo and conditioner. He had bought two shower poofs for him and Ryder to use. Knox's shower was not as big as Ryder's but had ample room for two people. The smell of the bath products was masculine and calming. Knox was sure Ryder would like it. When he had rinsed everything out of his hair and off his body, he stepped out into the steamy room and toweled off, enjoying the way the scents permeated the air.

Knox pulled on his socks and underwear and selected a clean pair of jeans from the drawer in the dresser in the bedroom. He threw the jeans on the bed and gave in to a sudden urge to rearrange the dresser. He emptied two drawers in case Ryder wanted to leave clothes in Barstow. He then walked to the closet and made space on the rack of hanging clothes for the same purpose. Would Ryder even want to leave clothes here? He didn't care. If Ryder wanted to do that, the option would be available to him. Knox selected one of his best snap-up shirts, a dark gray short-sleeve with embroidered gold and orange flowers at the top of each side on the front. He casually inserted his arms in the shirt, leaving it un-snapped as he stepped out of the small walk-in closet. As he passed the mirror, he glanced at his image and paused to recognize how sexy this look was for him. Socks, black Krakatoa boxer briefs that accentuated his package, and the open shirt – his chest hair gloriously exposed – was a good look for him. He would remember this while getting dressed while Ryder was in the room.

Turning his attention back to getting dressed, he pulled on his jeans and snapped up his shirt, putting his belt through the loops and tucking in his shirt before buttoning up his jeans. He slipped his feet into his boots, grabbed his phone, and walked to the living room. He sat in his favorite chair and turned on the TV. He hated nervous-waiting and had no idea how to pass the short time until Ryder arrived. He picked a mindless reality show on one of the streaming channels and scrolled through social media on his phone. It wasn't long before he heard from Ryder.

(Ryder) landed

(Ryder) will get a car and be to you in 20 min

(Knox) See you soon

(Knox) excited

(Ryder) so excited

Knox turned off the TV and stood up. He paced around the house until he noticed a black Mercedes sedan pull into the driveway. The driver's side door opened, and Ryder got out, putting on his black felt cowboy hat as he got out of the car. Ryder was dressed in black jeans, a black golf shirt, and black boots. Knox had not thought that Ryder could get any more attractive than he had seen him on the ranch, but this was a new level of sexiness. Ryder looked simultaneously like a supermodel and someone very important. Knox opened the front door as Ryder walked up the house.

"Can't miss that this is your place with that truck in the drive." Ryder smiled, a black leather overnight bag slung over his shoulder.

"Welcome to Barstow. Come on in." Knox held the door open as Ryder entered, not bothering to look around but staring directly at Knox as he walked.

Knox closed the door and removed Ryder's hat, placing it neatly on the crown on a side table. Knox placed his hands on Ryder's hips and pulled him close. Their lips met with a gentle kiss that quickly escalated to heated passion. Ryder hooked his fingers into the front of Knox's shirt and ripped the snaps open, pushing the shirt off Knox's shoulders before running his hands through Knox's chest hair. Knox unbuckled Ryder's belt, releasing the button on his jeans and pushing the zipper down. He reached his hand into Ryder's underwear and wrapped his fingers around Ryder's cock, which had been hard since he saw Knox standing in the doorway. Knox pulled gently as Ryder moaned. The level of passion that had been building during their brief separation was unmistakable.

"I've missed this. Not as much as I've missed being around you, but this feels nice." Ryder said, looking into Knox's eyes.

"Same, Ry." Knox agreed. "I want fuck you and then hold you tight. Then we can get our day started."

"I like that plan," Ryder said.

Knox removed his hand from Ryder's pants and moved him over the sofa, both kicking off their boots on the way. Knox sat on the sofa and made Ryder stand before him. Knox spread Ryder's shirt and started kissing his belly, moving in slow circles across and around the trail of dark hair that disappeared into the band of his underwear. Ryder rested his hands on Knox's shoulders, softly caressing his neck and earlobes with his thumbs. Ryder let Knox worship his body. He recognized the longing in Knox that he himself had endured over the past two days and wanted to give Knox this gift.

"I've missed your touch," Ryder whispered.

"I've missed touching you," Knox said, pausing to look up at Ryder's beautiful face.

Ryder looked down at him and moved his hands to caress Knox's handsome, rugged face. Ryder leaned down and kissed Knox, first on the lips, then on the nose, then moving to his forehead before standing completely upright and letting Knox continue to enjoy his body. Knox pressed his forehead into Ryder's stomach, sighing before he resumed the light kisses.

Eager to get to the prize but not wanting to ruin the experience, Knox slowed himself, taking deep breaths as he explored the dusting of dark hair on Ryder's thighs. Knox ran his hands the length of Ryder's legs, remembering the lines in the musculature and patterns of hair. Ryder played with Knox's hair, running his hands through the thickness and then down to his back, lightly fingering the patches of hair on his shoulders and across the muscles that rippled while Knox's hands and arms moved along the length of Ryder's body. Knox used his forefinger to trace the outline of Ryder's cock as it pushed against the fabric of his white underwear. He tested his memory of the shape and size, remembering what it felt like inside him. Remembering what it felt like to be inside Ryder while he stroked his cock.

Knox inserted the fingers of both hands into each side of the waistband of Ryder's underwear and pulled down an inch, allowing Ryder's dark pubic hair to escape the fabric. Knox kissed at the mound just above the head of Ryder's erect penis, which begged to be let free. His kisses moved to the fabric that covered the head, licking it with his tongue until the fabric of the underwear was soaking wet. Ryder's hands gripped Knox's shoulder tightly. His sounds became more intense as Knox edged his cock.

"Knox, Knox, Knoxman, you're bringing me close. And you haven't even touched it." Ryder said, his breath short and measured, trying to keep himself from releasing his load into his underwear.

Knox moved his attention back to Ryder's belly, moving his mouth up to his right nipple as he stood. When he was facing Ryder, Knox placed his lips millimeters from Ryder's and hovered there while he dropped his own pants and underwear. Knox's now-trembling cock pressed against Ryder. Knox pushed down on his own penis so that it was positioned between Ryder's thighs, the head pressing up against the soft fabric that still covered Ryder's loins. Knox ran his hands up Ryder's torso, not pausing but continuing up and over the shoulders, causing Ryder's open shirt to fall to the ground behind him. Knox slid his hands inside the back of Ryder's underwear and massaged his smooth butt cheeks as he allowed Ryder's lips to touch his.

Ryder's mouth explored Knox's like a man in the desert who has finally been given water. The hunger was unmistakable. The need was clear and evident. The desire was unfathomable. Knox pushed down on Ryder's underwear. The white cloth fell to Ryder's ankles as he grabbed Knox's cock and pushed him back to the sofa, never letting his hand leave Knox's dick.

"Get the lube or put it in dry. I don't care. Just do it." Ryder said frantically.

Knox reached to the end table and deftly took a packet of lube, opening it with his teeth in less than a second. He let the liquid fall on Ryder's fingers, which firmly gripped Knox's hard cock. Knox tossed the empty packet on the floor as Ryder made Knox wet and slick. Ryder moved his feet to be flat on the sofa on either side of Knox's muscular thighs. He lifted his hips and lowered himself onto Knox with one quick motion. Knox grabbed Ryder's cock to steady him. As Knox pushed himself all the way into Ryder, he felt like he was going to cum.

"Be still," Ryder said. "I'm close, and I don't want to cum yet."

Knox stopped moving and removed his hands from Ryder's body until

Ryder started slowly rocking his hips. Knox ran his hands across Ryder's chest and up to his shoulders. He pulled down, forcing himself fully inside. Ryder's hips rocked faster, the urgency unstoppable. Knox loosely gripped Ryder's pulsing cock, letting Ryder control the sensation. Knox tightened his grip, and Ryder shot his load onto Knox's chest. His body convulsed and rocked on Knox's cock. Ryder collapsed on Knox's chest, his breath heaving from the intensity of his orgasm. Knox rubbed his back and held him tight, stopping the movement of his hips while Ryder recovered. Soon, Ryder lifted his torso and grabbed Knox's head with both hands, kissing him deeply as his hips started a slow rhythmic rocking on Knox's hard cock that still filled his hole. Knox matched his rhythm, placing his hands on Ryder's hips to increase the movement. Ryder's hands moved to Knox's chest, getting wet and sticky in the drying ejaculate. The sensation of his own jizz on his hands enhanced his eagerness to please Knox. He rocked harder and faster, bringing Knox to climax. Knox gasped and shook with the force of the orgasm. Ryder did not stop, continuing to milk Knox's cock until he was told to stop. Knox remained still inside Ryder as the waves of pleasure enveloped him. He collapsed back on the sofa, his hands holding to the side of Ryder's hips. Ryder lowered his legs so that his knees were on either side of Knox, then he folded into Knox's chest, kissing lightly and making noises that sounded like soft whimpers of happiness. Ryder was still breathing hard, evidence of the intensity of his orgasm. Knox rubbed his back, his arms, his head, ending with his face. He pushed Ryder's head back and kissed him lightly as his softened penis slipped out of Ryder and rested, satisfied, between his thighs.

"Sex with you is… intense," Knox said. "Different from anything I've ever experienced."

"I know," Ryder said. "It's the same for me."

They rested where they were for a while, folded into one another. Knox asked about the flight, and Ryder asked about the drive. Their answers to each other were brief, too exhausted to have a discussion but finding it necessary for the connection to continue. Knox suggested they shower, which they did. Ryder really liked the scent of the body care products, continuing to bring the loofa to his nose as he lathered Knox. They seemed just as comfortable in Knox's shower as they had in Ryder's. When they had showered and toweled off, Knox went into his closet and returned with two pairs of lounge pants and two t-shirts. He threw one set to Ryder, telling him to put them on. Ryder complied without questioning Knox. Then, Knox gave Ryder a tour of his house.

"It's just two bedrooms and two baths," Knox said. "It's perfect for me and what I do for work. It's like my sanctuary when I'm not driving, just like my truck is my sanctuary while I'm on the road."

"You're my sanctuary," Ryder said, walking up behind Knox and giving him a hug from behind. Knox smiled and tilted his head back against Ryder's.

"So, what are we going to do today?" Ryder asked.

"Well, I'm going to cook dinner for us, and we're going to eat in front of the TV while watching a movie of your choice. Then we're going to make love again and go to sleep. Tomorrow, I'm going to show you around Barstow. I want you to see what my boring life is like." Knox laughed.

"Your life is your life, Knox. I'm just glad to be a part of it." Ryder said.

Knox ended the tour in the kitchen and opened the door to the garage, flicking the light switch before stepping back to let Ryder go in first.

"This is what I drive around town," Knox said, motioning towards the pristine 1969 Mustang Mach 1.

"This is incredible!" Ryder exclaimed. What's the color called? Seems like Ford called it something coral."

"Calypso Coral," Knox said. "I added the black racing stripes.

"I love it!" Ryder said. "You never said anything about this during our late-night talks. I just assumed you drive the truck everywhere."

"There's a lot you still don't know about me, Ryder. And I'm hoping you're willing to find out all of it." Knox said.

"I'm in for the long haul with you, Mr. Trucker, man." Ryder gave Knox a playful kiss on the cheek. "But I want to sit in this thing. Can we have sex in it? Wait, have you had sex in it?"

"Yes, Yes, and No." Knox chuckled. Yes, you can sit in it. Yes, we can have sex in it. No, I've never had sex in it. I've never been with a guy I felt worthy."

"Cool. I'm getting hard thinking about it." Ryder said as he opened the passenger door and slid onto the cream-colored seats. He marveled at the wood accents and commented on the large instrument in the center of the dash and directly in front of where the passenger would sit.

"That clock is a signature feature of the 1969 model year." Knox educated Ryder.

"Amazing. I've never seen one of these in this condition." Ryder said.

"I take of things that are mine," Knox said, looking longingly at Ryder, hoping he would get the not-so-subtle reference.

"I'm a lucky guy," Ryder said, staring at Knox, his eyes moist.

"Let's go inside. You can play with this tomorrow. I might even let you drive it." Knox teased.

"Wait, you refer to the car as "it." You're not one of those guys that gives their cars women's names?" Ryder teased back.

"No. Absolutely not. I've always found that practice stupid. I may occasionally refer to it as the 'stang, but that's about it." Knox laughed. "The rig has a name to honor the tradition of trucking, but it's a firm no to naming cars."

They went back into the house, and Knox asked Ryder if he wanted beer or wine, which started a conversation about what was for dinner. Knox was making beef stroganoff, which Knox kept saying as "strokin off," making Ryder laugh. They decided on red wine. Knox did not have the cellars of the Garcia family, but he did have a few good bottles, so he opened a nice Paso Robles red blend and poured generous amounts into two short glass tumblers.

"No wine glasses, so we're drinking it like the Italians," Knox said.

"I'm not that high maintenance." Ryder joked. "Seriously, Knox, I'm really not. I know my family has a lot, but for me, it's more about the quality of the people I'm with that determines the quality of the things we share."

It took a moment for Knox to process what Ryder had said. He took a sip of wine and gathered the ingredients to make dinner while he thought about it. It made sense. If true, it was the reason he felt such a strong connection to Ryder. God, he hoped it was true.

"This is a very fancy and complicated dish," Knox said, attempting a British accent. "Pay close attention. You might have questions as we enjoy this delicious dish from a bowl while seated in the entertainment room."

"Wait, I thought we were eating in the living room. We're eating in the bedroom?" Ryder joked.

"Funny, man." Knox gave him a side glance as he thinly sliced the beef.

Knox lightly sauteed the thin pieces of beef in a small amount of olive oil with a thinly sliced onion. He added a can of condensed French onion soup, a can of sliced mushrooms, and a can of beef stock. Black pepper and a dash of hot sauce completed the first step.

"This just needs to simmer for a few minutes. Let's find a movie to watch." Knox took Ryder's hand and led him to the living room.

"I can pick anything?" Ryder asked.

"Yes. Literally anything. I won't judge. At least not tonight. I'll save judgment for tomorrow. I don't want to risk not getting laid tonight." Knox said.

"Nothing you can do will keep you from getting laid tonight. That, I promise." Ryder smiled as he used the remote to scroll through the options on the screen.

Ryder selected a horror movie with a supernatural twist about a cabin where a group of friends get picked off one by one to satisfy a demon.

"Seriously?" Knox said, looking hard at Ryder. "I guess we didn't discuss this. I LOVE horror movies."

"Really?" Ryder said. "Me too!"

"Okay, Ryder, stop being so perfect. Just stop it." Knox teased, poking at Ryder, who fought back by flailing his arms like a schoolgirl in a fight. They both laughed so hard that Knox fell off the sofa, causing them to laugh more.

Knox returned to the kitchen to check on dinner. Ryder followed behind him. Knox stirred the pot, the sauce of which had reduced to a nice thickness. He turned the burner to low and started a separate pot of water to cook the egg noodles. While he was finishing dinner, Ryder asked a valid question.

"What happens when we find something that we don't like?"

"When that happens, because I'm sure it will, I think we should each tell why our position is important to us. Then it's the job of the other to respect that. We think we will need to find a way to compromise, but I don't have a lot of experience with that in relationships, so I'm going to need your help with it. And your patience." Knox said seriously. Knox thought about bringing up the topic of eventually including other guys if they got bored of one another but decided the conversation would hold until another time.

"That's fair," Ryder said. Can we revisit this conversation after that happens for the first time?"

"Sure," Knox said, knowing he had made the right choice to delay discussing all of his fears at one time.

Knox took a small container of sour cream from the refrigerator and placed it on the counter beside the stove. He drained the egg noodles and placed generous amounts in two bowls that he had arranged on the counter beside the stove. He opened the sour cream and dumped the entire container into the pot.

"Secret ingredient," Knox said, looking slyly at Ryder while stirring the mixture to a creamy consistency.

Knox spooned large amounts of the stew over the noodles, retrieved spoons from the drawer, stuck a spoon in the middle of each, and handed one to Ryder. Knox tore off two paper towels to use as napkins before heading to the living room.

Ryder sat cross-legged on the sofa and hesitantly tasted the stroganoff.

"This is delicious!" He said as he shoved another large spoonful into his mouth. "I mean, this is seriously really good!"

"Glad you like it," Knox said, smiling as he watched Ryder inhale the food. "Slow down, though, there's plenty."

"But it's sooooo good!" Ryder responded, his mouth empty, but not for long. "I mean, it could use some Garcia beef, but…"

They both laughed at the comment, knowing that beef from the ranch would make everything better.

"We just need to make this at the ranch, then." Knox smiled.

Knox picked up the remote and pressed play to start the movie. The ate in silence while finishing the bowls of stroganoff and noodles. Knox paused the movie, took the bowls to the kitchen, quickly rinsed them and placed everything in the dishwasher. He took the bottle of wine back to the living room and refilled their glasses. Before sitting, he got a blanket from a basket under the end table and draped it over their laps as he sat down. Ryder immediately cuddled up next to him, curling his legs under him and placing his head and hand on Knox's chest. They watched the movie, commenting on things that were funny but should have been scary and things that were supposed to be funny that were scary.

When the movie was over, Knox moved Ryder off him and turned so that his back was against the arm of the sofa and his feet were in Ryder's lap. Ryder placed his hands on Knox's feet and rubbed them casually.

"Thoughts on my life so far?" Knox asked."

"I like it," Ryder answered. "I like it a lot, and I like that you're in it. The way our lives are different makes us such a perfect couple. I think we complement each other. Don't you agree?"

"Yes, I agree. I was worried all this might be too simple for you." Knox said cautiously.

"Knox, please stop judging me. I'm not that kind of guy. Just because my family has money does not make me any certain way. I'm just who I am like you are who you are. Do you love me as I am? Be honest with me." Ryder was getting irritated.

"Ryder, calm down. Yes, I love you for who you are. I love everything about you. I love your life, your family, you, all of you. Your personality, your body, your legs, your hands, your cock." Knox laughed. "I'm sorry, Ryder. I'm just scared. That's all."

"It's okay. I'm scared, too. I like this. Let's go back to what we agreed at One Horse. Let's just go with it. Deal?" Ryder moved his hands up Knox's legs to his thighs.

"Deal," Knox said, moving his feet to the floor and standing up.

He walked around the sofa and headed towards the bedroom. "Coming?" he said, looking back over his shoulder.

Ryder jumped up and followed him. They went to the bathroom, where Ryder had placed a small toiletries bag on the counter. He pulled out his toothbrush and toothpaste and proceeded to brush his teeth. Knox did the same, sharing the one sink with him in a rhythm that looked choreographed. Knox walked to the toilet and peed, returning to the sink, where he washed his hands. That was the extent of Knox's bedtime routine. Ryder, however, pulled out several small jars of face and eye cream, which he used to moisturize his face. He pulled Knox over and repeated the routine on him. This felt good for Knox. He liked having someone care for him like this.

Knox removed his loungewear and left it where it fell on the floor. Ryder did the same. They situated themselves under the covers of Knox's bed with each of them on their backs. Their hands touched, and Knox entwined his fingers through Ryder's.

"I'm glad you're here," Knox said.

Ryder rolled towards Knox, placing his hand on Knox's furry chest. "Me too." He said.

They made love that night slowly. Their passion melted into need, want, and desire, with each of them achieving content satisfaction. They slept peacefully, this time with Knox falling asleep first with his head on Ryder's chest.

When Knox woke, Ryder was finishing his yoga routine in the space beside the bed. Knox watched him move through the positions. He could not foresee a time when he would tire of watching this man do this. When Ryder was done, he got back in bed and snuggled up next to Knox.

"I trust you have good coffee?" Ryder said.

"Oh yes. You do know that about me, don't you." Knox said rhetorically. "Come with me to the kitchen, and I'll get us some coffee and breakfast."

Knox walked naked to the kitchen. Ryder followed. Knox opened the refrigerator door and grabbed a loaf of multigrain bread, removing four slices before twisting the top of the bag, tucking it under and placing it back in the fridge.

"You keep your bread in the fridge?" Ryder asked.

"Yep. I don't go through it fast enough, and it molds. It lasts longer in there." Knox said matter-of-factly.

"Makes sense." Ryder agreed.

Knox put the slices of bread in the toaster oven and turned it on. While the bread toasted, Knox pressed the button on the Gaggia to wake it up, grabbing two heavy mugs from the cabinet above the machine. When ready, he pressed the button for a double espresso lungo and waited while the smart machine did its thing. Knox handed the steaming cup of coffee to Ryder, who took a sip and then started the machine again to make his own.

"This IS really good coffee," Ryder said.

"I take my coffee very seriously. That's why I was so happy that you have a good machine at your place." Knox said.

By the time they both had their mugs of coffee, the bread was golden brown. He removed it and placed two pieces each on two plates. He opened the fridge again and took out a small container of plain hummus. He used a spoon to load the bread with generous dollops of hummus, which he then sprinkled with Tajin.

"I usually have oatmeal with unsalted butter and coarse sea salt. People have told me that's weird, so I decided on hummus toast, my second favorite, before forcing you to try the oatmeal." Knox admitted.

"Then we must have the oatmeal tomorrow," Ryder said. "I want the full Knox Creed experience."

"Then breakfast is served," Knox said with a flourish of his hand, gesturing towards the plates sitting on the counter. Knox handed one plate to Ryder and took the other plate for himself, walking with it to the living room window. Knox stood at the window, naked, looking out at the truck and the Mercedes parked next to it.

"They look nice together. Like Cyber Wolf has a little sister." Knox laughed.

Ryder stood next to Knox, holding his plate and taking bites of his toast.

"Do you always eat breakfast standing naked at the window?" Ryder asked?

"Huh?" Knox looked toward Ryder, the question pulling him away from other thoughts. "Uh, yes, I guess I do."

"Okay, just checking," Ryder said, continuing to stand beside Knox while eating his toast. "I like this." And in that simple act, Knox felt another layer of his anxiety peel away. Ryder wasn't just tolerating his world; he was genuinely finding joy in it. That was a game changer.

"Yeah, I really like the hummus with the Tajin," Knox replied.

"I wasn't just talking about the toast, Knox." Ryder smiled at Knox, who blushed at being caught off guard by the double entendre.

"Thanks for saying that, Ryder, I know I have some weird habits."

"I love your weird habits. They make you who you are." Ryder reassured him.

Knox popped the last bit of toast in his mouth and took Ryder's empty plate from his hand. Ryder leaned forward and kissed Knox's upper lip, removing a small dob of hummus that had not made its way into Knox's mouth. Knox grinned, "I usually don't find that until much later."

They walked back to the kitchen and cleaned up things from their simple breakfast. Knox suggested that they get dressed and go for a drive. Ryder dug around in his bag and retrieved a fresh pair of underwear, socks, jeans, and a neatly folded snap-up short-sleeve shirt in a blue plaid with white piping. Knox dressed in his typical jeans and shirt like Ryder's but in a light gray color. After they had put on their boots and hats, Knox instructed Ryder that the Mercedes would need to be moved in order to get the 'stang out of the garage. Once Knox had backed it into the street, Ryder could pull the Mercedes into the garage and join him. Ryder did as Knox had instructed, and soon, they were on the road. Ryder loved the muscle car sound of the Mustang. He could feel the power vibrating through him as Knox shifted gears. Knox drove to the end of his street and pulled over.

"Wanna drive?" He looked at Ryder.

"Hell yes, I want to drive," Ryder said excitedly, opening his door and running around to the driver's side before Knox could even get out of the seat. Ryder barely waited for Knox to buckle his lap belt before he released the clutch and gave the car enough gas to make the backend fishtail.

"Woohoo!" Ryder yelled, sticking his left hand out the open window and waving it wildly in the air. Knox grinned at the fun Ryder was having. "Where to, Knoxman?" Ryder asked. Knox gave Ryder directions as they drove around Barstow. There was not much to see, but Knox showed him anyway. They drove past where Knox shopped for groceries, the gym where he sometimes worked out, and they drove down Hwy 247 towards the road to BarsTech and past SlashXRanch. Knox told Ryder stories about having a beer there and a few of the hook-ups that had resulted. Ryder was fascinated by the options that Knox had as a trucker and told Knox that, considering the way he looked, it was no surprise that anyone would go home with him. They talked briefly about BarsTech, and Ryder listened as Knox talked but asked very few questions.

They ended up back in Barstow at a regional chain restaurant called Black Bear Diner, which was one of Knox's favorite places to eat. When the waitress arrived at the table, Knox ordered for both of them. Two glasses of an IPA from a local brewery and two parmesan sourdough cheeseburgers. Knox told Ryder that it was his favorite and turnabout was fair play since he had been forced to eat that delicious meal at the Chris's in Fritch. They both laughed at Knox's comment. Ryder was happy to allow Knox to order for him, and the choice was delicious.

While they were eating, Knox got a text from Chuck at BarsTech.

(Chuck) Hi Knox

(Chuck) I hope you are rested from this last haul

(Chuck) Let me know when you might come in to discuss the next one. No need to bring the rig since this will just be a planning meeting

(Knox) Hi Chuck

(Knox) I can be there tomorrow morning at 10 if that works.

(Chuck) Perfect. See you then.

Knox apologized for texting while they ate and explained what was going on to Ryder.

"I need to go in and talk to him about this next haul. Are you okay waiting at the house?" Knox asked.

"Of course," Ryder said. "How long do you think the meeting will take?"

"I'm guessing about two hours," Knox replied.

"Sounds good. I'll have some lunch ready for you when you return." Ryder smiled.

"You're just too perfect. I think I'll keep you around." Knox teased.

They finished the meal, and Knox drove the Mach 1 back to the house. When they were back at home, Ryder asked Knox if they could cuddle in bed, no sex, just talking and touching. Knox agreed, laughing to himself that cuddling with Ryder always led to sex. They kicked off their boots and removed their jeans and shirts, lying down on the bed in just their underwear and socks. They faced each other, and Ryder reached up and caressed Knox's face.

"I just want to tell you what a beautiful man you are," Ryder said, kissing Knox softly on the lips.

"Thanks, you know I feel the same about you, Ryder," Knox said.

"I know. Sometimes I just want to tell you." Ryder said. "How are we going to handle this next haul? I suppose I can meet you in places unless you think it's better to do it on your own?" Ryder asked hesitantly.

"First, I don't need to do it on my own. Second, my choice would be to have you with me during the entire drive." Knox said forcefully.

"I would need to make arrangements to be with you for the entire trip," Ryder said. "But I can try. Let's see what the trip looks like first."

"Agree. I'll know more after meeting with Chuck tomorrow." Knox said. "Right now, though, I just want to enjoy my time with you."

Knox pulled Ryder close and kissed him. They spent the next two hours kissing, caressing, rubbing, and talking. But not having sex. It was the first time that either of them had ever achieved such deep satisfaction with another person without having sex.

"What's for dinner?" Ryder asked.

"If you're okay eating at home, I was planning on grilling chicken and having a Caesar salad." Knox offered.

"Sounds perfect. Can we cook together?" Ryder inquired.

"I'd like that," Knox said.

They got out of bed, took off their underwear and socks, and dressed in the lounge clothes from the night before. In the kitchen, Knox retrieved a package of chicken breasts from the refrigerator, opened the package and placed the meat on a plate. Ryder patted the chicken with a paper towel to dry it off, washing his hands before discussing with Knox what seasonings to use. From the limited selection in the cabinet, they decided on salt, black pepper, and garlic powder. Ryder sprinkled generous amounts of each onto the chicken and used his fingers to rub everything into the meat. After washing his hands again, he placed the plate of chicken back in the fridge and went out the back door from the kitchen, where Knox kept a small gas grill.

Knox lit the grill and used a scrubbing brush to clean the grates while the grill heated. When it was hot, Ryder retrieved the chicken from the fridge and used tongs to place the boneless breasts on the grill. Knox closed the lid and noted the time on his phone. Ryder followed Knox back into the kitchen, where they placed the dishes and tongs in the dishwasher and washed their hands yet again. Knox looked around in the cabinets and found a wooden salad bowl that he rarely used. He wiped it out with a damp paper towel and opened the fridge door to get the lettuce and some shredded parmesan cheese. Ryder rummaged in the cabinets and found a bag of croutons and a new bottle of salad dressing.

Knox looked at the time on his phone and quickly walked out the back door to the grill, where he turned the chicken before coming back into the house. Ryder was busy tearing the lettuce into large chunks in the salad bowl, tossing it with cheese and dressing and then placing it in the refrigerator. Knox gathered two large shallow bowls, forks, and paper towels, which he used to set the small table at the end of the kitchen. On impulse, he rummaged in a junk drawer and found a small votive candle, which was lit and placed in the center of the table with a bottle of red wine, two glasses, and a corkscrew.

Knox took the chicken off the grill and brought it back into the kitchen, moving it to a small cutting board where he sliced it thinly with a butcher knife. He arranged the sliced chicken on a plate and placed it on the table. Ryder took the bowl of salad from the fridge, tossed croutons on top and got a clean set of tongs from the drawer, which he placed directly in the salad bowl.

They worked in perfect harmony, preparing the meal. They spoke rarely and touched each other frequently. Knox opened the wine and poured it into the glasses.

"This is nice," Ryder said

"Yeah, I like the grilled chicken and salad combo," Knox responded.

"The food is good, but I wasn't talking about just the food," Ryder said.

"I know." Knox agreed. "I like this too."

They finished dinner, cleaned up the dishes, and watched a house-hunting reality show for an hour before heading to the bedroom. Knox fell asleep in Ryder's arms, feeling safe and content. And without having sex.

Knox woke the next morning to an unusual sensation. His cock was hard and was being stimulated, but his hands were on his chest. As his mind caught up with his body, he realized that Ryder was sucking his cock. Not just sucking it but relishing in it. Worshiping it. Knox moaned to show that he was awake. Ryder moved his mouth and hand more quickly up and down Knox's shaft. Knox came before he was even fully awake. Ryder swallowed it all, continuing to rub Knox's balls and kissing the inside of his thighs. Eventually, Ryder moved up to Knox's chest and rested his head there.

"Thank you for letting me do that," Ryder said. "I woke up and reached over for you and saw that you were hard. So, I took advantage of that."

"I should be thanking you," Knox said. "I've never been woken up by a guy sucking my dick. It's always been a fantasy of mine. And it was hotter than I imagined."

"Take care of me later? When you get back from your meeting?" Ryder asked.

"You can count on it," Knox promised.

Knox kissed Ryder before getting out of bed and walking to the shower. He showered and got dressed. Ryder met him in the living room with a travel mug of coffee and protein bar for the road.

"Seriously, Ryder, stop being so perfect," Knox said, kissing Ryder before heading out the door.

"Be back in a couple of hours," Knox said.

Knox approached the gate to BarsTech, keenly aware of the noise the car made in the vastness of the desert landscape. Janet stepped out of the guard building and held out a hand for the car to stop, her hand on the butt of her pistol in its holster. Knox cranked down the manual window and held out his ID.

"Knox! No rig today?" Janet asked.

"Nope. Planning meeting. This is my regular vehicle." Knox replied.

"It's beautiful," Janet said. "Go on it. I'll see you when you pick up your next load."

"Thanks, beautiful," Knox said, noticing Janet blush as he drove through the gate.

As he approached the buildings, Knox realized that he wasn't sure if he should park in the parking lot or pull into the loading bay. His confusion was resolved when the loading bay door rolled up. He pulled forward and parked the Mustang where he would normally park the truck. Chuck was waiting beside the car before Knox could even open the door.

"Nice car," Chuck said.

"Thanks." Knox smiled at Chuck.

"Let's talk. This is an unusual one." Chuck said as he walked to the lounge. "Make yourself some coffee and have a seat at the table."

Knox made the coffee and sat at the table. Chuck sat down next to him, spreading three pieces of paper out before them. One was a map, the next a list of locations, and the third a list of talking points that Chuck had made to help him with the brief.

"We have an order from a very important client." Chuck started. "The client requires a single delivery. This means that you will drive to the delivery location, wait for unload, then drive back here."

"Sounds simple enough," Knox said.

"You would think." Chuck laughed. "The delivery is in Thompson, Manitoba. In Canada. The road distance is 2,165 miles." Chuck let the number sink in.

"One way?" Knox asked.

"Yes," Chuck said, waiting for Knox to process the information.

"I don't know those roads well, but I'm guessing there are not a lot of charging stations in northern Manitoba," Knox said. "So, that's a problem."

"You are right. We would need to modify your truck with a device that would recharge the batteries." Chuck said.

"That would change the EV industry if that device existed," Knox said.

"It would. And it might, in the future. For now, it is a…let's call it a prototype that works, is reliable and would extend your range for at least a thousand miles." Chuck explained. "It would require you to leave your truck with us for several days, then we would train you on the device."

Knox was silent.

"Tell me what you're thinking," Chuck said, sounding worried.

"Well, I'm wondering why this needs to be trucked. Why can't you send it by train, or plane, or teleport it, since you have these magical devices here." Knox was being serious, with a tinge of sarcasm.

"All valid questions," Chuck answered. "There are custody issues with trains and planes. And we haven't perfected the teleportation device yet." Chuck winked at Knox. "For us to guarantee the delivery, it must be delivered by vehicle. When you deliver the load to the location in Manitoba, the custody transfers. We know that the client will deliver it to the final destination by train and boat, but we are only ensuring delivery to them in Manitoba. Do you think you are up for it?

"When would I need to leave?" Knox asked.

"Delivery needs to be within the next sixty days. So preferably within the next thirty days." Chuck contemplated.

"Can I take a friend?" Knox continued.

"Who would that be? Your new love interest?" Chuck smirked.

"Actually, yes," Knox said.

"What's his name?" Chuck asked.

"Ryder. Ryder Garcia." Knox said.

"Wait. Of the Texas Garcia's? the Garcia's that are the largest landowners in the State of Texas?" Chuck's tone changed.

"Yes, why?"

"It's not important, but yes, I think that would be okay," Chuck said, waving his hands as if the matter was inconsequential.

"Then yes, I can do it," Knox said.

"Excellent. When can you bring the truck by?" Chuck responded.

"Two days from now." Knox offered.

Okay. Drop it off, and we will have someone take you back to your house." Chuck said, gathering the papers. "We will need to have a complete training and briefing at least a week before you leave."

Chuck escorted Knox to his car. As Knox pulled out of the loading bay and drove home, he started to get nervous about mentioning this to Ryder. Knox could make the run alone, but it would be so much better with Ryder alone. Knox arrived back at the house, parked the Mustang, and entered the house to find Ryder sitting naked in the bed, watching TV.

"Fuck me first, then tell me about your meeting," Ryder commanded.

Knox forgot about the meeting, taking off his clothes as Ryder turned over and got on his knees to present his hungry hole to Knox. By the time Knox walked a few feet to the bed, his dick was hard and ready. Ryder lubed up his hole and pushed back as Knox positioned his cock at the right angle. Knox grabbed Ryder's shoulder with his right hand, placing his left hand on Ryder's hip and moving his cock in and out in a steady rhythm. Ryder reached his right hand back and grabbed Knox's hip, pulling him tighter into him.

Ryder lifted his torso up and back against Knox's chest, reaching his arm back to bring Knox's face close to him as he turned his head to kiss him. Ryder tilted his hips back and forth in this position, holding tightly to Knox's head. Ryder released Knox and fell forward, where he placed his chest and head on the bed as his left hand stroked his own cock. They continued to move in perfect rhythm, their hands moving along each other's bodies as they took pleasure in both the company and the sensations. Ryder came hard, vocalizing that he had been waiting for this all morning. Ryder's breathless voice made Knox thrust harder and faster. Ryder reached his cum-wet hand between his legs and fingered Knox's balls, his forefinger finding purchase at the entrance to Knox's hole. Ryder pushed in slowly, using the remaining jizz on his finger as lube. Ryder pulled forward with his finger, increasing the pressure with each movement of Knox's hips. Knox came with a force that pushed Ryder flat on his belly. Knox collapsed onto Ryder's back and remained inside him until his penis deflated and fell out naturally. Knox rolled Ryder over and pulled him to his chest.

"We have to talk." He said.

Knox recounted what Chuck had told him. Ryder listened quietly.

"Can you come with me," Knox asked.

"I'm not sure, Knox. It's a lot of time and distance. There's so much that I need to check on. Can I give you an answer in a few days?" Ryder sounded doubtful that he would be able to make it work.

"Of course." Knox said. "Let's forget about this for now."

"Okay. I'm going to go back to the ranch tomorrow and see what I can do. Until then, let's just spend the day together."

"Okay, Ryder. What do you want to do today? Knox asked.

"Can we just hole up here in the house? Watch TV, cuddle, fuck, eat, repeat?" Ryder leaned up and smiled at Knox.

"I like that idea!" Knox said, poking Ryder playfully. "Let's start with that lunch you were going to make me."

"Already done and in the fridge," Ryder said as he hopped up out of bed. "Follow me, Knoxman."

Knox followed Ryder to the kitchen. Ryder had made a simple pasta salad and two sandwiches with a variety of leftover veggies and hummus.

"You did all this in the two hours I was gone?" Knox marveled.

"Yep, gotta take care of my man," Ryder said in an exaggerated Texas accent.

"You're perfect, Ryder. Seriously, I don't deserve you." Knox became unexpectedly emotional.

"Yes, Knox. Yes, you do." Ryder said, hugging Knox and kissing him softly. "Now, let's eat.

"They stood side by side, naked, looking out the front window while they ate their lunch.

After lunch, they got into their lounge clothes and settled on the sofa to watch TV. The day continued with them moving from the living room to the kitchen, to the bedroom, and back. Having sex, eating, and watching TV in all three places. When bedtime came, they were exhausted and fell asleep quickly, this time with Ryder taking the position of the big spoon.

The morning brought a somber and silent breakfast of toast with butter and coffee, having forgotten about the oatmeal as Ryder gathered his things to leave. Taking Knox up on the offer to leave a few things, he neatly folded a complete change of clothes and stored them in the dresser drawer. Knox held him tightly before walking out the door.

"I don't want to let you go," Knox admitted.

"I don't want to go. But I need to figure this out." Ryder said, hugging Knox tighter.

Ryder walked out the door, followed by Knox. He threw his duffle in the back seat of the Mercedes and sat down in the driver's seat. He started the car and rolled down the window. Knox placed his hand on the door and leaned in to give Ryder one final kiss. The kiss lingered in the air of uncertainty.

"I promise I'm going to try to make this work, Knox," Ryder said. "Knox, you need to know that if I can't come, it only means that I'll be waiting for you when you return. That's all it means."

"I know, Ryder. Please try. This is going to be difficult without you." Knox sounded panicked. "I love you, Ry."

"I love you, Knoxman." Ryder smiled, a single tear falling down his cheek.

Ryder rolled up the window and drove off as the sun set over the not-so-spectacular landscape of Barstow.

Knox stood in the driveway, his hands in the pockets of his jeans. Tears streamed down his face. He hated the uncertainty. He hated that he loved Ryder so much. He hated that Ryder loved him. He turned and walked to the porch, entering his house with his mind swirling with possibilities. He did not know how his story with Ryder Garcia would continue. But one thing he did know – Canada was calling.

For Shayne, the details tell you why.

About Gray Wilder

Gray Wilder is the naughty side of author Gray Taylor. He lives in Albuquerque, New Mexico, with his husband, Shayne, and their corgi, Indigo. You might find him writing at a local coffee house or running in the Bosque. If you see him, please compliment his kilt and his beard – he loves that. And don't forget to ask him what he's writing next.